ev...

Ryan said
did take her
gentleman.

A wolf in man's clothing—casual, ordinary-looking clothing, right down to his own athletic shoes.

A wolf...

"There's not much to explain," he said. "You saw me. I'm a shapeshifter who changes into a wolf sometimes."

"Then it was real, not some kind of hypnosis or mind control?" Although even if it had been, she'd have no idea why he'd have done it to her.

"No, it was real."

She slipped a little on some leaves beneath her feet, possibly because of the distraction and unease his words caused within her. He caught her, and she was very aware of his touch.

A human's touch.

But still...

PROTECTOR WOLF

LINDA O. JOHNSTON

First Published in Great Britain 2017
By Mills & Boon, an imprint of HarperCollins*Publishers*
1 London Bridge Street, London, SE1 9GF

© 2017 Linda O. Johnston

ISBN: 978-0-263-93009-2

89-0617

Our policy is to use papers that are natural, renewable and recyclable products and made from wood grown in sustainable forests. The logging and manufacturing processes conform to the legal environmental regulations of the country of origin.

Printe
by CP

Linda O. Johnston loves to write. While honing her writing skills, she worked in advertising and public relations, then became a lawyer...and enjoyed writing contracts. Linda's first published fiction appeared in *Ellery Queen's Mystery Magazine* and won a Robert L. Fish Memorial Award for Best First Mystery Short Story of the Year. Linda now spends most of her time creating memorable tales of paranormal romance, romantic suspense and mystery. Visit her on the web at www.lindaojohnston.com.

Protector Wolf is dedicated to wolves of all kinds, as well as people who love and protect wildlife. And like my other Alpha Force Nocturnes, *Protector Wolf* is also dedicated to shapeshifters and the readers who love them.

Plus, despite this being repetitious, again my special thanks to my wonderful agent, Paige Wheeler of Creative Media Agency, and to my delightful Harlequin editor, Allison Lyons. They're so great in helping to keep the stories of Alpha Force an ongoing miniseries. *Protector Wolf* is number eight!

And, as always, thanks to my amazing husband, Fred, whom I acknowledge in each of my books because he inspires me. My hero!

Chapter 1

Lieutenant Ryan Blaiddinger strode quickly down the sidewalk.

Beside him were his dog, Rocky, and his aide, Staff Sergeant Piers Janus. The two soldiers were dressed in civilian clothing—nice slacks and button-down shirts. They were here in Fritts Corner, Washington, undercover.

According to the map on Piers's phone, the park they sought was only a block away. Ryan scoped out the whole street—fairly narrow, considering it was the quaint town's main avenue. Some of the buildings appeared to have been constructed more than a century ago, with spires, decorative windows and wide porches that led into restaurants and other retail establishments.

"We're almost there," Piers said, staring at the phone in his hand. Piers was short and a bit stocky, and despite his being in his early twenties his blondish hair had begun to thin. But he was a damned good helper—in many respects.

Piers held Rocky's leash, and the dog bounded along with him.

The dog with thick brown-and-black fur who resembled a wolf.

A wolf who looked a lot like Ryan…when he was in shifted form.

The air was brisk but dry on this Thursday afternoon in September. Cars drove by in both directions, with no hint of any traffic jam in this small town. People passed by as well, and a few headed in the same direction they did.

Interesting that on the day of their arrival a public meeting was scheduled about the very topic they'd come to check out.

But maybe it wasn't too surprising. After all, though there had been sightings of wild wolves for years in various areas of Washington State, even identification of some small packs, the latest new sightings had been right around here, in this area southeast of Tacoma.

And when Ryan, sounding as offhand as he could, mentioned wolf sightings to their hotel's receptionist a short while ago when they checked in, she had immediately perked up and told him that a naturalist had just come to town and was going to talk on that very topic in less than an hour.

That was really interesting since wolves previously hadn't been spotted around here much for a long time, the receptionist had acknowledged. Lots of people in town were fascinated by the situation…though some weren't too happy about it.

There. The open-air park, mostly green, rolling lawn with a few trees, was finally off to their right. A large crowd stood on the grass facing a raised podium that appeared old and worn, perhaps even constructed around the same time as the rest of the town.

On it stood a tall and slender woman. A screen behind her contained a photo of a wolf, projected there by some modern equipment that clearly wasn't as antique as the town.

"The pictures I've shown you are from other areas in Washington," she was saying into a microphone so her deep, energetic voice projected around the area. "It's so exciting that wild wolves have been returning to this state. Of course WHaM has been keeping up with the Washington Department of Fish and Wildlife's postings online, as well as US Fish and Wildlife, which has jurisdiction for their protection around here. We're thrilled—and tracking them, too, taking a census including the official estimate of nineteen packs in the state. Plus, we encourage the media to let the public know. Any media people here?" A few hands were raised. "Great!"

WHaM. That was Wildlife Habitat Monitoring, Ryan knew. He needed to talk to this woman after her presentation, and using his cover of being with the US Fish and Wildlife Service—not the state's—should make it easy for him to find out everything WHaM knew about the latest wolf sightings.

Of course their agenda was far different from his. Wolf sightings to them would be just that—evidence of the continuing but slow return of wild wolves to increasing locations in this state, fewer here than in the eastern part. And some had already been destroyed after attacking livestock, though not in this area.

Ryan was here on his first lead assignment representing Alpha Force. Rocky and Piers had come along as his backups. He was the only commissioned officer present— and the only member here of that covert military unit of shapeshifters who was actually a shifter himself.

For the moment, he eased his way through the large

group of onlookers, men, women and children of all ages,
knowing that Piers would follow with Rocky. Rocky might
garner some attention since he looked so much like a wolf,
but that was because he was Ryan's cover dog. He had been
chosen because of his resemblance to Ryan in shifted form.
That way, in case anyone noticed him while shifted, they'd
be told it was Ryan's dog they'd seen. Him as a shapeshifter? What a laugh.

Or so went the cover story he'd been provided by Alpha
Force.

He finally reached the front of the crowd after excus-
ing himself and smiling and looking apologetic to lots of
people along the way.

What did they all think of the slow influx of wolves
around here?

Were any of them shapeshifters, too?

Ryan would find that out while he was here. Quickly.
It was a major part of his assignment.

And if there were other shifters? Well, he'd determine,
once he'd found and spoken with them, exactly what that
might mean with respect to their lives here...and, potentially, to Alpha Force.

Right now, though, he moved over to give Piers and
Rocky room to stand beside him. The woman was still
talking, speaking with such excitement that it appeared
contagious. Lots of folks in his area were cheering and
clapping.

Which meant he'd better take time to listen.

"Wolves are such wonderful creatures," she was saying—and that warmed his insides immediately. This close
he could see how attractive she was, with a curvaceous
body and a face pretty enough to put her onstage for something other than a wildlife proponent rally. "They're smart,
loyal to their packs, loving to their families and more.

They're—" She had been scanning the crowd with her gaze as she spoke, sometimes waving her slender arm beneath its black WHaM T-shirt up toward the screen behind her, where the pictures of wolves had now turned into a rotation. But now she stopped.

She was looking down toward Ryan, which gave him immediate pause—until he realized she was instead staring at Rocky.

"Is that a wolf among us?" she asked, this time looking right into Ryan's eyes, or so it appeared from this distance.

He smiled and called out, "No, he's my pet, a shepherd-husky mix for the most part, I think. But I wouldn't be surprised if there's some wolf ancestry in there, too."

"Me, neither," she said. But cocking her head so her long, pale brown hair slipped to the side, she held the microphone back up to her mouth. "Okay, folks, you'll need to see that adorable dog before you leave here this afternoon, especially if you've never seen a wolf before. But one thing I should mention is that wolves are wild animals and should stay that way." She paused, and again stared right into Ryan's face so intensely he felt as if she was almost touching him. Maybe slapping him. But she looked away again before she said, "Everyone, never, ever, try to turn a wild animal into a pet...especially wolves."

Maya Everton wanted to jump right off that stage and confront that guy. No, what she really wanted was to meet that wolf-dog face-to-face, hug it, feel its soft fur.

And then let it loose, as wolves should be. Only she realized that, even if that canine had once been wild, as a pup or older, it could probably not survive in the wild now.

Maybe she could talk to his owner later, find out the dog's background, so she could hopefully feel content that she was wrong, that this truly was a canine with dog genes that had never actually been a wild wolf.

"Okay," she was saying despite her thoughts twisting in so many ways. "Has anyone here seen any of the wolves that have visited this area?"

A woman way toward the back of the generous crowd waved her hand. Maya was thrilled that so many people had shown up to see her, to hear her talk about WHaM and its excellent work keeping track of wild animal sightings—wolves and more. But the latest influx of wolves was a big deal here. Newsworthy, and they needed to be protected. WHaM maintained a comprehensive file on all the wolves sighted recently in this state—more in the eastern areas than here, though that might be changing. Her organization had been in close touch often with the Washington Department of Fish and Wildlife, and had a good relationship with them.

Like other wildlife, wolves weren't appreciated in all areas of the state, especially those where some had apparently attacked local farm animals. But around here, they had a fresh start.

She called for the woman to come up to the microphone and describe her experience. While Maya waited for that lady to make her way through the crowd, she looked again toward that wolf-dog. Gorgeous.

His owner wasn't bad-looking, either—as long as Maya could regard him without anger. Well, for now she'd give him the benefit of the doubt.

The woman soon joined Maya onstage. She introduced herself as Ivy. Ivy appeared in her fifties, with a lined face and a huge smile. "I live near here," she said, "but a distance out of town. It was so amazing. I heard some howling in the dead of night and looked outside, only to see a couple of wolves jump over my fence, run through the yard and then out again. It was light enough under the full moon that it didn't matter that I'd forgotten to turn on my porch lamps."

"Really? That's so exciting!" Maya really was impressed, wishing something similar had happened to her. She'd had to seek out every wild animal she'd seen herself without any miraculously appearing. "And did you let anyone know officially?" She thought she recalled a report on the Washington Department of Fish and Wildlife site, or WDFW, that could have been a description of what had happened to this woman but she wasn't sure.

"Absolutely. I researched online what to do and filed a report there with Washington's fish and wildlife department. Only—"

She stopped, and her face seemed to age visibly.

"Only what?" Maya prodded gently.

"Only the one thing I forgot was to grab my camera." Tears rose in her eyes.

Maya couldn't let her leave the stage feeling bad, so she said, "But you took a picture in your own mind, I'll bet. Will you ever forget what they looked like?"

"No, never." The lady smiled, and Maya gave her a brief hug, encouraging her to rejoin the rest of the audience.

Her presentation was pretty much over—at least for this day. "Thank you all so much for coming," Maya said. "And just remember some of the takeaways I suggested to you. First, you should all be proud, as Washington residents, that wolves are returning to your state and this area, and should continue to as long as you treat them well. And second—keep up with what we're doing at WHaM in our tracking of wildlife and otherwise. Provide reports to us, too, and photos if you happen to take any. But be sure to report, as Ivy did, to the Washington Department of Fish and Wildlife, and maybe the federal fish and wildlife department, as well. And if you care to make a contribution to help us keep WHaM going, that would be more than welcome. Just visit our website that's on our flyers. I've got a boxful right here on the stage."

"There's something else you should all remember," yelled a voice from the audience. Maya's gaze lit first on the guy with the wolf-dog but he was scowling in concern. He hadn't been the speaker.

"What's that?" she asked, feeling as if she was setting herself up for some kind of bad situation.

She proved to be right. A couple of men and a woman separated themselves from the middle of the crowd and made their way onto the stage beside her. She felt her brows go up and a slight smile make its way to her lips, even as she continued to figure this wasn't likely to be anything good.

One of the men, maybe her age of late twenties, wore a plaid shirt and a huge, snide grin. He put his hand out for the microphone. Reluctantly, she handed it to him.

"You all know me," the guy said to the audience. He turned back to Maya. "But you don't. My name's Carlo Silling. I've lived in Fritts Corner all my life. This is my town, and those wolves getting close aren't a sign of wonderful things to come, no matter what you and your wham-bammers seem to think. You don't live here. You're not subject to the danger that wild wolves can present to people, as well as any livestock they raise. They're just that—wild animals. And I'd suggest you leave this stage, leave this town and let us take care of our own bad luck."

Ryan felt himself freeze with tension as his hands curled into fists at his sides.

He'd been staring at that guy Silling as he'd come on-stage, as well as the others who'd accompanied him. The malicious, menacing way they regarded the naturalist whose name he'd learned was Maya Everton made him want to rub those expressions right off their faces.

"I agree with Carlo," the woman yelled to the crowd. "I'm Vinnie Fritts—and this is my husband, Morton." She nodded toward the man in a yellow shirt beside her. "You all know us and how long we've been around Fritts Corner—Morton's family especially. Who needs wild animals here to hurt people and ruin our wonderful town's reputation?"

Ryan stood then and, grabbing Rocky's leash from Piers, maneuvered from the front of the crowd and onto the stage.

Time to express their cover story.

"You're all certainly entitled to your opinion," Maya was saying. She had somehow retrieved her microphone and was glaring at the three interlopers. "But the reality is that if you stay away from wildlife, particularly wolves, they're likely to stay away from you, too. You do need to be careful on behalf of your pets, though, since they can often resemble prey. And—"

The guy Carlo reached out and grabbed the microphone again, even as Maya attempted to hold on to it. "Yeah? Well, what if that lady Ivy happened to be in her backyard that night she saw those wolves? Or—"

This time, Ryan was the one to grab the microphone, even as the other guy, Morton, started to stride toward him.

That was when Rocky growled—and the guy stopped.

"See what I'm saying?" Carlo yelled out to the crowd.

Ryan smiled as he spoke into the microphone, not pleased to see those who'd admitted to be with the media continuing to take pictures. Oh, well. His cover was solid. "This is my dog, Rocky," he said, "who only resembles a wolf. He's well trained in many ways, including my protection. Threaten me, and he threatens back. But look, everyone. The appearances of wolves in this area clearly started months ago, even longer. I'm unaware of any farms or dairies around here. Have any people been hurt?"

That wolves had been seen, per Ivy's story, around a month ago under the light of a full moon, intrigued him— but he'd check more into that later.

Maya strode up to him. She was as tall as she had appeared from below, though she wasn't close to his height of six-two. He'd noted the fear and dismay on her face as he'd gotten close to the stage, but now she'd recovered all her aplomb as well as a huge smile that she leveled on him. "Thank you, sir," she said. "And thank you, pup." She turned toward Rocky, standing beside Ryan, who nuzzled her hand and wagged his tail just like any well-trained, friendly dog.

"That's his way of saying you're welcome," he told her unnecessarily, loud enough that the audience should be able to hear. He was gratified to hear a bit of laughter.

"So, as this gentleman asked," Maya continued, "has anyone been hurt since the wolf sightings started?"

Apparently not, since no one responded in the affirmative even though the low roar of the crowd's voices grew louder.

"Great. Anyway, please keep in mind what I said before. And thanks to all of you for coming."

"You're welcome," shouted a female voice. "Thank *you* for coming. And I totally agree with you."

"Me, too," chorused other voices in the audience.

"That's so wonderful," Maya called back. "You're totally in the right."

"So are you, and WHaM," yelled a skinny guy in the front row, doing a fist pump.

"Thanks," Maya returned, smiling down at him for a second before turning away.

Ryan was amused that Maya ignored the others onstage as she approached the table where her computer equipment rested. He joined her there, Rocky at his side.

"I'm Ryan Blaiddinger, with the US Fish and Wildlife Service," he told her. "Count me with those who liked your presentation. And I want to hear more."

"That's great, Ryan," she said. "Glad to meet you. You can join us." She once more picked up the microphone from the table and spoke into it. "Hey, everyone," she called to the now-disbanding audience. "I just got an idea. Can anyone suggest a bar in town where we all can meet?"

A bunch of people spoke out once more, this time making suggestions. The decision was to go to Berry's Bar, a nearby establishment that sounded fairly large and accommodating.

"See you there?" Maya said, turning back to Ryan.

"You can bet on it. In fact, Rocky and I would enjoy walking there with you now."

"Of course, though I need to drop some of my things off at my car. I want to learn more about your wonderful wolf-dog." Her tone had turned soft and loving as she gazed down at Rocky—making Ryan wish for a moment that she'd been speaking about him instead. Which was ridiculous. She was a potential information resource for him, and that was all. And of course Rocky was one special dog.

"Good. Ready to go now?" Ryan glanced toward Piers, who stood near them. His assistant nodded briefly. He was ready to go—and to have Ryan's back, if needed. Maybe Maya's, too, since for now, at least, their goals seemed aligned.

"Just a minute while I gather up my stuff and turn this

area back to the park personnel," Maya told him. "Then I can join you."

The idea of her joining him for any reason sounded much too good.

He was going to have to be careful in this lovely wild-life lover's presence.

Chapter 2

Maya had encountered controversy before. She thought about that even more as she moved about the stage, first watching the local park attendants pick up their gear, then packing up her notebook and tablet computers, printed files, WHaM brochures and other items she'd brought.

The crowd below dissipated noisily, leaving the grass they'd been standing on bare, but she didn't hear any arguments among them. Maybe the pro-wolf people and anti-wolf people had gone their separate ways. Good. She hoped to meet with a lot of the pros shortly. Maybe some of the media, too.

But as much as she disliked it, controversy was sometimes part of her job. Despite the growing numbers of outspoken people who liked wildlife, those who despised it—or wanted to kill it, whether or not using the protection of livestock or humans as their supposed rationale—never seemed to get smaller. That was why she not only took census but also spoke before groups, partly to make sure the pro-wildlife faction recognized that the other mind-set existed and knew they had to oppose it.

Usually, her talks and that knowledge helped to make those on her side a lot more outspoken right along with her. They often contributed donations to WHaM, too, which helped the nonprofit.

Finishing her organizing and packing, she glanced to-ward the steps off the stage and saw that the nice, helpful—and great-looking—guy Ryan stood there with Rocky, waiting for her. She couldn't help smiling. Now, there was a man with proof right beside him of his position on this important subject.

It was almost time to head to the bar. She'd intended to stay in Fritts Corner for only a few days, but now she might hang out longer. Of course, that depended at least in part on who showed up at the bar this afternoon and how they acted.

Maya intended to get to know some of the people around here, particularly the few locals who had already been generous with donations. This wasn't the way she'd hoped to get them together, but it should work.

Now, she walked toward the steps, following the park guys whose hands were full of the town's electronic equip-ment they had collected. Her arms were full, too, and she stopped at the top of the steps to rearrange what she car-ried so she wouldn't fall.

She shouldn't have been pleased to have Ryan reach up to steady her—but she was.

"Thanks," she told him as he held her arm.

He didn't immediately let go, either, as she reached the last step. She made herself pull gently away, not wanting to encourage him to think she had any interest in him ex-cept as an animal advocate.

Although…did she want him to be interested in her in any other way?

No. Of course not.

"My car is parked just past the bar," she told Ryan. He was watching her with very deep brown eyes. She hadn't looked at him this closely before but couldn't help appreciating how good-looking he was, with angular planes on his face and dark brown hair cut short. She turned slightly to try to prevent his recognizing that she'd been studying him. "You can just go to the bar, and I'll meet you there after I put some of this stuff in my trunk."

He reached toward her and lifted one of her tote bags and a few other things she held, lightening her load tremendously. "I'll carry these. You lead the way."

She couldn't help looking at him again then—continuing to appreciate his tantalizing appearance as well as his gentlemanliness.

Still holding a few things she wanted to carry with her, including her tablet computer, she headed across the grass to the sidewalk, and then in the direction of the bar and where she had parked her car. Both Ryan and Rocky stayed beside her. The three of them pretty much took up the whole sidewalk, but other people didn't seem upset about stepping aside to let them pass. Maya shot each of them smiles—and they smiled back at her as they seemed to enjoy Rocky.

"Nice town," Ryan said. He was watching the people, too, so his reference to the town seemed to mean its inhabitants. At this angle, she was glad to look around nearly everywhere but toward him.

"It sure is. I like the people—most of those I've met anyway—and this area is definitely charming."

She'd enjoyed sightseeing before, on her way to the

park. She just hoped the town maintained its charm by continuing to be supportive of the return of the wolves.

For right now, talking in generalities about this area seemed pleasant enough as they walked. They soon reached her car, after passing Berry's Bar on the way. It looked crowded inside despite the time being early afternoon. Were these all people from her talk wanting to discuss wildlife some more? She hoped so.

She opened the trunk of the sedan she had rented and Ryan put his armloads of her stuff into it. She did the same with what she was carrying.

Ryan closed the trunk. "I'll be interested in how things go at the bar this afternoon. And I enjoyed your talk before. But I wanted to say something before we're with the crowd." He stood in front of her, Rocky still at his side, and frowned, which removed some of the allure from his good looks.

"What's that?" She felt sure she wouldn't like whatever he had to say.

She was right.

"I know about your organization, and I like what WHaM stands for. I've heard about how you go talk to groups like this while you confirm and count sightings of endangered animals. But—do all the talks wind up with results similar to yours? I mean, not only did you get people there who are excited about the prospect of a new influx of wildlife, but those who are against it. Outspokenly against it. Doesn't that harm your position and your organization?"

"No," she said flatly. She turned away, starting to walk toward the bar, and Ryan and Rocky joined her. "Well… maybe." She didn't look at them. "Controversy sometimes stirs up people who didn't even know they had an opinion. So far I think that's been helpful."

"Maybe," Ryan said. "But it can also cause problems

both for your group and for the animals—potentially risky for both of you. I'd suggest you back off a bit, though I'd like to know more about your intentions. Let's talk about it another time."

They'd reached the crowded sidewalk in front of Berry's Bar. "Sure," Maya said, realizing that the idea of getting together with the gorgeous, sexy man to talk appealed more than a little. But…could it be risky? She hoped not. Should she back off? That wasn't her.

What they would talk about might only rev up the controversy she knew was there.

Ryan saw Piers as soon as he entered behind Maya, with Rocky at his side. He'd told his aide to get here ahead of him and save some seats.

Were dogs allowed in here? If questioned, he would just claim that Rocky was his service dog. He even had paperwork in his pocket that would confirm that—if the person asking didn't dig too deeply.

Inhaling the strong, predictable scent of alcohol, he waved, and Piers waved back, gesturing for him to join the group sitting on stools at the bar. Ryan therefore maneuvered through the crowd—and away from Maya.

Which in some ways he hated to do.

The woman was beautiful and sassy and loved wild animals. What wasn't there to like about her?

The fact that she might be putting herself—and his role here—in danger?

Could be. That was why he had asked her to back off.

Sure, there was likely to be attention regarding each new wolf sighting around here, especially if they continued and grew in numbers. But he needed a bit of quiet in his own search regarding the inherent nature of those incoming wolves, not people talking and arguing, or worse.

And he didn't get the sense Maya would pay any attention to him.

"What's wrong?" Piers asked quietly as he reached the bar.

"Nothing, I hope." But his aide knew him well. "We'll talk later," he amended.

"Fine."

Ryan ordered a dark beer, which was also what Piers had in front of him. He decided to confront the situation of Rocky right off and requested that the bartender, a sizable fellow with a full head of hair and a beard, bring a bowl of water.

"Sure thing," the bartender said. "Nice-looking dog. Is he yours?"

More or less, Ryan thought. He certainly treated his cover dog as his own. "Yep," he said. "Rocky is one really good boy."

"I bet." When the bartender brought a metal bowl half-filled with water to the customer side of the bar and laid it at Ryan's feet—next to several pairs of feet belonging to other patrons—the guy asked, "Have you ever been to Fritts Corner before?"

"No, though I really like this place." He was laying it on a bit thick, but what the heck? "I'm here because of the latest wolf sightings. I work for US Fish and Wildlife."

"Really?" The bartender's whole, round face lit up. "Were you at the talk at the park before? I was here working, but I heard about it."

"I sure was." Why not go for broke—maybe lay into some of Maya's contentious ground? "There were some arguments. Not everyone is glad there are wolf sightings around here. How about you?"

"I'm definitely for them," the guy said with no hesitation. He held out his hand to Ryan to shake. "I'm Buck

Lesterman. My family recently bought Berry's Bar, and I'm happy with everything to do with wildlife."

Which was what Ryan had been looking for. Was this guy a shifter? Were any members of his family?

Or was Ryan just hoping too hard to find some evidence of shifters in this area?

Could be that all the recent wolf sightings were just that—sightings of actual wolves. Well, he would know more tonight.

"Glad to meet you, Buck. I'm Ryan, and this is my friend Piers." They shook hands, too, then Ryan continued, "Not sure how long I'll be in town, but I'm glad I've found this place."

"Hey, bartender!" called a guy nearby.

"'Scuse me," Buck said. "Got to get back to work."

That was when Ryan heard voices raised behind him, and he turned.

Maya sat at a table, hands on her hips. Across from her were the three people who'd come onstage to give her a hard time, and they didn't appear any friendlier.

Time for Piers and him—and Rocky, too—to join her.

As they moved in her direction, so did a few other people Ryan believed he recognized as having been at her talk.

Were they for, or against, her position?

This discussion was getting out of control. Too bad Maya couldn't have just invited the people from her talk that she wanted to come here.

Fortunately, some of the people who'd been on her side were in the crowd, too. In fact, the tall, skinny fellow who'd been at the front and called out something favorable had made his way through the people who were giving her a hard time. Now, standing beside her table, he waved at her and asked, "Can I buy you a snack to go with your drink?"

His brown eyes were open wide beneath shaggy blond brows, and his huge smile looked hopeful.

"Thanks," she said, facing him and using the opportunity to look away from the others, "but I'm good." She appreciated that he'd been on her side, yet she felt a bit uncomfortable under his happy stare—even though it was way preferable to the potential argument that had just started.

"You certainly are," he said. He held out his hand. "I'm Trevor Garlona. Trev. And I want to know all about you and WHaM."

"Thanks," she said. "But—"

"Hey, I'm talking to you." The voice across from her sounded familiar—the woman who'd just challenged her. "Don't you ignore me. And why are you even still in town?"

Maya turned again in her seat just a little. She had already recognized the woman who had confronted her after her talk. That woman now stood at the opposite end of the table from where Maya sat with a glass of wine in front of her. Some other people who'd been at her presentation had just gone up to the bar to order their drinks.

That guy who'd introduced himself as Trev moved in the direction she now faced, although other people, including that woman, didn't get out of his way. He squeezed in and looked at her, though, from behind them and raised his glass of beer as if toasting her.

She didn't toast him back, but neither did she try to get away. Not yet, at least.

She felt a little relieved to notice that Ryan had joined her, too, and stood at her side. She wished he'd come here sooner. Despite his attitude before against how she worked, she wanted to spend more time with the great-looking guy. Talk to him more about wildlife.

Especially now, while she was being confronted again. What was this woman's name? Vinnie? Vinnie Fritts, wife of a man who had the same name as this town and whose family had apparently lived here a long time, had maybe even founded it.

She wasn't that old, though—maybe midforties. Her hair was a wavy mass of brown that appeared cut and styled to remain exactly so on her head. She wore bright pink lipstick and dark-rimmed glasses. Surprisingly, the whole package went well together.

Now, if she only had a sense of consideration of others and their opinions...

"Do you have any pets at home?" Maya countered, focusing on Vinnie. "Or small children?" She took a sip of her dry white wine in an attempt to bolster her floundering courage but it didn't help. At least she didn't think she was projecting any nervousness in her tone of voice.

"No. Our kids are in college, and no way would we have animals in our house."

That figured.

"Well, I appreciate your coming to my presentation," Maya lied. "And everyone is entitled to their own opinions. But since you don't have pets or young family members at home, I doubt that you have to worry about anyone being attacked by the wolves—assuming these wolves run away from confrontations with nonprey creatures, as most do. And—"

"And you're trying to convince us that you're not only entitled to your opinion..." said the man in the pale yellow shirt just beyond her who hadn't spoken before. It was Morton, Vinnie's husband whom she'd introduced at the talk. "...but that you know everything, and everyone who lives around here should support your ridiculous position?

Now look, lady. This is my town. My family's town, and I intend to protect it. Understand?"

"No," Maya said quietly. "I don't." She noticed then that most conversations in the bar had ceased. It was a lot quieter than when she'd entered. She didn't see any of the people who'd admitted to being with the media there, though.

"We don't want any damned predatory creatures around here." The man spoke through gritted teeth. He appeared older than his wife, maybe in his fifties. His hair was thin, his brows gray and curved over his angry brown eyes. His arms were crossed over a chest that appeared sunken—but his fragility did nothing to ease Maya's fear of him.

She figured that this man hated wildlife—or, worse, wanted to wipe it out. She might not like the idea, but there were laws protecting some species in specified areas, and requirements of licenses before hunting those that were more plentiful and might actually need to have their numbers limited for the good of the rest of the species. She wasn't a vegetarian, and she could understand hunting for one's dinner.

But she had a sense that this guy just despised animals enough to kill for sport. And if that was true, she would despise *him*.

Right now, though, she did not want to continue this confrontation.

"Look," she said, "I recognize that we have very different positions on this."

"Ya think?" Morton asked sarcastically, his hands now on his hips. "Hey, here's what I think. I'll be the one to change my mind, suddenly love wolves. Want to hug them all." He glanced toward Ryan, who stood with Rocky beside him. Morton moved then, approaching the dog with his hand out. "Well, aren't you just the greatest creature on earth?" He reached out and shoved Rocky's muzzle.

The dog didn't even growl, which made Maya very happy. But the man's gesture didn't.

"Don't you hurt him." She hissed between her clenched teeth, "He's a lot nicer than you are."

"That's for sure." Ryan placed himself between his dog and the jerk of a man who'd touched him. Ryan's friend Piers also stood at the dog's side and faced down Morton as well as Vinnie and Carlo, who'd joined him.

"What a great dog that is," said a male voice from behind Maya, and she realized that Trev had moved again.

"He sure is," said someone else, a woman this time.

"Leave him alone," came another voice. When Maya turned to see who was there she was both glad and surprised to see at least half a dozen people behind her, apparently backing her up. She recognized some, maybe all of them, from her talk.

"Back off," said yet another one.

"This isn't over," Morton said, sidling away from Rocky and all the people now confronting him. "Not unless you leave and stop trying to get people to love those damned wolves. They're nasty and vicious and don't belong around here."

"Sounds like you're describing yourself," Maya couldn't help saying in return.

She caught Ryan's eye, then recalled that he had suggested she was endangering herself by her attitude in standing up to these people who didn't see things her way.

But instead of scowling or looking angry, he had a half smile on his sexy face and shook his head slowly as if amused by her.

That made her want to run over and hug the handsome guy—but she stayed still.

Instead, it was Morton Fritts and his gang who stomped out of the bar.

Chapter 3

Good. They were gone.

Ryan continued to stand near Maya, with Piers and Rocky at his sides—and all those nice people behind her who'd spoken up in support of her.

Bartender Buck Lesterman had joined them, too. Interesting.

This group seemed to be filled with wildlife advocates who appreciated what Maya said and stood for, which was a good thing in Ryan's estimation.

But were any of them shifters? All of them?

There'd been hints of an influx here thanks to the wolf sightings, and Alpha Force members had heard those rumors.

If some or all of these folks were shifters, then Maya had helped Ryan start to meet his goal. He owed her for that.

But for right now…

He regarded the group across from them, then strode forward, hand outstretched, purposely avoiding the guy who'd spoken with Maya and offered her a snack, apparently flirting with her. For some reason, that irritated Ryan, even if the guy turned out to be a wildlife advocate.

"Hi," he said to the first of them. "I'm Ryan Blaiddinger, with the US Fish and Wildlife Service. Thanks to all of you for your support of conservation of the latest arrival of wolves around here." He felt Maya stir behind him and figured she wasn't thrilled that he'd taken over the position she probably intended to fulfill.

"Good to meet you, Ryan," said a petite woman with long and fluffy light brown hair streaked with deeper color. Hair that resembled a wolf's?

Ryan knew he was reaching a bit in an attempt to convince himself things were as he hoped.

But he might not be wrong...

"I'm Kathie Sharan," the woman continued. "This is my husband, Burt. We just recently moved here and bought the Corner Grocery Store down the street. We used to live in Montana, and there are wolves there, too. We've no problem with some showing up in this neighborhood. It's kind of cool, in fact."

Could that actually be why they'd moved here?

"Hi, Ryan." Burt, tall and thin with deep brown hair and a hint of a beard, edged next to his wife and held out his hand. His grip was firm as he shook Ryan's. "I hope you'll come visit our store while you're in town. You, too, Maya." He turned toward where she stood and held out his hand to her, as well.

A couple of other people near them also issued greetings that Ryan returned. Maya, too, and also Piers when Ryan introduced him as another employee of the federal fish and wildlife organization. And all of them made a fuss over a clearly pleased Rocky.

Even bartender Buck did so, as did the guy who'd been flirting with Maya—Trev Garlona. He'd introduced himself, as well.

So at least some of these wolf advocates had recently moved here and purchased businesses, intending to stay.

Of course Ryan could be completely wrong. They might have had different agendas when they decided to settle in Fritts Corner, nothing at all to do with wolves—or shifting.

But he had a feeling he would get to know some or all of them a lot better.

Maybe starting tonight.

For now, though, he needed to prepare, perhaps even to rest. He soon said goodbye to the gang of wolf supporters who'd joined them, and they all headed back to their seats—after Buck promised to refresh their drinks. The place remained busy, and the sound of conversations picked up once more. Other bartenders had remained active, so Ryan also inhaled the scent of different kinds of alcohol.

All seemed well again.

Even so, he asked Maya, who had also turned to go, "Where are you off to now?"

The people who'd given her a hard time were no longer in the bar. They surely wouldn't be waiting outside to give her a hard time—would they?

He'd rather be there for her, though, just in case.

"I'm heading back to my hotel," she said. "I may even take a nap. It's stressful to give a talk, and to act happy and energetic and all…anyway, I'm glad how things have turned out so far and really appreciate your support."

"You're very welcome," he said, knowing his face mirrored her large smile. "How about if we walk with you?"

"Which hotel are you staying at?" Piers asked. He was now at Ryan's side and had taken Rocky's leash.

"The Washington Inn," she said, unsurprisingly naming the largest one in town.

"So are we," Piers said.

"Great," Ryan said. "Let's get on our way."

Maya saw Trev waving goodbye as she prepared to leave, and she briefly aimed a wave back at him. But her mind was on something else altogether.

Ryan, Rocky and Piers were all staying in the same hotel as she was.

How close was Ryan's room to hers? That question kept intruding into Maya's mind as they walked out.

No matter. They could be next door to each other and still be worlds apart.

They had to be. Sure, he was a great-looking guy. A nice guy who clearly wanted to walk with her to protect her in case those nasty folks who'd confronted her were still around. He didn't have to say so for her to know that.

But other than their love of wildlife, they most likely had nothing in common. Even if they did—well, she'd been involved with a guy not long ago who'd professed to love wild animals but acted like a jerk when it came to maintaining a relationship with a human being. He'd even publicly slammed WHaM.

She didn't need anything like that—especially since she'd soon go home to Denver and figured a guy with the US government would return to the DC area, far from her.

"I don't see your buddies out here," Ryan said. "Guess they decided not to harass you again."

"I sure hope so," she said. "Maybe they can start picking on each other instead." She admired the few buildings they passed. "This is such a cute town. Where do you live? Is it anything like this?"

"We live near Washington, DC, not Washington State," Ryan responded. Near it? Not in it? That made Maya wonder where, but before she could ask he got in his own question. "And you? Where are you from? Colorado? Isn't that where WHaM is headquartered?"

She acknowledged that it was, and they talked a bit more about her organization as they continued down the block, with Piers behind them.

Rocky trotted between Ryan and her, and she got a truly warm and fuzzy feeling about this short walk and the males near her, including the dog. In a minute they had reached her car and said goodbye.

And because she didn't have far to drive, she arrived at the Washington Inn about the same time as the two men and the dog did. Or maybe, driving slowly, she had unconsciously planned it that way.

The inn, like so many other buildings in town, was quaint, with multipaned windows and circular turrets. The concrete exterior looked substantial, though, and Maya figured it was either a much newer structure than it appeared, or it had been remodeled recently.

She parked in the lot beside it and walked quickly to the front—just as the others arrived, too. She joined them.

"Hi again," she said, waiting while Ryan stopped at the grassy area near the front with Rocky. "So where are your rooms?" she asked Ryan casually, as Piers preceded them inside.

"First floor, toward the back. It's a good spot to take Rocky into the yard if he needs to go. How about you?"

"Third floor," she said, "around there." She pointed toward the right, glad that the windows there indicated multiple rooms so she didn't exactly tell him which was hers.

They proceeded up the walkway to the steps and, crossing the porch, entered the quaint-looking lobby. There were
only a few people there, mostly in line at the reception
desk. Piers stood nearby reading a newspaper. He joined
them.

Ryan lifted his arm with the loop of the dog leash over
it and Piers slipped it off him. "You can put him in my
room," he told Piers. "I'll be right there." He then said to
Maya, "I'll walk you to your room, just in case."

In case her new enemies were around, she assumed.
She hadn't seen any sign of them on the road and didn't
really need Ryan accompanying her—she hoped—and
yet she didn't object.

They soon were in her room, which was as charming as
the rest of the inn. He even went inside, glancing around,
walking past the bed with a fluffy, lace-trimmed coverlet.

She had a momentary urge to ask him to stay. Just to
talk a little longer, of course. About wolves and other wildlife.

Not about a wild life. The guy was one delicious-looking
man and had started to get her internal juices flowing when
they were together. But he was mostly just a nice guy with
similar interests to hers. And he'd given no indication he
thought of her in any sexual or other way—a good thing.

That meant she didn't have to worry about any interest
on her part that could lead to disaster, as her recent relationship had.

Even so, she found herself asking, "So do you have any
plans for this evening?"

She couldn't quite read the odd look that quickly passed
over his face, replaced by a smile that almost appeared
pleased. "Sleeping," he said. "I intend to order in pizza
later for Piers and me. I brought food for Rocky. I'm already a bit tired and may do some hiking tomorrow, so I'll

go to bed early." He looked her over. "No offense intended, but you appear a little sleepy, too. Maybe you should do the same thing."

That had been what she was considering…unless they worked out a dinner date, which would undoubtedly be a bad idea.

She noticed that he didn't suggest that she join them for pizza, either.

"I just might do that," she said. As he walked to the door of her room she added, "Have a good evening. And thanks again for all your help."

Rocky was well trained, but even so he wasn't staying alone in Ryan's room that night.

No, right now Piers drove all three of them, in the sedan they had rented at the Sea-Tac International Airport, along the remote, twisty roads outside Fritts Corner, beyond the park and beneath the forest's overhanging trees to a clearing they had previously scouted out.

Near an area where wolves had been spotted over the past months.

The ride was bumpy, and Ryan was conscious of every jolt. It was getting close to twilight now.

It was nearly time.

And since this was the night of a full moon, Ryan would be shifting.

But thanks to that wonderful elixir that had been formulated and modified over time by Major Drew Connell, the founder of Alpha Force, and other members, Ryan would not only have some limited choice as to when the shifting started and a lot of choice about when he shifted back, but he would additionally retain his human cognition.

Unlike the other shifters he anticipated meeting on this night.

"Here we are," Piers said, stopping the car. Rocky, in the backseat, let out a small woof, as if he understood where they were and what was about to happen.

This wasn't his first time, after all, to be around when Ryan shifted—and it wouldn't be his last.

Piers parked, and Ryan immediately exited the car. There was hardly any light in the sky, and the clearing was vast enough that Ryan knew the full moon would soon appear.

There were plenty of times in his past when that would have caused him to shift into a feral wolf as soon as darkness fell. But now—

Now, he couldn't have been more delighted that Alpha Force had found and recruited him into its amazing military unit. He was starting to give back, including by being here. And he loved it.

If he was correct about the nature of at least some of the people here, he might even be able to give back more to his cherished organization by recruiting others who, in turn, could add to its very special mission.

He'd already done some of that while being trained and working directly with other shifters located by senior Alpha Force officers.

Piers pulled the large backpack out of the trunk and approached across the hard dirt of the clearing to the area several feet from the car where Ryan had stopped. Ryan began to remove his clothing, even as Piers extracted the cooler in the backpack and from it one of the vials of elixir that they had brought. He also pulled out the light that, turned on, resembled the light of the full moon, although, since it would not be necessary tonight, he returned it to the backpack.

"You doing okay?" Ryan's efficient assistant now stood

there with the vial in one of his large hands, assessing his superior officer.

"I'm fine, Piers. And how are you?" Ryan kept his tone light, even though he knew exactly what he was about to go through.

The elixir helped shifters in so many ways—but nothing could totally eliminate the discomfort of a shift from human to animal form—and back again.

"Okay, buddy. The moon's a-rising. Let's get this thing started, okay?" The stocky young guy grinned as if he couldn't wait for his superior officer's shift to start. And maybe he couldn't.

Ryan was now nude. He felt the pulsing sensations inside him that presaged a natural shift.

It was definitely time for the elixir.

"Bring it on," he told Piers, reaching out for the vial.

His initial shift was over. He was standing again, this time on four canine legs, the discomfort behind him.

Just in time, he thought—since he heard a howl in the distance. Followed by another, and some barks. They all sounded far away, but he would have heard them even without his enhanced hearing.

Shifters? Most likely. Natural wolves might howl and bark like that, of course. But why would they do so tonight? And not just one or two now, but several of them.

Ryan could tell—thanks to that enhanced hearing—not only the direction from which the sounds came, but he had a sense of distance, too.

The others were likely in the hillsides here, beneath the trees, farther from town, perhaps farther along the road where Piers had driven them only a short while earlier.

Rocky remained in the car. Piers had returned to it to

sleep, to wait for Ryan's return early in the morning, when he would naturally shift back on this night of the full moon.

He also had some choice about when to change back, even under the full moon. But if he did not choose when, it would occur once the sun started to rise.

Another set of excited howls. They caused more excitement in Ryan, as well.

Time for him to run through these woods, let his wolfen side loose. Revel in his very special gift, his talent, the other, only partly human feature of his life.

His shifting ability.

He felt his mouth move as he allowed himself to express his emotion in what would have been a smile had he not been shifted.

He aimed one glance toward the car where his companions now sat and waited for him.

And then he ran into the woods.

Maya hadn't been sleeping deeply, though she had been in bed for a while, reading at first, then nodding off.

But her mind had been tossing around all that had happened to her that day.

Her talk. The confrontations with those wild animal–haters.

The support she had received from Ryan, backed up by some of the other people in this small town near which wolves had begun to appear again.

And—

Hey. What was that? Was she imagining things because she was thinking about the local sightings of wolves?

Maybe, but she thought she'd heard not only some canine barking but also a howl. Yes! She had. It was followed by another.

And now there were even more of them, somewhere

way in the distance. But close enough to be heard here, right in the downtown area of Fritts Corner.

She froze. If she heard them, so did those wolf-haters. She wasn't in any kind of law enforcement. She had no weapons.

But might the US Fish and Wildlife Service be able to help?

She hadn't gotten Ryan's phone number, not even his room number, but she felt stressed enough to use the hotel's phone to try to call his room even now, in the middle of the night. She did reach a hotel operator—after waiting several minutes. And then, when she was connected to his room, no one answered.

She tried the same with his friend Piers, but again no answer.

He'd said he was going to bed early—but maybe the sounds had awakened him, and now she couldn't join up with him to check things out.

Heck. Maybe there was nothing she could do. Maybe the wolves wouldn't really be in danger.

But if nothing else, she could bring her camera—just in case.

She'd already risen from her bed.

Now, she threw her clothes on, grabbed her purse and camera, and rushed out the door.

Chapter 4

He loved it, reveled in it, this unleashed, unfettered ability to run on four powerful legs, beyond the park, up hillsides and within woods that were entirely new to him, in darkness lit only by the full moon.

To chase in the direction where he would soon see others who were like him in one way or the other: wolves that were born as canines, or that were humans in shifted form.

Those whose howls he still heard—

But he nearly stopped running as he heard something else. Voices that weren't wolfen but human.

Male and female voices in the distance, low but audible to him, with his highly enhanced keen hearing while in wolf form.

And that wasn't all. He knew who was talking. He slowed his pace and inhaled and smelled, from the same direction, those humans with scents he had first sensed that day but not as intense as he could inhale now, as a wolf.

The smells included those of the two people named Fritts. And more. Another human scent emanated from that same area.

But they weren't the only ones.

A different scent, but no sound, came from near them, as well. An aroma that was entirely familiar—now—to the wolf who was Ryan.

The scent belonging to Maya.

None of the humans should be here, not with wolves of any origin around, here in the woods in near darkness—except for that brilliant moon.

Most especially not Maya.

Was she not aware of the potential danger from the wolves she also revered and wanted to protect? She had sounded so wise, so knowledgeable before, when she had spoken to an audience and talked with individuals. But did she ignore her own wisdom when wolves were around?

And if they were shifters, without having access to his special Alpha Force elixir they would not have human cognition. They could be just as dangerous as wild wolves to mere people.

And what about those other people? Would they present a danger to the wolves—and, perhaps, to Maya, too? Or were they themselves in danger?

He turned to move more purposefully in the direction from which he scented Maya.

If Maya wasn't cautious, he would have to be so on her behalf.

He wanted to protect them all, the wolves and the woman, and perhaps the other people, as well. If the wolves harmed them, then other humans might hurt those wolves.

But there was only one of him. And if he had to choose who to protect, he knew which it had to be.

* * *

Maya had arrived at the edge of the woods, and now debated what to do.

She had known from the moment she had heard the distant howls and barks, while still inside the hotel, the direction in which she had to go, and she had hurriedly driven that way. When she parked her car and got onto the sidewalk at the park where she had given her presentation, she'd stopped to listen even more.

The sounds now came from somewhere to her right, in the woods beyond the park. She had hurried in that direction.

At the time, she had felt somewhat surprised to find herself alone here. Surely other people heard the sounds and could figure out where they came from. And some of the people who'd attended her talk had seemed fascinated, too, by the reappearance of wolves in this area.

Plus some had claimed to be part of the media. Were they interested in wolves or not?

Was she the only one who hoped to actually see them? Or was everyone afraid?

Well, no matter. Although…well, she wouldn't have minded some company.

Too bad she hadn't reached Ryan. She couldn't help assuming he was already outside, also trying to get a glimpse of the wolves. If so, they could have joined up, banded together, safety in numbers. And being with him in the middle of the night would be practical, nothing to do with the fact she found the man attractive.

No matter. For now, all she really hoped for was to see those wolves herself.

The air was cool, and the intermittent sound of the soft wind, plus occasional cars in the distance, were the only sounds she heard at this moment as she stood there.

Still at the edge of the park, she looked beyond the streetlights behind her into the near darkness of what lay ahead. The only light came from above, the brilliance of the full moon.

She carried a special flashlight that she could make as bright or dim as she wanted, as well as a state-of-the-art small camera that took still photos and videos. Mostly what she wanted was to observe and film the wolves from a distance, without them getting too interested in her.

Another howl sounded, followed by some yips and a couple of additional howls. How many wolves were out there?

She would have to be very cautious. Those wolves would sense her before she could get close. And there was no way she could communicate to them that she loved wildlife, only wanted to see and photograph them.

This was probably a bad idea—but it might be her best opportunity to see them.

Here, at the end of the park, the grass gave way to low foliage at first that soon rose to become mountainous woodlands, with trees relatively close together and dry underbrush below. The area was fairly dark, since the treetops erased the light from the moon above.

Maya gave herself one more chance to stop, to back off. But only for a minute. Then, she pulled her flashlight out of her purse, set it for its dimmest setting and started out.

And heard another wolf howl.

She smiled and carefully started forward. She heard her own footsteps on the dried underbrush but not much more. Was she still heading in the right direction?

At least she went in a straight line, so she would be able to find her way back. Even run back, if she had to...

She reached a clearing. Was that a human voice she heard somewhere ahead, off to the side?

Maybe she should go back…

But that was when she heard the crackling sound of dried growth being stomped on by feet—canine feet?

Was she really going to get to see a wolf? Yes!

And in fact, there one was. She upped the intensity of her flashlight as she aimed her camera at it, just as another wolf joined it.

They were both running toward her. Still filming, she looked around. Fortunately, she stood beside a nice, wide tree trunk. Maybe she should get behind it—

But the wolf at the front growled, ran even faster toward her.

Was it going to attack?

"I just wanted to see you," she cried aloud, knowing how ridiculous that was. As if the creature could understand she was on its side, doing her job, learning about it. Quickly, she moved so the tree was between the wolf and her. But where was the other one?

She heard some barks then that sounded angry. Feral growls, just as another wolf emerged from the woods and attacked the wolf that approached her. The third wolf, behind that one, leaped into the fray, as well.

"No. Please. Don't hurt each other," Maya cried out, but she wasn't stupid. Not entirely, she thought. She used the opportunity to light her flashlight beam to the fullest and run back through the woods in the direction from which she'd come.

She glanced back once, though. The fight had wound down, at least somewhat. One wolf—the attacker?—was facing the other two, crouched as if ready to leap onto them again and growling deeply.

The others stood warily but did not appear as if they were ready to attack again.

Which made Maya smile, at least a little, as she turned again and hurried toward the edge of the park.

Yes, she'd been foolish. But she'd seen wolves. Three wolves. And she'd gotten videos of them.

She wasn't hurt, and the canines appeared to be okay, too. This was definitely a memorable night.

He remained in a crouch, growling and teaching the others he faced who was alpha, at least for now.

Their scents were strong, and not entirely wolfen.

Then they, too, were shifters. That didn't make them less feral, less likely to attack him.

And it wouldn't have prevented them from attacking that foolish human woman.

But at least he had been able to save her from harm.

And soon, tomorrow, when he had shifted back and was in human form, he would find an opportunity to chide her, and more.

To warn her never to put herself in such a situation again.

He was unlikely to be there the next time.

The other wolves had apparently had enough. They both issued loud warning growls back to him, then turned and loped back into the darkness of the forest behind them.

Good. He, too, returned to the darkness but in a different direction.

He wanted to get a better sense of these surroundings and where the wolves by blood might be—and whether these shifters might be in any danger.

Only later, when morning started to arrive, would he shift back.

She was out of the woods, so to speak, and onto the lawn constituting the park. Maya smiled, stopped walking and turned to look back at the dark woodlands she had just left.

The wolves were still there, somewhere. Hopefully, none of them had been injured by the others.

She had seen them, photographed them, and she was fine. More than fine.

Too bad she had no way of rewarding that one wolf who'd confronted the others and allowed her to get away. He surely had an agenda of his own that had nothing to do with her, but she still appreciated it.

With a sigh, she turned and started walking briskly back to where she'd parked. Good night, wolves, she thought as she got into her car.

There were some other cars on the road now. She even saw a few people exit a bar on the far side of the street, though not the one she'd visited before.

Had anyone else heard the wolves?

Did anyone else in this town really care?

Surely the answer was yes, at least those who'd come to her presentation or commented on it afterward, like that bartender she had met. What was his name? Lesterman?

Or maybe the other people who'd been there, the Sharans, and that lady, Ivy, who had seen a couple of wolves. They'd at least seemed interested.

And her new *buddy* Trev. He'd at least expressed some interest in wildlife at her talk. Had he heard the wolves from wherever he was? Did he give a damn?

Then there had been Ryan, and his friend Piers. They'd surely have been interested.

She'd thought she heard some human voices. Could it have been theirs? Were they also out here checking out those howls?

If so they'd surely left Rocky in one of their rooms. The dog might have been particularly at risk when wolves were around.

She parked behind the hotel and went inside.

She felt so happy and excited that she wished she could shout about her amazing evening to the world.

Or at least to people who might give a damn.

But it was way too late to call Ryan in case she had guessed wrong and he was in bed at this late hour. Nor could she call any of her colleagues at WHaM, since this area was on Pacific time and everyone else would be an hour or more later.

With a sigh, Maya made her way through the empty, dimly lit lobby and headed up to her room for the night.

And figured she wouldn't sleep at all.

But she did sleep, though not at first.

Once she'd gotten into the antique-style bed in her hotel room, Maya had visualized those wolves once more. All three of them.

Were there more in the area? The return of wolves to various parts of the state of Washington had been slow and sparse, especially around here. Even so...

How many? Despite her duty to take census, she didn't intentionally begin to count wolves, like sheep, but she knew there were more than three.

Finally, smiling to herself, she actually relaxed. And slept.

Still, when she woke, the same visions and questions captivated her mind.

Well, somehow she would find a way to use it all, to continue to inform locals who were otherwise unaware that wolves had returned to the area—and how wonderful it was. First thing, she would check her video to see how it looked, since she would show her results to as many people as she could.

And expound even more about wildlife—probably without revealing she'd put herself in danger.

But wouldn't it be fun to let the world know she'd been saved by one of those wolves? Sure, but then she'd have to let everyone know that she'd felt threatened by the others.

Somehow, she finished showering and dressing and prepared to visit the local world again today.

She looked at her video, thrilled at what she'd captured, yet a bit uneasy that it did show the wild and potentially dangerous nature of those feral canines. But, heck, that was who and what they were. People could admire them as wildlife, stressing the *wild* part. She certainly did.

She didn't exactly have a plan, but first thing would be to find somewhere to grab breakfast, hopefully someplace busy. Maybe she could start expounding on her latest lesson about the visiting wolves there.

She pulled on a nice blue shirt over jeans, then looked out her hotel room window. Sun shone between an irregular blanket of clouds. She looked down through the partial brightness toward the street, trying to recall what restaurants she'd seen in the area—and noticed that Ryan and Piers were out there walking Rocky on the Washington Inn's narrow lawn next to the sidewalk.

Hey, no matter that she hadn't reached them before. Now, they would be good targets for starting to tell her story about the night before. They'd at least be interested.

She put her camera into her purse and headed out the door. Not wanting to wait for the elevator, she walked the couple of flights of stairs down to the decorative lobby and hurried through it to the door, then outside and down the walkway to the sidewalk. She looked around and saw the men and dog still on the lawn but near the end of the block. She headed briskly in their direction, noting that a few other people milled around outside the charming structure, probably additional tourists who were staying there.

Now wasn't a good time to stop and be friendly and

talk up wildlife to strangers, she realized—despite how strongly the urge shoved at her.

Before she could get to Ryan, though, Trev exited a car parked at the curb and hurried up to her. "Good morning," he said. "How are you today?" He aimed his geeky grin at her again, and she briefly smiled back at him. He was dressed in a white button-down shirt tucked into blue jeans.

"Okay," she said. "Have a good day." She turned away, ready to hurry off toward her goal.

"You, too. You know, I heard about your organization WHaM before. I saw online, on the WHaM website, that you were going to give a talk here, and that's why I came to town."

She stopped for a moment. "Then you don't live in Fritts Corner?"

"No, but I wanted to hear you."

"That's very nice," she said, meaning it. She'd have to tell her coworkers that the small mention they'd put up on the website was achieving what they wanted, at least a little—attracting people to learn more about them, and wildlife. "Then you care about wildlife?"

"I think about wildlife a lot," he said.

"And did you hear the wolf howls last night?"

"I did, from my hotel room. They must have been pretty close to town."

"You could say that," she said.

"Hey, would you join me for breakfast?" He looked so eager that she considered saying yes to this wildlife aficionado who'd come here because of WHaM. But that wasn't how she wanted to spend her morning.

"Sorry, I can't. I have other plans." And she did, even if they didn't work out the way she hoped. "I hope to see you later, though." Maybe. Especially if she had an opportunity to give another talk on behalf of WHaM.

For now, she said goodbye to the guy, who appeared disappointed. She felt bad, at least a little, as she strode away. But if he truly was flirting with her, and not just because he liked WHaM, she didn't want to encourage him.

And right now she wanted to find out if Ryan and Piers had heard the wolves, too. They were the ones who'd been defending her and cheering on the return of those canines to this area. And if they had heard the wolves—well, she would enjoy the opportunity to describe her own adventure last night to them.

Should she tell others, too? Maybe. What she could do, after she reached Ryan and his crew, was to talk loudly enough that people around them could eavesdrop and hear it all.

Before she reached them, Ryan looked toward her. She couldn't quite interpret his smile, though. Oh, yes, there was a smile on that really great-looking face of his, and yet it didn't look exactly humorous or welcoming or glad to see her, the way she expected. Well, hoped, at least.

Instead…she couldn't quite interpret that smile, but the first thing she thought it conveyed was irritation, maybe. Scolding? Wry, certainly.

"Good morning," she called out, feeling somewhat annoyed herself. Why should she have to interpret this man's expressions?

"Good morning, Maya," Piers said. The smile on the shorter, heavier guy's face looked a whole lot more friendly. "Did you have a good night's sleep?"

"Yes, I did. But not before—"

"Have you had breakfast yet?" Ryan interrupted. "If not, why don't you join us?"

Somehow his words, and his now-challenging expression, definitely turned Maya into the one who was irritated. Maybe she should tell him she already had plans and go find Trev again.

But she really wanted to tell them about her night and at least find out if they'd heard the wolves.

She first hurried toward Rocky. "Good morning, boy." She greeted the friendly wolflike dog by patting his head and scratching behind his alert ears. "And, no." She turned to face the men. "I haven't had breakfast yet. I'll be glad to join you. I had a very interesting evening and would love to tell you about it."

"And we'd love to hear about it," Ryan said. The expression on his face didn't change.

"How about Andy and Family's?" Piers gave the name of a restaurant Maya had noticed a couple of blocks from the hotel, the opposite direction from the park.

"Sounds great to me." Maya strolled around Ryan to stand beside Piers. She'd walk beside him, and hopefully Rocky, too, till they got there. Her conversation with Piers was likely to be a lot friendlier than if she spent the time with Ryan. Although she'd like to understand why. "Let's go!"

Chapter 5

As he walked along the sidewalk behind his three companions toward his upcoming breakfast, Ryan wondered if this was a good idea.

Oh, yes.

What he'd really wanted to do, upon first seeing the lovely, upbeat—and foolish—woman was to grab her by the shoulders and shake her and tell her she could have been killed.

But he would give too much away by doing that. No, he'd have to be a whole lot more subtle, yet still find a way to get that chastisement across to her.

The sky was somewhat overcast this September day, the air a little brisk, although it would warm up later. He felt warm enough now, though, partly because of his suppressed anger—and concern.

What would have happened if she'd been attacked by the

wolves? Those wolves would have undoubtedly been considered feral and dangerous and possibly hunted and killed.

And would Maya have survived such an attack? To his surprise, that mattered as much to him as—maybe more than—whether the wolves who might be fellow shifters would have gotten out of the situation okay.

They reached the restaurant. Unsurprisingly, Andy and Family's was family style, and on this Friday morning it was crowded.

"Hey, there are a lot of people here," Piers said unnecessarily. He'd turned to look back at Ryan, clearly giving him the opportunity to decide to go elsewhere.

"The food must be okay." Ryan gave a brief nod to his aide. He was fine with staying here to eat.

"Probably." Piers glanced toward Maya, who was still beside him, but instead of giving her the opportunity to say no Ryan moved past her to the glass front door.

Sure, they'd have to wait even to tell the people seating customers how many of them there were. But at the moment, having a lot of people around to eavesdrop on, after last night and the full moon and those howls and barks, could be pretty interesting.

And maybe he and Piers would be able to determine what to do next, who else to get chummy with, to confirm that at least some of those wolves were shifters.

They needed to go chat with the people they'd suspected were shifters anyway. If they had more ammunition, all the better.

But he believed he had a good idea of the wolves' human identities thanks to their scents while he—and they—were shifted.

Would the Sharans be here for breakfast today, for example? It didn't matter. Ryan had believed it was their scents he'd smelled last night. But he wouldn't confront them here anyway.

He'd also had Piers check online to learn if there'd been any indication that the media—those who'd claimed to be members yesterday at Maya's talk or others—had mentioned Maya, or last night's wolves, in any paper or blog or broadcast somewhere but he had found nothing. Not yet, at least.

"What's the wait time?" Maya asked the middle-aged lady holding menus who'd come by to check on how many people there were in each party.

"We're pretty fast," the lady said. "Probably no more than five minutes. You can wait right here and we've got an area on the back patio where we can seat you with your dog."

Five minutes up here, in the crowd, with lots of gabbing people even before they took their seats. That could work in their favor, Ryan figured.

"Let's wait," he said, looking first at Piers. He turned to Maya and asked, "Are you okay with that?"

"Sure," she said, then repeated, "Let's wait."

Standing behind the rest of her group in the waiting area line leading up to the rows of tables, Maya couldn't help looking around at this crowd. The place resembled nearly every other busy family style restaurant she'd ever eaten at, with servers in the aisles and tables filled with people of all ages, some dressed as if they were heading to work on this Friday morning, and others as casual as she was in her shirt and jeans.

No, not all ages, she contradicted herself. The kids were fairly young. Their older counterparts might already be at school for the day.

But the conversations created a low-key roar, and she

also heard the clink of silverware on plates and the clunk of glasses on tables.

Hey, if she didn't know better, she'd wonder if her visit with wolves had elevated her own senses the way theirs were—like her hearing. But she had no doubt they'd enjoy the aromas around here more.

In fact, she looked toward Rocky. Sure enough, his canine nose was elevated and sniffing and—

She glanced up to find that Ryan was smiling at her, and this time it seemed genuine. Surely he couldn't read her mind...could he?

"You hungry?" he asked. "I am."

Apparently he couldn't   although his question was definitely pertinent here. And her answer, partly thanks to the low-level aromas she could inhale, was, "Me, too. This is a good place to be hungry. But what about Rocky? Will he also eat here?"

"He had his breakfast back at the inn," Ryan said, "but I won't be surprised if he talks one or more of us into giving him some of what we're eating, too."

"Bet on it." Piers was also smiling but his gaze drifted around the busy dining area as if he hoped to glom on to a table they could request. Which would have been unlikely even if they didn't have Rocky along, since, although a few more people had been seated since their arrival, there were still a couple more groups ahead of them.

Maya made herself tear her gaze away from Ryan's great-looking, angular face with just a hint of beard shadow, as if he hadn't fully shaved that morning. Though those dark brown eyes looked a little tired, they seemed to be studying hers. Why? Hadn't he slept well—and had he been out looking for wolves? And now, was he trying to figure out if she was telling the truth, that she really was hungry?

Absurd. And yet she thought she sensed some kind of question, or message, in his expression.

Her mind began churning around possible ways to lead into a conversation with him, get him to reveal what he'd done last night and what he was thinking. But before she got very far the restaurant hostess invited the last groups ahead of them in line to follow her.

They should be next to get a table—at least assuming the patio area designated as appropriate for Rocky to join them had a vacancy.

Rocky. He'd been sitting, examining the air around them and behaving like a well-trained dog, despite his resemblance to wild wolves. But something, maybe the movement of the people ahead of them, apparently got his attention, and he stood.

Ryan immediately tautened the leash attached to his collar, drawing closer to the dog. "Easy, boy," he said.

Maya noticed then the people hurrying toward them from between the nearest tables, people who'd been at the bar yesterday and indicated their support of what WHaM stood for. The Sharans. Kathie and Burt, right?

Kathie was ahead of Burt and she looked first at Rocky, then at the people with him.

"Hi," the short, attractive woman said as she reached them, smiling toward Maya. "So you brought that adorable dog who resembles the wolves you talk about to breakfast with you?" She moved her hand slowly in Rocky's direction as if making sure he knew she was friendly.

Rocky started to rear up on his hind legs, but Ryan, pulling the leash gently and also pushing him with his other hand, got him to settle back down. "Sit, boy," Ryan said, and the dog obeyed, though he began sniffing the air even more than Maya had noticed him doing before. Interesting. She didn't smell even a hint of a difference in the food aromas around them and wondered what Rocky smelled.

He pulled sideways again when Burt, a beefy guy with a short chin and long nose, got close and put out his hand, too, as if he also wanted to pat the dog. Rocky seemed pretty interested in these people. Maybe they were the reason his sniffing had grown more pronounced, and Maya wondered what they had just eaten.

"I'm delighted to have Rocky's company for breakfast," Maya said. "Oh, and Ryan's and Piers's, too." She lifted her eyebrows as she passed her gaze over the two men, waiting for their reaction.

Surprisingly, neither was looking at her. Ryan had one hand on Rocky and was watching him, and Piers was regarding the couple who'd just joined them here as they'd been leaving the restaurant.

Maya sensed something going on that she didn't follow, but no matter. She'd ask about it later.

For now, she wanted to say something nice to these friendly folks who appeared to love wildlife. "You said before that you own a grocery store, right?"

Kathie nodded. "Yes, we do. We sell pet food there, too." She grinned as she looked toward Ryan, obviously knowing who was in charge of Rocky.

"We brought enough for a while," Ryan responded, "but we'll still check out what you've got."

"Well, I'm sure I'll need some snacks while I'm here," Maya said. "I'll definitely come to visit your store." And buy something there, in support of these people who seemed truly in favor of the idea that wolves had returned to this area.

The hostess returned then. "We've got a table for you on the patio, where your dog is welcome," she said, menus still plentiful in her arms.

"We'll let you go now," Kathie said. "We've got to get back to the store anyway."

"See you there later," Maya said, earning another smile from Kathie.

But before Kathie and Burt had taken more than a few steps, another woman stepped in front of them, blocking them—Vinnie Fritts.

Rocky, still under Ryan's control, remained standing— and growled, not a good thing, Maya thought.

But Maya considered growling herself, and more, when Vinnie began talking. "How dare you bring that damn dog here!" she spat toward Ryan. "And how dare any of you say that it's a good thing that wolves are back in this area? What happened last night is at least partly your fault, damn you."

Maya didn't really want to ask but said anyway, "What happened last night?"

"Those damned wolves. Did you hear them howling? My husband did, and he decided to go check them out, make sure the town was safe. And it wasn't. *He* wasn't."

Maya had a sinking sensation that she knew what was coming, but she had to ask again, "What happened?"

"Morton was attacked. Mauled. Fortunately, he's going to be okay, no thanks to you. But those horrible creatures don't belong here. One way or another, they have to go."

Ryan couldn't help it. His first reaction, rather than sympathy—feigned or otherwise—was to glance at the Sharans. They were blocked from leaving by Vinnie but now faced her back as she looked furiously toward Maya.

He felt fairly certain that the Sharans were the wolves he'd confronted last night to protect Maya, shifters with no human cognition or control. He couldn't recognize their scent for sure while he, and they, were in human form, but he did sense that they weren't ordinary humans—and Rocky's reaction to them also suggested a different aroma from a regular person's. The dog hadn't acted that way when they'd been around the Sharans before, but he might sense now that they had recently shifted. Did all cover dogs have that ability? Ryan wasn't sure.

The Sharans' reaction was what his should have been. Both maneuvered around Vinnie so she could see them. They began expressing how sorry they were to hear of Morton's injuries. No admission that they'd had any part in them, of course. But they acted like concerned fellow townsfolk.

Even if they were the cause of the man's injuries, they might not even know it, since they wouldn't have had human awareness—but might they have recalled their attack anyway?

Ryan recalled a lot of what he'd done while shifted before he had joined Alpha Force and learned about the elixir—mostly visualizing, not consciously thinking about what he'd done, or analyzing it.

But would the Sharans? Assuming it had been them. There were probably some truly feral wolves in the area, too—and possibly more shifters.

"Thanks," Vinnie muttered at their sympathetic words, but she still kept her focus on Maya.

Heck, Maya was the last one here who should get any blame for a wolf attack. Ryan moved around this group so Rocky was behind him. He whispered to Piers, as he passed, to take the dog to the table the hostess had found for them. "We'll catch up."

Then he joined Maya at her side. Her expression appeared stricken. Horrified. And remorseful.

"I'm so sorry," she finally managed to say to Vinnie.

"But—well, I did remind people that wolves are wild. I gather that poor Morton was outside, and—"

"Like I said, he went out when he heard those howls last night. He wanted to make sure that those damned wolves, wherever they were, were not about to hurt anyone. I don't know exactly how it happened. Maybe he was protecting another person. Maybe he just happened to cross the wolves' path at the wrong time. But fortunately he yelled and ran and somehow got away from them. I'd been worried about him so I called Carlo Silling and he picked me up in his car and tried to follow where the howls were, too. When we heard Morton yell we went after him and got him to the hospital."

"Is he going to be all right?" Maya asked.

"Yeah, we think so. No thanks to you."

At Maya's cringe, Ryan stepped between Vinnie and her. "That's enough. We're all sorry that your husband was injured, but Maya's right. She did warn people that wild wolves are...well, wild. She didn't encourage anyone to face them."

But with herself...? He looked down at her then, attempting to put a chiding expression on his face, but only for a moment.

For now.

"Yeah, they are," Vinnie said. "They're dangerous. They don't belong here. And if they stay around here, near Fritts Corner, well, yeah, they're supposedly protected under the law. But I know we can get around that if we figure out which ones attacked my husband. And if that kind of thing happens again you can be certain we'll do everything possible to make sure none ever gets near this town again."

She pivoted and nearly knocked over some people in line behind them who weren't hiding the fact they were eavesdropping.

"That's such a shame," Kathie Sharan said. "No one likes to hear that, especially not those of us who care about wildlife." She looked at Maya, and Ryan thought he saw tears in her eyes. In both women's eyes, in fact.

"But she shouldn't threaten any protected species," Burt Sharan interjected, putting his arm around his wife.

"No, she shouldn't," Maya said, "though I can certainly understand her position." Her head drooped—and Ryan found himself beside her, his arm around her the way Burt had done with Kathie.

He felt something amazing, something indescribable, when Maya turned and put her head on his shoulder. He faced her, held her even closer, wanting to comfort her— and more. His whole body was reacting to her closeness. And it didn't hurt knowing that this woman was someone who gave a damn about wolves.

But Ryan's shoulders stiffened at that thought. She cared about wolves, sure—but what would she think about people who turned into wolves, and back again?

Most regular humans, unless they'd had contact with shifters, didn't believe in them. And once they had something like that, which they considered weird and paranormal and scary, happen within their consciousness, they backed away.

Might even become particularly fearful of those creatures, real or shifted.

Even so, for now, he didn't loosen his grip.

But he couldn't help wondering how Maya would react knowing that the wolves who'd nearly attacked her last night were likely shifters.

Or that he was a shifter, too.

Chapter 6

How could she be so very aware of this man's nearness? His arms around her.

His lower parts hard as he pressed against her.

Absurd to even think about it. He was simply being nice. Kind. Sympathetic.

She shouldn't need sympathy. Morton Fritts did. She felt just terrible about what had happened to him, as if it was her fault.

But she hadn't brought the wolves here. She was merely an advocate, excited that a wonderful protected and endangered species appeared to be making a resurgence here.

Enough of a resurgence that she, perhaps acting foolish in her delight, had nearly been attacked, too.

If anyone should have been mauled, it was her.

"Thanks," she finally said in as decisive a voice as she could muster. She pulled back, immediately feeling somewhat bereft as Ryan no longer held her, no longer touched her. But it was better this way. "Let's go find our table—although I'm not very hungry now."

"Don't let any of this get to you." Ryan's tone sounded like an order, and she looked up into his face. His brows were knitted, but there was something in his expression that suggested caring. She started to smile, though a bit weakly she figured—but then he added, "Of course I gather you also did something as foolish as Morton Fritts, but you're just lucky you weren't hurt, too."

She took a step back, bumping into someone standing there in line. She excused herself but didn't take her gaze off Ryan.

How did he know that? She hadn't left a message when she'd tried calling him at the hotel. And all she'd really said on the subject this morning was that she'd had an interesting night.

Still, under the circumstances—the howls and barks in the distance and her obvious love of wolves—he could certainly have guessed what she'd done.

And since he apparently hadn't been in his room when she called last night, maybe he had done the same thing. And maybe he had seen her, though she hadn't seen him.

She needed some answers. "Yes," she said, "I'm lucky, and maybe you are, too. Did you do anything after you heard those howls last night?"

When he frowned and opened his mouth to reply, she shook her head. "Let's go sit down and order breakfast—and we can each tell our reactions to those sounds and what we did about them."

Okay, so he'd gone a little too far in his initial chastisement of Maya. So what?

He didn't have to get into specifics.

As they made their way between tables, with him in

front, Ryan spotted Piers sitting at a table outside just beyond the glass door. He couldn't see Rocky at first but
figured the dog had been there long enough to relax and
lie down on the patio.

"There they are," he said and finished leading Maya
to the table.

Rocky stood up, and Ryan couldn't help smiling at the
way Maya immediately went over and petted him before
taking her seat facing Piers. That was a good thing, since
one of the remaining chairs had its back to the far patio
wall, and if Ryan sat there he'd be able to keep an eye on
the crowd.

Ears, too—although he hoped he didn't regret too much
that he was there as a human, with limited ability to eavesdrop. But if someone happened to mention the word *wolf*
he was sure he would hear it.

Piers picked up the menus near him on the tabletop.
Ryan noticed he'd already gotten a cup of coffee. As he
handed a menu to Ryan, Piers looked at him quizzically,
as if asking what he'd missed.

But he'd heard the worst of it before heading to the table:
Morton Fritts had apparently been attacked by a wolf.

Ryan didn't want to bring that up now. There was nothing they could do over breakfast to research which type
of wolf had attacked the man, let alone fix that situation.

As a result, he just gave a brief shrug and opened his
menu. "Great! They have a good selection, and I'm hungry." Which he actually was, after his busy night on the
hillside.

Not to mention the energy used for shifting. That
burned a lot of calories.

As he read the menu, he did hear the word *wolf* and several times with his heightened hearing. He allowed himself to glance in those directions. Other seated diners, both

here and inside, seemed to be discussing the events of last night—at least the howls, since he heard that word a few times, too.

He also heard the word *attack* at least once...

News had apparently spread about Morton Fritts. Not that it was likely to be hushed up for any reason—not even by shifters, if they were the source of the problem. They could discuss it while in human form, but would they know who did it—shifters or not? And if shifters, which ones were involved?

But with all the various conversations, many of which seemed to be on that subject, and the fact that there was a curious woman at his side so he couldn't simply sit there listening, Ryan gave up on the possibility of learning much that was useful right away.

Nor did he get any sense, via scent or conversation, that anyone here was a shifter—not that his belief was conclusive.

He decided to order eggs with sausage and toast. Good thing he figured that out fairly quickly since their server, a thirtysomething woman who looked like she'd been at this for a while, came right over to their table for their orders.

Maya asked for only toast and decaf. When the server was gone, she looked toward Ryan. "Did you go outside, too, after you heard the howls?"

Ryan knew he had to be cautious about how he responded. But he'd already hinted that he was aware she hadn't stayed in her room.

Not that she'd recognized him. Sure, he had chased the other wolves away from her, but he didn't think she had a clue that any of them were shifters.

Before he responded, though, he glanced toward Piers and grinned, knowing his aide would take his cue and keep any answers on his part consistent with Ryan's.

"Yes, we did hear those howls and all and went out for a little while," Ryan said. "As representatives of US Fish and Wildlife, we wanted to gather as much information as we could. We wanted to listen, to try to determine how many animals, presumably wolves, were howling and from what direction. We left Rocky in our car since he wouldn't necessarily follow a safety protocol and stay with us rather than pulling away to chase whatever was making those sounds." He glanced down at the dog, who once more was lying on the patio.

Ryan then shot a glance toward Maya, just as the server came with her decaf and his high-octane coffee. She also refilled Piers's cup. "Your food will be up shortly," she said, then left.

"Did you hear any more when you were out there?" Maya asked. "See anything?"

"A few more distant howls and barks, but that was all—and we didn't see any wolves or other wildlife." He didn't need to tell the truth, of course. In fact, nearly everything he said was a lie. He happened to be one of those wolves. "How about you? Did you go outside to check things out, too?"

He needed to tread somewhat lightly here, but he'd already suggested he knew that answer.

"Yes," she said. "I wanted to see the wolves, so I followed the sounds as best I could."

"I gathered they were on the hillsides beyond the park. Was that what you determined?"

"Yes," Maya said. She sucked in her lips slightly as if in worry, and if Ryan read her expression correctly she was recalling all that had happened.

"And did you see any?" Her response would be what determined how he followed up.

"Yes," she said almost curtly. He gathered she didn't want to continue after that.

But Piers, great aide that he was, was the one to ask, "Really? What did you see?"

Her eyes narrowed, and then she looked down at the table. "They were beautiful," she said almost reverently.

Ryan shouldn't feel so happy to hear her words, her attitude. Maya might be one gorgeous woman with a laudable attitude toward wolves—but she had no idea who and what he was, along with the probability that there were at least a few others in this area.

She might not be so pleased about the proximity of wolves if she did.

"How many wolves did you see?" Piers continued. "Where were they? I assume you didn't get near any of them, right?"

Piers hadn't been close enough to see the encounter among Ryan and the two other wolves he believed to be shifters, but Ryan had filled him in once he had shifted back to human form—including how he had kept the wolves from attacking the lovely and foolish human who'd tracked them down.

"Well…" Maya looked toward Ryan as if attempting to judge how much he knew. He'd already suggested that she might have done something as foolish as Morton Fritts and was therefore lucky she'd not been hurt.

But he wasn't about to tell her why he believed that to be true.

He looked straight back into her soft hazel eyes. "Why don't you tell us what you did and what you saw?"

"Because I'm both happy and embarrassed about it."

Their food arrived then, and Maya looked pleased at the interruption. But a short while later, when they'd all taken their first bites of food—and Ryan had given Rocky a taste of his sausage—he said, "Okay, tell us about your night."

She took a deep breath and raised her light brown eyebrows as if she actually did feel discomfited about her anticipated response. But she described having followed the howls and other canine sounds into the woods, using her flashlight and camera—and being confronted by a couple of wolves.

"But then there was a third one," she said, "who distracted the two that seemed as if they might attack me. I ran away then."

"I hope you sent thoughts of thanks to the wolf that helped you," Piers said, taking another sip of his coffee before glancing toward Ryan.

Ryan couldn't help a small smile although he aimed it at his own cup rather than toward his aide.

"I definitely did," Maya said. "He might have saved me from…from being mauled like Morton Fritts."

"Quite possibly," Ryan agreed. "You need to be careful. In fact, once we find out the details of the attack on Fritts, I'd suggest you give another presentation on behalf of WHaM, or just in general if that's better for you. You should emphasize to people to stay far, far away from wild animals, because they are wild. They don't know even to stay away and not hurt wonderful people like you who give a damn about them." Unless they happen to be shifters with access to the Alpha Force elixir, he thought, but of course he wasn't going to mention that.

"That sounds like a good idea." She looked him straight in the eyes again.

Damn, but she was one beautiful woman. He was attracted to her. Very attracted. Would like to do more, a lot more, than just have breakfast with her…and save her from other wolves.

But any thoughts beyond encouraging her to be a wildlife proponent were inappropriate.

And so, after exchanging gazes with her, he gave a
goofy grin and dug back into his breakfast.

Oh, that look on Ryan's face. It was as if he forgave her
foolishness in seeking out the wolves—yet he cared about
her, was glad she was okay.

Or was she reading too much into it?

Maya reached over and picked up her last piece of toast,
slathering a little apricot jam on it. That gave her an excuse not to look directly at Ryan, at least for this moment.

But she remained fully aware of his closeness. And how
she felt glad about that.

But only because the guy also liked wildlife. And
maybe he seemed a little attracted to her just because he
was glad she was out there promoting the return of wolves
to this area and championing all creatures.

"I like the idea, too," said Piers, sort of interrupting the
mood, but that was a good thing.

Maya took a decisive bite of her toast. She had no intention of getting interested in any man, let alone one who
lived outside Washington, DC.

And just the fact that Ryan appeared to love wildlife,
too, didn't mean they shared anything else in common. Or
that the way they cared could coincide.

She had gone through that before with her ex, who'd
turned out to be the opposite of what she'd believed. She
had even developed what she'd believed to be a relationship with him, a reporter who seemed to support her pro-
wildlife position.

But just the opposite. He had turned on her in a number of articles lambasting WHaM for not just documenting
and counting an influx of wildlife but acting as advocates,

too. She'd been hurt and angry and determined not to get involved with someone like that again.

US Fish and Wildlife undoubtedly had a different agenda from WHaM, despite their few similarities.

And Maya figured she had a different agenda from Ryan—although his suggestion about a modified topic for her next talk actually made sense.

"So how long are you staying in town?" she asked Ryan, turning back to face him again. Maybe he was leaving today and she wouldn't see him again.

That should make her feel relieved, shouldn't it? But it didn't.

"Not sure yet," he replied, which did in fact give her a sense of relief. A small one.

Being in his presence, getting to know him better—would that be a good thing?

Possibly…but only as long as they helped each other in their quest to ensure that wolves remained welcome and safe in this area.

And hopefully didn't attack any more people. But neither of them could guarantee that.

She, though, by giving another talk on staying far away from them might be able to help, at least a bit.

But would she convince herself…?

"How about you?" Piers asked. "How long will you be here?"

"I'd originally thought just a couple of days," she said. "But it sounds as if there is a lot more I can do here, both by informing people and maybe even finding out about the wolves here and how dangerous they might be. If they attack people, that's bad for them as well as for the humans near them. It gives people an excuse—maybe even a good one—to hunt the wolves, even though they're protected in this area."

"I think we're on the same wavelength," Ryan said, his tone decisive and his expression now not particularly warm but highly businesslike—a good thing.

"Then let's work together," she said. "Find out about that attack last night and try to determine the wolves' location. And despite the danger those wolves may present—well, I'm hoping to find a way to make sure they're left alone."

"Sounds good to me," Piers said, nodding, then looking toward Ryan.

"Absolutely," he agreed.

Chapter 7

Maya found the rest of their breakfast quite pleasant—until it ended and she got into a small squabble with Ryan about who was going to pay for her meal. She allowed Ryan to win after he convinced her that the federal agency he worked for might not directly make contributions to WHaM but would be glad to assist it in at least this small way.

On the way out, she noticed that Trev was sitting at a table near the door with another man and a couple of women. Good. Though he'd said he wasn't from this town, he apparently had friends here—and hopefully was putting in a good word with them about WHaM and wildlife.

And those friends included women. Hopefully he was flirting with them, so Maya didn't need to feel so uncomfortable with this nice fellow wildlife lover.

She split up with Ryan and Piers on the sidewalk outside and Maya gave Rocky a goodbye hug. She considered doing the same with the guys—Piers first, although it was really Ryan she wanted to touch again. But she hugged neither man.

"Where are you off to?" Ryan asked. She had wanted to ask him the same question but had decided not to since it might seem too personal.

"Oh, I need a few things so I think I'll head to the grocery store." She left unsaid that she hoped to learn more from the Sharans about the people in town who were happy that wolves were back. Not to mention whether they'd heard more about what had happened to Morton Fritts.

"Sounds good. But are you also going to follow up with our suggestion and arrange to do another talk in the park — one about staying away from wild animals?"

"Yes," she said, "I'll do that later this afternoon. And if you give me your cell phone number, I'll call and let you know how it goes."

All three exchanged numbers, and Maya wished she'd thought of doing that yesterday, after they'd met and learned of their joint appreciation of the wolves' return. Considering all that had happened since then it seemed even more necessary that they keep in touch as long as she remained in Fritts Corner.

The men then led Rocky in the opposite direction from Maya along the fairly empty sidewalk. The street didn't have much traffic, either. But Fritts Corner wasn't a particularly large town. As far as Maya was concerned, its only claim to fame was the proximity of the influx of wolves.

She headed toward the grocery store, figuring she didn't need to drive since she wasn't intending to buy a lot of stuff anyway. Her main goal was to get any information that the store owners could convey.

On her way, she passed what was probably the only hospital in this area, the Fritts Medical Center. Its appearance was much starker than most of the town's other buildings, six stories high and squared-off redbrick construction.

She wondered if Morton Fritts had been treated for wolf injuries in this facility—and whether he remained there.

How could she find out what happened, where he was attacked and whether the wolves who hurt him could be the same ones who might have harmed her if the other wolf hadn't come along?

Asking him directly, or his wife, didn't seem the best idea, but she'd give it a try if she saw them again.

She walked the few blocks to the Corner Grocery Store fairly quickly. It looked a little larger than other retail establishments like clothing stores that she'd passed. Its design appeared somewhat quaint as well, and the front consisted of long windows that showed off the well-stocked interior.

The place looked relatively crowded, too, with people in all the aisles and lined up at the couple of cash registers near the front. Was that because it had a good supply of healthful produce, reasonably priced food—or simply because it was the only grocery in town? Maya hadn't seen any supermarkets since she'd arrived here.

Was the place too busy for her to approach the owners, who'd seemed so interested in and happy about the nearby wolves? She just wanted a better sense as to whether the townsfolk like the Sharans felt any differently about the situation today, after the sound of howls and more had infiltrated the town last night—and someone had been attacked.

And did the Sharans know the Frittses well? They had expressed concern for Morton at the restaurant, but for the wolves, too.

Was there any media coverage? Maya hadn't seen anything so far on the internet via her cell phone about her talk, or even the attack—although she hadn't spent a lot of time looking. Were there any social media reports that she wouldn't know about?

The thing was, she had a whole lot of questions without any answers—at least not yet. And so she entered the store.

A young man exited as she came in. "Welcome," he said, grinning at her.

Why was he welcoming her? Was he an employee? Related to the owners?

She saw Kathie Sharan as soon as she got inside. The woman chatted with some people near the closest cash register, and Maya approached.

"It's a terrible situation," she heard one of the group say, a senior woman in a loose dress. "And it should have been good for everyone."

"Well, we still don't have much information," Kathie responded. "Maybe Morton was goading those wolves."

Aha. A conversation exactly on the topic Maya wanted to discuss.

"Hi," she said, taking a few strides forward. "Sorry to be eavesdropping, but you won't be surprised to know I've been listening for the word *wolf* a lot these days." She grinned toward Kathie, who smiled back.

"Oh, hello, Maya," she said. "Everyone, this is Maya Everton. She's the very nice lady with WHaM who talked at the park yesterday about the return of wolves to this area."

"Do you know what happened last night?" the older woman asked. "I've always loved animals and was so excited—but maybe having wolves come back is a horrible situation."

"Now, Yola," Kathie said, "as I mentioned, we don't really know what happened. You've lived here a lot longer than I have but I think it's wonderful that even a few wolves have been sighted around here."

"That's right," Maya said. "And of course all of you know a lot more about the area around Fritts Corner than I do, but I realized afterward that maybe I'd given the wrong idea at my talk. I love wildlife, but a lot of it is truly wild. I'm hoping to give another talk to make sure people understand not only to avoid attempting to turn wild animals into pets, but I also want to stress that no one should try to confront any wild animals, especially those that could harm them."

The older woman, Yola, appeared a little mollified. "Morton is a bit...well, egotistical. Maybe he did think he could go find out about those wolves and confront them, maybe even try shooing them away from this area, without their reacting against him."

"And might he have had a weapon?" asked another member of the crowd, a thin guy with shaggy gray hair.

"You're new here, too," Yola said. "Yes, it's entirely possible that our Morton went to check on those wolves carrying something that could hurt them."

"And potentially protect him," Kathie said. "Which would have been fine as long as he just scared the wolves off without injuring—or killing—them."

"Well, however it happened," Maya said, "I'd really like to know how the confrontation went. And I'm terribly sorry Morton got hurt."

"Me, too," Kathie said fervently.

Her husband, Burt, joined the group just then from someplace within the store. "All of us are."

The conversation continued a short while longer—but no one appeared to have any more information than Maya had. None of them could identify the people at her talk who'd said they were with the media. According to this group, there weren't, in fact, any local TV or radio stations, although when things happened here major networks sometimes sent reporters from Tacoma or other not too distant towns. Or sometimes they just showed up here, which might have been the case during Maya's talk—although she wondered if the wolf-haters invited them.

"I'm not going to be the one to contact any," Burt said, "but I wouldn't be surprised if those reporters return and start nosing around again."

"Especially if the Frittses notify them about the attack," his wife said, her expression troubled.

Maya's concerns eased, if only a little. Apparently the Sharans, and hopefully other locals, weren't totally turned against the wolves by this difficult situation.

And maybe, once the facts—whatever they were—came to light, the wolves would somehow be exonerated.

Although…well, she had somewhat brought the confrontation she'd had with a couple of them last night on herself.

She had a sudden urge to return to that area now, in daylight, to see if she could find evidence of where the wolves had gone. Would there be paw prints? Other indications?

But she still needed more information. So, after she bought a few things to justify her presence at the store, she just might head to the Fritts Corner Police Department to see what information they were releasing to the public about what happened last night.

She wondered where Ryan was. Had he already gone there to learn what he could on behalf of the US Fish and Wildlife Service?

She'd find that out later, too.

For now, she'd probably just head back to her hotel.

But as she reached the grocery store's door, she saw

Trev standing outside talking to one of the women who'd been at breakfast with him.

The fact he had company like that was a good thing. But was it a mere coincidence that they'd wound up at the very place she had headed after her meal?

Drat. She realized that the guy was making her uncomfortable, even though he'd done nothing but be friendly and cheer on WHaM—and her public talk about local wildlife.

She was undoubtedly worrying too much.

But she hoped whatever flirtation he was now carrying on with this lady—a short, slightly plump but definitely pretty girl wearing a bright-colored scarf over her sweater and carrying a huge purse—continued and got Trev to forget about her.

Though not about saying nice things to the world about WHaM.

Was he one of the people now becoming a skeptic thanks to the attack on Morton Fritts? If so, Maya could certainly understand it, even with a person who'd come from somewhere else to learn how WHaM wanted to promote the presence of the newest local wolves.

Maybe she'd have to speak to the guy—or at least be sure he was there if she talked to the public again.

"So what next?" Piers asked Ryan as they walked back toward the hotel from the restaurant.

"I texted a brief description of what happened last night to Major Connell first thing this morning but that's my only communication with him so far since we arrived. I think it's time to give a call to our commanding officer at Alpha Force and give him more detail."

"Good idea," Piers said. "But we need to find someplace more private than our hotel room. I've heard voices in the hallway from my room, so someone might be able to eavesdrop. The old place has some charm to it, but I doubt that soundproofing was topmost in the minds of the people who built it."

Ryan held Rocky's leash, and the wolf-dog stopped to sniff the stonework at the front of a drugstore—possibly where other dogs had lifted their legs. Ryan turned to look at his aide. "I've been trying to come up with a good idea about where to go for it," he admitted.

"How about back to the park?" Piers stopped, probably since they weren't going in that direction. "We can keep walking with Rocky there as we talk and avoid any nosy folks that way. Better yet, maybe we'll find someplace where no one else is hanging out."

"Good idea."

They were soon at one end of the rolling lawn that constituted most of the park till it met the forested hillside. It was distant from the aging podium where Maya had given her talk. Maybe that was a good thing, Ryan thought. He'd have to mention her—not that his mind ever seemed to deviate far from her and her attractiveness both in looks and the way she talked about wolves. But he'd keep his talk about her to a minimum.

As Ryan had predicted, the park wasn't empty, but most people, many with dogs and/or kids, paid them no attention.

Ryan headed for a bench beneath a pine tree and sat down, Piers right behind him. Rocky seemed fine with it, too, lying down on the grass at the end of his leash. If anyone got close, they could walk away.

"You ready to call?" Piers asked.

"Do it," Ryan responded.

His aide pulled a cell phone from his pocket, pushed a few buttons, and Ryan heard it ring. Clearly Piers had put the call on speaker, so they'd have to remain remote and discreet, but that didn't look like it would be a problem, at least for now. The nearest people weren't close, and none came in their direction.

"Hey," Drew Connell said nearly immediately. "I've got Patrick here, too." Lieutenant Patrick Worley was the major's second in command at Alpha Force. "Tell us what's going on."

Briefly, keeping his voice low and continuing to look around to make sure no other person in the park was coming closer, Ryan described what had gone on last night: the full moon, which they of course all knew about. Hearing wolves howl and bark, also no particular surprise but perhaps indicating that Ryan wasn't the only shifter in the area. Describing his own shift with Piers's assistance along with the Alpha Force elixir, with no artificial light under the full moon.

He then told how, while on the prowl, he had seen the woman who'd given a talk to the public the day before in the same park where they now sat—the woman representing the wildlife championing organization WHaM—out and about in the woods beneath the full moon. A couple of wolves had prepared to attack her, and he, in shifted form, had driven them off.

Then, the next morning, he and the rest of this town of Fritts Corner had learned that a local citizen, one not pleased about the influx of wolves, had apparently been attacked.

"We don't know yet if those two wolves I went after were shifters, although their scents indicate the possibility to me. We also don't know if they, or possibly other shifters, attacked Morton Fritts. Shifters or not, apparently we may have a problem here with wolves too prone to attack humans—although we of course don't yet know whether Fritts was doing something to provoke them."

"Better find out soon," replied Drew. "Either way."

"Yeah, we want to talk to Fritts but haven't been able to yet," Ryan said.

"And if they're shifters," Piers said, "we have a month till the next full moon to learn what we need to and ensure nothing like this happens again."

"That's a big if," Patrick broke in over the phone. "First, even if they are shifters, we don't know if they have access to anything like our elixir. We've recruited a few shifters who had done some experimenting, or their families had, and the formulas they came up with sometimes let them shift more at will than just under a full moon—and they had varying degrees of human cognition, just nothing nearly comparable to what we've got with the Alpha Force elixir."

"And even if there are shifters in the area," Drew said, "you still need to figure out if wild wolves conducted that attack and were perhaps provoked enough to do it again—without waiting for a full moon, of course."

"Of course," Ryan agreed. "Well, we'd thought we would only be here for a week or so, but looks like we'll just have to see how long it takes. I assume that's okay, Major Connell?"

"Just call me Drew unless we're in a formal meeting." Ryan heard the smile on his commanding officer's face and grinned slightly himself. "Like I've said before, we've got too much between us in Alpha Force to maintain formality. But we—you—have responsibilities. Keep us informed about what you learn, and be sure to figure out as quickly as possible the details of what happened last night. If you have to stay till the next full moon or even beyond, that's fine, too. But be cautious—and conduct your own shifts whenever you think it's best for tracking any nonshifting wolves in the area to learn what you need to."

"Yes, sir." Ryan's grin grew into a larger smile. "Er, yes, Drew."

"Watch it, Lieutenant," Drew responded. "Er, Ryan. And a couple more things."

"Yes?"

"Keep an eye on that WHaM representative as long as she's there. We won't want someone embracing and promoting the idea of wildlife to be injured by a wolf, no matter whether it's a shifter or not. And as we discussed before, if you do find shifters in the area, be sure to check them out to see if any are worth recruiting into Alpha Force. Our unit, as covert as it is, is strong and growing."

"Will do, with both of them." Of course the idea of keeping an eye on Maya sounded good to Ryan. Too good. He'd have to rein in his inappropriate interest in the lovely woman who liked wolves. Way back. Watch her, yes. Learn from her, sure. But nothing more than that.

"I'll do my part to help him," Piers added. "Rocky will, too."

"Go to it, then," Drew finished—a good thing since some kids tossing a basketball between them headed in the direction of the bench.

"Will do, and we'll keep you informed about anything useful that we learn. Oh, and if you happen to hear any more about shifters in this area—"

"We'll keep you informed," Patrick said.

Chapter 8

Her visit to the local government offices of Fritts Corner had only been partly productive. Maya grumbled internally as she left the lovely, quaint and picturesque set of old-fashioned buildings and stood on the nearly empty sidewalk watching the traffic while deciding where to go next.

At least she had received the okay from the city manager to do another talk in the park. She'd obtained her first authorization from that office as well, but this time she'd had to request a meeting with the manager himself, Perry Fernander.

And Mr. Fernander, politician that he was, had concerns about anyone taking a positive position about the wolves any longer.

He'd sat behind his desk staring grimly at her from beneath shaggy gray brows and shaking his head. "I haven't talked directly to our injured citizen Morton Fritts," he'd said, "but of course the town of Fritts Corner is now concerned about the nearness of those wolves."

"I understand," Maya had told him, and she *had* understood—but without more information she didn't want to hold any wolves, or herself, responsible. "What I want to talk about is staying safe when potentially dangerous wildlife is in the area." A good thing for the people, sure—but also to protect the wolves and their abilities to roam freely.

Fernander had stared at her a moment longer, then nodded. "That could benefit us all. I'll give the city's approval, but you'll need to let me know when you want to give that talk in the park."

"Soon, but I want to check a couple of things." She'd noted his contact information and left.

When did she want to give it? Well, she hoped to confirm a time when Ryan and Piers could be there—perhaps also with Rocky—and lend her at least some moral support. Maybe the Sharans, too, since they still seemed to appreciate the idea of wolves returning to this area. They could also let other pro-wolf people know.

And, okay, sure. She might not want to get extremely friendly with Trev, but he'd been nice to her and expressed his interest in wildlife. He had also apparently been making friends here. Did they have the same affinity to wildlife he did? She hoped so.

Plus, as she'd considered before, she hoped Trev—and lots of locals, too—hadn't changed their minds about the good things resulting from the latest influx of wolves.

She might need to figure out where Trev was staying, since he had indicated he was a visitor like her, and expressly invite him to her next talk. Then, she had to choose a time that he, with his new buddies, could attend, too.

Then there were the Frittses. One thing that had encouraged her when she was in the city hall building was that, while she'd been in the waiting room, she had overheard a receptionist talking on the phone, apparently with a concerned citizen who wanted to stay safe from the wolves.

"Now, I can't tell you for sure," said the thin woman with glasses and a nasal voice, "but what I heard was that Mr. Fritts went up the dirt road at the far end of the park's hills once he heard those howls. He had some kind of large stick with him, I gather, and he was all set to shut those wolves up by pounding at them and scaring them into running away from our area. But when they attacked him—"

She'd shut up then when a couple of uniformed cops walked into the reception area.

Really? What Morton Fritts claimed didn't sound too likely, Maya thought. But what if it was true? And what if instead of his chasing them with his stick they'd felt frightened and attacked the human threatening them?

A stretch, she realized...yet she had an urge to go up that trail now, during the daytime when it was light outside and the wolves might be sleeping. Or if they were hunting they'd surely make noise and she could get out of there.

But what if, after he was attacked, Morton Fritts had dropped his weapon and left it there? It would likely have his fingerprints on it—and Maya could photograph it.

Or maybe there would be other evidence that could show that the wolves only acted for their own protection and weren't the initial aggressors.

It would be an explanation that she—and WHaM— could use to perhaps reduce the animals' bad reputation here...

And it wouldn't hurt to give some proof of the goodness of wolves to the representatives of the US Fish and Wildlife Service who happened to be in town, as well.

That would give her a good excuse to see Ryan again—

not that she really needed one beyond the talk she now planned about wolf safety. Oh, and human safety, too.

But for now…

She hurried back to the hotel to change clothes.

As much as Ryan disliked what he'd done, he at least had more information. He had used his power as a representative of the United States government—or at least one of its agencies—to have his contacts in DC get in touch with local authorities to extract what information they had about the attack on Fritts.

Now he mulled it all over again as he walked silently with his cover dog and aide through downtown Fritts Corner.

The story his supposed superiors at US Fish and Wildlife—actually, some members of Alpha Force—had conveyed to the police chief was that they needed all information available to collect statistics. They wouldn't guarantee any reprisal against the wolf or wolves at fault but might allow it locally, the way those that had attacked livestock were being treated elsewhere in the state.

Ryan would need to stay on top of it all and prevent anything similar around here if some other agency or regional authority decided to try to take action against the local wolves. After all, no matter why or how Fritts had been attacked, he had survived it.

If he hadn't, protecting any wolves, especially those involved, would be difficult—no matter what their backgrounds.

Worst-case, if these wolves were wild, Ryan would use some contacts Alpha Force had within US Fish and Wildlife to ensure they were trapped and relocated to a habitat much farther from human habitation.

And if they happened to be shifters—well, things would be handled quite differently.

But the real Fish and Wildlife Service had been informed about this attack. They probably would have been anyway, yet now Ryan felt somewhat responsible for whatever happened to the wolves—shifters or not—who were involved.

Now, he, along with Piers and Rocky, passed through the park that had become so familiar to them. The podium where Maya had given her last talk was in front of them, and just beyond that were the forested hillsides—their destination at the moment.

Was she going to be able to give another talk there—the kind they'd discussed, where humans would be warned to be careful? They should know that anyway.

In any event, Ryan had entered the forest from the other end last night, to prevent being seen by anyone even before his shift began.

He had left the area the same way, after changing back.

He recalled very well the way he had gone after the wolves menacing Maya.

Maya. Where was she now?

He had no doubt she was using her own skills and knowledge to look into the realities of last night and how Morton Fritts had been hurt. She was a lovely, gregarious woman who loved wildlife—very attractive to him.

Not that he, or any member of Alpha Force, could let any interest like that go further. But he appreciated her.

And hoped she was learning something she could share with him. Something to protect wolves, despite the glitch caused by the attack on Fritts.

But for now... "You ready?" He looked at Piers, who'd been equally silent on their trek from the hotel and held Rocky's leash.

"Yeah. But do you really think we'll find anything helpful—even you, with your special…abilities?" Piers had lowered his voice along with only hinting at what he was talking about, like Ryan's special, acute senses even when he was in human form since he definitely wasn't shifted now.

"Guess we'll just have to find out."

They started up the nearest dirt path at the end of the park. Ryan inhaled deeply. Would there be any residual odors from those wolves—any that he could pick up while not shifted?

Would there be anything else indicating where Fritts had been attacked…and what kind of wolves had done it?

This probably was useless, but waiting longer made even less sense.

"Yeah," Piers said. "Meantime, now that we're alone here—except for Rocky—tell me what you hear and see and smell, would you?"

Ryan smiled. His aide had told him many times that he'd volunteered to be a nonshifting member of Alpha Force because he found the concept of shapeshifters fascinating. But would he want to be one if he had the ability to choose?

"No way," he'd spat out when Ryan had asked. "I'd never be able to be as good at it as you."

Which had only made Ryan smile all the more.

He looked down at his cover dog now. Rocky was busy doing his dog thing, sniffing the undergrowth and lifting his leg now and then to leave his own canine scent.

What would the wolves think about that? Although, if they had been shifters, they probably wouldn't know anything about it since the likelihood was that they wouldn't shift again for a month.

Of course Ryan, in his human form, inhaled the odors of wildlife and more around here—including the scents that his own dog was leaving, though a whole lot less acute than if he'd looked just like Rocky.

They neared the clearing where Ryan had jumped in last night to prevent Maya from being attacked.

Which was when he smelled it. Smelled *her*. And not just the residual aroma from the night before.

"C'mon," he growled to his aide and cover dog. He pulled quickly ahead and emerged from among the trees around him, right into that clearing.

"Maya," he said. "What are you doing here?"

Maya gasped and jumped sideways.

She'd been keeping her mind open to sounds, had enjoyed hearing many different types of birds and became aware of leaves blowing in the slight breeze.

But she had listened especially for any noise that could be wolves. And not only wolves. She had done her research before her journey to this area. Although they might not be present right here, there were often sightings of other kinds of wild animals in Washington State, including bears, cougars and coyotes, as well as more usual small mammals such as rabbits and raccoons.

Any of them, if present, could create rustles in the dried leaves on the ground or other noises.

But she hadn't been listening for human voices.

"I could ask you the same thing," she shot back, turning to look at the source of that question.

Although she wasn't exactly shocked by the sudden appearance of Ryan or Rocky or Piers. They were, after all, wildlife advocates, like her.

Still…the tall man who was Ryan now stood beside her, almost as if attempting to intimidate her.

Well, that wasn't going to work. In fact, she had a sense that this guy, and maybe his friend and dog, would do their utmost to defend her if a wolf did happen to show up right now.

"We're still trying to collect all the facts about that attack last night," Ryan said. "We learned it might have occurred around this part of the hillside so we decided to check it out. The more we know, the more likely it is that we'll be able to prevent more attacks from happening."

"Hey, we're on the same wavelength," Maya said, a sense of warmth shooting through her.

"Maybe." Ryan's scowl didn't exactly intimidate her—or even turn her off. But she knew he intended to convey something that wasn't being said.

Something like, *stay away from here, got it?*

Although—how had he determined to come to this particular spot? Surely he hadn't eavesdropped on the same people she'd heard talking at city hall?

But if he had learned about it, that meant more information was getting out—whether by gossip or more official channels.

"But look, Maya," Ryan continued. "You told us that you were nearly attacked last night. What's to say that the wolves around you then aren't still in this area? If they were defending what they consider their turf, or maybe they're even breeding now—they could attack again. And the other wolf that challenged them might not be around then, or might even join the attack. What about the talk you're giving to tell people to stay far away from wildlife?"

"I figured I'd do what I wanted till I give that talk," she retorted. "Once I do, I'll have to live with what I said in case someone catches me disobeying myself." She shot him a huge grin.

Although Piers, too, was smiling, Ryan wasn't.

"Well, obey yourself starting now," Ryan said. "If nothing else, hang out with us while we're up here. Otherwise you could get hurt—or worse. Then think about how people around here would react to the new influx of wolves—maybe justifiably so."

He was right. Maybe her own type of research and showing love to wild animals wasn't the wisest way to go just now.

"Okay," she conceded. "I'll stay with you, and we'll leave this area—right?"

"Yes, let's get out of here," Ryan said. He looked at Piers, who also nodded, and, as if he understood, Rocky rose from where he sat, too.

"Let me show you something before we go," Maya said. At the time Ryan had startled her by talking, she'd thought she had seen something at the edge of the forest.

A slight clearing, with leaves somewhat trampled.

And if she wasn't mistaken…

"When you startled me, I'd just seen that. It might mean nothing, but…well, I was looking for any evidence about what happened when Morton was attacked. We've all heard from different sources that this area could be where it happened. It's a large enough hillside, and there are quite a few animals around that are carnivores. Even so—"

As she'd spoken, she had moved back to the area at the edge of this clearing where she had seen some tromped-down leaves…and more.

And pointed now toward a spot on the ground.

A reddish-brown spot.

A spot that could be blood.

Chapter 9

Out of the corner of his eye, Ryan saw Piers glance toward him as if awaiting his confirmation about the composition of the dark spot on the ground.

He had already inhaled almost instinctively. Despite the lessening of his senses in human form, he did catch the scent of what the spot appeared to be: blood.

Not that he could inform Maya of his certainty.

But even though it was blood, she was right. He couldn't be sure it was human blood, and even if it was, that the blood belonged to the man who'd apparently been a victim of an attack last night.

Ryan, while in human form, had met Morton, had inhaled his scent, but that wouldn't tell him what his blood alone smelled like. Even if he shifted and inhaled this aging and foliage-tainted scent, he might have a better idea but wouldn't be sure.

For now, he would just act like a regular human—at least to the extent he could.

"Wow," he said to Maya. "That certainly looks like it could be blood—but you're right. We've no way of knowing if it could be Morton Fritts's. Even so—"

"Even so," Maya repeated, pulling her camera from the bag over her shoulder and filming the spot, then pulling back to take in more of the area. "We can inform the authorities."

Enough time had passed that, even though Ryan believed he also caught a faint aroma of canines in the area, he couldn't be certain. That could simply be his expectation—or imagination.

Either way, he didn't want the blood to be human, and if it was, he didn't want it to be the result of an attack by wolf, shifter or otherwise.

Or an injured, or dead, wolf's blood.

"Yes, we can," he said, "although since Morton apparently survived it would be better if he told the authorities where he was hurt. Maybe he already has. That might not matter now anyway. It's not like a crime scene where one human attacked another." On the other hand, he wasn't about to mention it but identifying which wolf it was, assuming Fritts had been mauled by a canine or two, would be particularly interesting to him—and to the rest of Alpha Force. He again traded glances with Piers, who was undoubtedly thinking the same thing.

Perhaps it was, in an unusual kind of way, a crime scene, after all—one involving another human in a non-human form…

"You're right. I guess the best thing would be just to mention it to the authorities, maybe show them the pictures I took, and let them decide if they want us to show them where this is. It could just be the result of a wolf or other predator catching its nonhuman dinner. And they're allowed to do that."

"Right." He looked at her. She appeared almost fierce as she nodded toward him, clearly willing to do a lot to defend the wildlife she cherished.

"And in any event, even if it happens to be Morton's blood we can't tell whether he acted aggressively first or just protected himself. The authorities might not care either way, but I certainly do."

"Me, too, of course." Ryan shrugged off the sudden desire to pull her into his arms for a hug. To thank her for her attitude. That was all.

Not because that sudden desire meant anything else…

"Okay, then," he continued. "Thanks for pointing that spot out to me. It never hurts to have information, even if it doesn't make sense to use it. Now, let's head back down to the park."

Maya found herself smiling nearly the entire hike down the hill. That was partly because of the company she was with: other wildlife lovers.

But in addition, Piers gave her the handle of Rocky's leash, and she got to be with the wolflike dog nearly the entire walk. She had to be careful, of course. Although Rocky stuck with her, he could topple her over if he ever decided to start running while she held the end of his leash.

But he didn't, good dog that he was. She patted him often.

Rocky and she led the group, and she heard Ryan and Piers behind her, talking. Which in itself was interesting. They discussed what else they would do for the rest of this day.

They also asked again when she intended to give her next talk, about staying away from wild animals for safety.

She informed them she had a phone number to call to set it up, and they agreed she should ask for a time tomorrow afternoon.

"I can give a call to work out the time as soon as we're back in the park and I get a better signal," she told them.

She looked forward to her next talk, especially considering all that had happened in Fritts Corner since she'd last happily discussed the resurgence of wolves into this area.

Now, that talk could have become a little controversial, but she was going to do all she could to encourage the incredible excitement of having some previously missing wildlife return—yet stress how people should react for their own safety, as well as the wolves'.

She would also need to make certain somehow that it was well publicized so a lot of people would know about it and, hopefully, show up.

And as many as possible remain pro-wildlife despite the now more obvious need to be careful.

They reached the area at the base of this portion of the hillside, then took time to walk around it into the park.

There, near the podium, Maya handed Piers the end of Rocky's leash and made the call she'd planned on. She reached City Manager Perry Fernander, and he OK'd the following afternoon at one thirty for her next talk.

"All set," she said as she pressed the button to hang up.

"Good deal," Piers said, and even Rocky, standing beside Piers with his leash slack, panted a little in a way that resembled a laugh.

"I take it you'll come," Maya said to Ryan, who also stood beside them.

The tall man's brows went up, although he didn't smile. "Of course not," he said, "despite my insistence on your giving this additional talk and scheduling it as soon as possible, and—"

"I get it," Maya said with a laugh at his sarcasm, and her insides seemed to warm at the idea that he would be there to listen, maybe to help her, or maybe to contradict her if he didn't like her approach.

But somehow she had an urge to impress him—even as they both did their best to help wolves.

For now, though, she called the police department, put the speaker on so the men could hear her conversation and told the dispatcher who answered about having heard about a possible wolf attack last night and seeing something today that could be blood near a path in the middle of a hillside, then described the general area. The woman put them on hold for a minute, and when she returned said the authorities had already been informed by the victim about what had happened and where. She thanked Maya, then hung up.

Which gave Maya some sense of relief. She had done her duty but didn't have to follow up anymore about that unnerving patch of darkened red on the ground.

But she wished she had more information—like where the attack actually had happened and what had provoked it...

And now, their hike was over and so was anything else she needed to do with these men, at least for the moment. It was late afternoon. They were about to split up, probably not see each other again until her talk tomorrow.

That disappointed her. She wanted to hang out with them—and the dog—even longer.

"Hey, you guys care to join me for dinner tonight?"

She noticed that Piers looked at Ryan, as if he'd go along with whatever the other guy said. Too bad, in a way. She would rather have just invited Ryan, but those two seemed always to stick together. Sure, they had a common employer and common goal, but...

Well, in some ways it might be better not to get Ryan alone. She found the guy much too attractive.

"Sure," Ryan said. "There's someplace we need to go first, but we could meet you. Any ideas where?"

"Not really." She pulled her phone from her pocket and looked at the time. "It's about four now. How about if we meet around six, in the hotel lobby? We can ask there for a restaurant recommendation."

"Sounds good," Ryan said.

They walked in the same direction, toward the hotel, for a few blocks, but then the men excused themselves.

"See you later," Ryan said, and Piers reached for Rocky's leash.

Their splitting up then somehow made Maya feel a bit bereft. But she felt really good that she'd see Ryan later.

They could talk more then about what she would say in her presentation tomorrow. Could discuss wolves even more. Spend a little more time together, even with Piers present.

And as they left Maya figuratively kicked herself for even thinking such thoughts. Ryan and she might share a love of wildlife—but nothing else.

"So where are we going?" Piers asked. He had ceded the handle of Rocky's leash to Ryan, who now upped the speed of their walk along the street in a different direction from the way Maya had gone.

"I'm hungry." Ryan resisted the urge to pivot around to determine if he could still see Maya. He would see her later anyway. And how much trouble could she get into while in town? "I need some snacks. How about you?"

"Oh, then we're going to the grocery store to sound the Sharans out about…well, whatever info we can get from them, right?"

"You got it." Ryan turned back to aim a grin at his aide. They'd learned that Maya had visited the grocery store earlier that day and said hi to its owners, but she wouldn't have any idea of Ryan's suspicions about them.

She probably hadn't the slightest idea that shapeshifters even existed except in books, movies and TV, and that was a good thing.

He needed to make sure she stayed safe, didn't create any waves that would give more credence to the claims of the locals who weren't wildlife fans and that was all.

Except for learning what he really needed to know while here…

They'd reached the block containing the Corner Grocery Store. The place was crowded this late afternoon. Not good, Ryan thought.

Its owners might have less time to talk if they were busy handling customers.

On the other hand, he had some ideas of what to hint about that could get their attention—fast.

"It would be best if you wait outside with Rocky," he told Piers. "He might not be welcome, and he's also likely to be bumped or have his paws stepped on in that mob."

"Got it. We'll go for a walk. But call if there's anything you need." He accepted the end of Rocky's leash back from Ryan, who then headed inside.

He stopped first near the entrance, close to the few cashiers, then went around them to the heart of the place when he didn't see either of the Sharans.

For such a relatively small grocery, there seemed to be a good selection of all kinds of products, Ryan thought. The aisles were barely wide enough for carts going in opposite directions, and those he glanced at had a lot of stuff in them.

This probably wasn't the best time to buddy up to the

owners—and hint strongly that tomorrow afternoon, around one thirty, they ought to be in the park again listening to Maya.

They'd been pro-wolves before, and should be again, but it was also a good thing for them to see their fellow locals' reactions once more, especially when Maya told them to stay away from wildlife around here for their own safety.

That should be something the Sharans promoted as well, whether or not they had anything to do with the attack on Fritts.

Or if they were the wolves who'd appeared ready to hurt Maya before he'd come along...

"Hello, can I help you?" A medium-sized guy with narrow shoulders who appeared to be in his early twenties had approached Ryan. Did he work here?

"Oh, I'm fine," Ryan said. "Just deciding what to look for." He paused. "And I had a couple of questions for the owners—the Sharans, right? I met them the other day."

"I'm their son, Pete," the guy said. He did in fact have his mother's light brown hair, not streaked as hers was but with a sheen to it—like a wolf's? His nose was longish, as well.

If he was their son, he was probably a shifter, too, assuming Ryan was correct and both older Sharans were. His scent suggested that as well, along with his physical resemblance to his parents.

Then Pete, too, should hear what Maya—and Ryan—had to say tomorrow.

And what had he done last night, while shifted beneath the full moon? Might he have been the one who'd attacked Morton Fritts?

"Good to meet you, Pete. Are you a champion of the latest presence of wolves in the area like your parents are? I met them at a talk given by a representative of WHaM the other day—Wildlife Habitat Monitoring. I'm Ryan Blaid-dinger, and I work for US Fish and Wildlife." He held out his hand while studying Pete's face.

His expression froze for an instant as if he was shocked, or at least uncomfortable, at being approached by a wild-life proponent.

Was that because, as a shifter, too, he tried to keep his opinions to himself to avoid any kind of strife with regu-lar humans?

Ryan didn't get the opportunity to push for an answer, though, since Kathie Sharan walked up and stood close to her son.

"Hi, Ryan," she said with a smile. "Welcome. I'm sure Pete's already asked, but can we help you find anything? As you can see, we've got a lot of stuff here—including people buying it." She blinked at her own joke, and Ryan gave a short laugh, turning his head to once again take in the crowd. He'd already noticed the many aromas of food—as well as the buzz of people talking. There were even scents of sweet, fresh baked goods in the air.

"Yes, I do see that. And I don't want to take up much of your time. Since I'm just visiting and staying in a hotel, I don't need much in the way of groceries except maybe some snacks. Jerky sticks, maybe, roast beef and bread for sandwiches, and some fruit. And I think I'll get some extra dog food for Rocky."

While he was in human form, he felt a lot happier eat-ing produce than while he was shifted—although he rarely had to eat while shifted anyway. But he wasn't about to ask them for beef products that he might love to devour. He couldn't really store and cook in his hotel room. Beef jerky was okay as a snack. So was sliced roast beef. But neither were his favorite food. And he tended to feed Rocky high-quality dog food.

"Sure. Pete, why don't you show Ryan where those are?"

"Thanks," Ryan said. "Oh, and I just started to tell Pete about the next talk Maya is giving in the park tomorrow. I'll be there, too. Since we heard about what happened to Morton Fritts, she's going to be describing how everyone, even wildlife lovers like us, can stay safer—like not getting too near them. And I wonder how close you and your family get to wildlife, and people, at times like last night. Full moon and all, you can certainly see what's out there a bit better than on other nights."

He looked Kathie deeply in her dark brown eyes, reading the shock on her face. Her son must have seen it, too—or maybe he was just reacting to what Ryan said.

"We don't know what you're talking about," he said quickly, planting himself in front of his mother.

"Really? Maybe not." Ryan smiled, then stepped out of the way as someone pushed a grocery cart a bit too close. "Although your even saying that suggests otherwise to me."

Their conversation, or maybe the way they were all regarding one another, apparently grabbed Burt Sharan's attention, since he was suddenly with them, as well.

"Is something wrong here?" the beefy guy demanded, his arms fisting at his sides.

"I don't think so," Ryan responded, although he knew the question hadn't been directed at him. "Just met your son, and I was telling Kathie and him that Maya plans to give another talk, this time about how to deal with wild wolves now that some are back in the area—hopefully to prevent any more incidents like the one with Morton Fritts. Although there's a possibility that couldn't happen again for about a month anyway."

He kept his expression innocent and calm as he looked

straight into Burt's shocked face. "What are you talking about?"

"Just the possibility of different kinds of wolves showing up around here—not just gray wolves, for example, but…well, others, too."

Burt grabbed Ryan's arm in a rough grasp. "Look, if you're insinuating—"

"It's okay, dear," Kathie said. "I don't think Ryan means anything besides letting us know that he's on our side—on the side of everyone who appreciates wildlife, including whatever wolves happen to show up. Right, Ryan?"

He'd already reached down and pried Burt's hand away. "Exactly," he said. "But I really do think it would be a good thing for all of you to come to tomorrow's talk. Can I count on you?"

He looked first into Kathie's face, and though it was pale she had raised her chin and appeared strong. She nodded.

Ryan then glanced at Burt. His face was flushed, but he no longer looked angry. Worried, maybe. Which was probably a good thing.

"Yeah, I'll be there. Pete, too." Burt glanced at his son, who nodded.

Pete's expression was unreadable to Ryan, but that was okay since all three of them might be shifters.

And the talk tomorrow would be to benefit all wolves, no matter what their background.

But Ryan had a pretty good idea what their background was—and hoped to be able to get them to admit it.

Which might only happen when he admitted at least part of his own background, too.

Chapter 10

Maya chatted with the concierge in the lobby of the Washington Inn. His nametag said he was Larry, and he stood behind a tall stand with a computer on top—probably the way he researched things that guests wanted to know for which he didn't have answers. He had little hair to frame his unwavering and respectful smile.

Maya kept sneaking looks toward the stairway. Were Ryan, Piers and Rocky up in their rooms? She'd only arrived downstairs a few minutes ago, just before the time they'd said they would meet, and she didn't even know if they'd returned after their outing this afternoon. She hadn't changed her clothes, but her shirt, jeans and athletic shoes felt appropriate for the casualness of their arrangement.

"I'm not exactly sure what the people I'm going to dinner with will want," she told Larry. "Do you have any kind of restaurant list?"

"Nothing official, but I've got a pretty good sense for what's close by, if you can give me some idea—"

"Oh, I should know shortly." Maya had just spotted Piers and Rocky heading down the stairway. They were followed by Ryan. The men had changed from their climbing outfits but remained dressed as casually as Maya, both in sweatshirts and jeans.

They soon had maneuvered through the fairly empty lobby and joined Maya near the concierge stand.

"What kind of food would you guys like for dinner? And I'm not asking Rocky, since I think I know what he'd say." Maya grinned. Of course a wolf-dog would want some pretty heavy meat.

"How about some kind of steak house?" Ryan asked.

Maya supposed that the dog's owner could share some preferences with his pet but still found that kind of amusing.

"Fine with me." As much as she liked wildlife, she had considered becoming a vegetarian early on but decided against it—although she did limit her meat intake, often preferring more salads to heavy foods like steak.

Larry gave them the name of a nearby dog-friendly place called, appropriately, House of Steak, and handed them a town map, where he circled the location. In a few minutes, they were on their way. There weren't many others walking on the sidewalk, but the weather was fine, a fairly warm evening in September.

Once again, Maya enjoyed being with this group, and not just because Rocky resembled one of the kinds of animals she especially appreciated.

She found she also appreciated being with others who liked wildlife as much as she, but whom she hadn't met through WHaM. And the fact they brought that adorable, wolflike dog along nearly everywhere only added to her appreciation of them.

They were seated on a sparsely occupied patio as soon

as they reached the restaurant. Rocky was the only dog present, but there were several other groups of people. Unsurprisingly, both men ordered steaks, which actually sounded good to Maya but she decided that a steak salad instead would be perfect for her. The men both ordered beer but she decided to stick with iced tea. They did, of course, request a bowl of water for Rocky.

When the server, a friendly and knowledgeable fellow, had left, Maya turned to Piers. "Why did you decide to join the US Fish and Wildlife Service? Obviously you care about wildlife, but why make it that official?"

She wanted to know the same from Ryan but thought it would be easier to ask Piers first to lead into the topic.

She caught the men trading glances that looked somehow strange, but only for a second. "My background is in science," Piers said. "I've always liked animals. I started out in the military, then decided to follow up this way."

"Same thing, basically, with me," Ryan said without her even having to ask him. She opened her mouth to ask for more detail but he continued, "And you? Why did you decide to join WHaM?"

This was something she loved to talk about. "The thing is, I'm a statistician by background, as well as a real animal lover. Even before, I loved observing and documenting and forecasting future numbers in different fields. But along the way I met other people as obsessed and adoring of wildlife as I am—so we got together and formed WHaM."

"Then you're one of the founders?" Ryan's tilted head and smile suggested he was impressed, which made Maya feel even better.

"Yep," she said. "A group of us decided that an organization was needed to document and try to maximize restoration of native wildlife throughout the country. We discuss ideas with each other and, when appropriate, make

suggestions to local governments. Of course we recognize
the need to make sure that the influx of wildlife occurs as
safely as possible for both animals and locals, so my talk
tomorrow is entirely appropriate for me—and so was the
one I gave yesterday."

"So what brought you here, to Washington?" Ryan
asked. "Although I'll bet I can guess."

"I'll bet you can, too," she replied. "We're all so delighted about the return of wolves to this state and wanted
to be part of it, though there aren't many yet and even
fewer in this area. And some, in other areas, are unfortunately being disposed of for doing what comes naturally
to them: hunting prey. But here I am, representing all of
WHaM—and maybe all wolves, too!" She shot them both
a smile—but noticed they glanced at each other again first.
What was going on? She had to ask. "Do you two have
some kind of opinion on WHaM or the wolves or whatever
that you'd like to share with me? Or some kind of official
opinion from Fish and Wildlife?"

"Not really, though of course the more we know about
your organization, and the more your organization knows
about Fish and Wildlife regulations and standards, the better for all of us—and the wolves here, too." Ryan spoke as
if he was a government guy, which he was, and Maya saw
Piers's head nodding, as well.

Their food arrived then. Maya wasn't surprised when
both men cut pieces of meat from their steak and fed them
to the now-sitting and clearly happy, tail-wagging Rocky.

For the rest of the meal, they talked in generalities,
sometimes about this town and any sights to see, sometimes about transportation here from Sea-Tac, but never
again anything personal about their backgrounds, even
though Maya attempted now and then to turn the conversation gently back to that subject.

No matter. She enjoyed her salad—and she enjoyed the company.

She even kind of enjoyed it when Ryan took over the discussion and began telling her what she ought to cover in her talk the next day.

Most of what he said made sense.

But it was her talk. If she chose not to do it his way, too bad.

There was something about this woman that really resonated with Ryan.

Maybe it was her enthusiasm about wildlife—particularly wolves.

Maybe it was her intelligence. Her determination. Her jumping right into a situation that fascinated her and finding a way to share it with the world. The organization she had helped to create was now known by nearly everyone involved with wildlife preservation.

And maybe his appreciation of her was spiced up even more by his attraction to her—physically and otherwise.

For now, though, as they finished their meal, he had already donned his nonexistent cloak of being in command, thanks to his false job with the federal government.

He allowed that once more to be the reason he treated her to this meal—and Piers, too, of course.

"Thanks," Maya said as they stood to leave. "And thanks also for your suggestions about what I should say tomorrow."

The smile on her face, as cute and appealing as it was, seemed false, as if she wasn't overly excited about his ideas on how to give her presentation.

But he didn't mind. He liked the idea of her being her own woman—on behalf of wolves. And he would be there. If she got into anything she shouldn't, whether a topic or approach or anything else, he'd be able to channel her back in the right directions. Even correct her.

And he felt certain that she wouldn't appreciate it.

Their walk back to the hotel was at a nice, leisurely pace, partly because Maya asked to be the one to hold Rocky's leash again. Ryan's cover dog acted as he should, taking his time sniffing out everything and taking care of what he needed to this night before they went to bed.

The air was comfortably cool, and the streets in this small retail area were fairly quiet. In all, it was a very pleasant time.

"Have either of you ever been to Washington State before?" Maya asked as they neared their destination.

"I have, briefly, when I was a kid," Piers said. "My family took a sightseeing trip to the Seattle area. It was fun, but I never really thought about coming back again. Glad I'm here, though."

"This is my first time here," Ryan responded, "but I like it, or at least what I've seen of it so far. I may stick around even longer than I'd first planned."

Like, until the next full moon, thanks to his belief now that there actually were shifters in Fritts Corner.

Or maybe he would leave and come back.

But at the moment, staying as long as Maya did felt best, at least until that next full moon.

When they reached the hotel, Ryan opened the door to the otherwise empty lobby. "Is Rocky staying with you tonight?" he asked Piers—another way of telling his aide that Rocky *was* staying with him that night.

"Sure thing. Good night, you two." Piers took the end of the leash from Maya and tugged gently till Rocky followed him up the stairs—but not before Piers aimed a knowing smile toward Ryan.

A very suggestive smile, but Ryan had no intention of

doing anything but acting gentlemanly and seeing Maya to her room.

To the door of her room, and that was all.

They walked up the steps together, side by side. Ryan had an urge to reach over and take her hand—to steady her on the steps—but he knew it would be a bad idea to touch her at all.

He managed to share glances with her now and then on their climb. Was there something in her gaze besides friendliness and appreciation of someone else who liked wolves?

He thought so. And the heat, the interest, he thought he saw there turned him on...no matter how inappropriate that was.

He tried to make his thoughts back off—*tried* being the operative word.

"It's only been a few days since I arrived here," Maya said, her upward pace slow but deliberate, "but it feels as if I've been here much longer." The smile she shot at him was sexy as well as sweet.

"Is that a good or bad thing?" Ryan asked. They had reached the hallway to the third floor, where Maya's room was. He again resisted the urge to take her hand. No reason at all to try to steady her.

"Good, I think. And I hadn't planned to stay long, but I may extend it depending on how things go at my new talk tomorrow. If people seem to take the position I do, that wildlife is wonderful but shouldn't be approached for one's own safety, that's great. But I'd still like to know what really happened with Morton Fritts."

"Me, too," Ryan said, really meaning it. Well, he would find out somehow, maybe tomorrow and maybe not, but one way or another he needed to know.

At her doorway, Maya reached into the small purse she

Protector Wolf

carried and extracted her room key—an actual key in this older place. She unlocked her door.

Ryan was about to tell her good-night and suggest they meet for breakfast again tomorrow—when she grabbed his hand and yanked him inside.

In moments, her arms were around him and he couldn't help but reciprocate. Their kiss was hot and long and damn sexy, with her pushing hard against him and teasing him with her tongue.

For a moment, he found himself eager to accompany her across the room to her bed.

But then reality set in. He certainly hadn't brought any protection along, and he wasn't about to make love with this amazingly sexy woman without making sure no offspring resulted.

Although the idea of surprising this wildlife lover with the kind of offspring they'd conceive...

No way!

Reluctantly but with determination he ended the kiss, even as his mouth, and the rest of his body, ached for more.

"Wow," he said, smiling down at her, appreciating the surprise on her sensual, clearly stimulated face. "Wow," he repeated. "Now that's a great way to say good-night. So, good night, Maya. Let's grab breakfast together in the morning again, okay? Same time as today?"

Before she could respond, he hurried out the door.

And wondered if he would be able to sleep that night— or if his body would be aching for what had been more than hinted about here, but he'd unfortunately had to end.

Chapter 11

The hallway on her floor was empty when Maya finally left her room the next morning to head downstairs and meet her breakfast companions.

She had taken her time getting ready so she was running a little late. She'd even considered calling Ryan to tell him she was going to skip the meal.

Mostly, she wanted to skip seeing him, thanks to her confusion over his reaction to their kiss the previous night. Only…well, the problem was that she did want to see him. Maybe look him straight in those deep brown eyes and attempt to figure out if her attraction to him was wholly one-sided.

She hadn't thought so, but…

Well, it wasn't like her to be so forward, either. Maybe he'd done her a favor.

She walked more briskly down the steps until she reached the lobby and looked around. Sure enough, the men and dog were waiting for her near the door.

Should she apologize for being late?

No. In a way, it was Ryan's fault—although she couldn't exactly explain it even to him, let alone to Piers.

She made her way through the small lobby crowd till she reached them—and neither man looked at her immediately. They were apparently engaged in conversation, something about what they should be looking for around here.

Here? In the lobby? In town?

Maybe they didn't even realize she wasn't on time. Of course, it was only five minutes past when they'd agreed to meet, which wasn't particularly bad, but still—

"Hi," she said, not looking at either of them but kneeling to give Rocky a big hug. She appreciated the fuzzy, warm feel of the dog, and the way he nuzzled her face. Too bad she couldn't just opt to spend time with him this morning and not the others.

When she stood again and saw both men looking at her, she tried to read the expression on Ryan's face. Maybe she was seeing what she hoped to, but she thought she saw a hint of regret, maybe sadness.

Yeah, and maybe she saw an expression like a scolded dog on his face, too.

"So, you guys ready to eat?" she asked.

"Sure," Piers responded. "Same place as yesterday?"

"Fine with me." Maya pivoted to head out the door. She assumed Ryan would follow.

Instead, he rushed slightly ahead and pushed open the door in front of her. Outside, he positioned himself beside her on the sidewalk as they headed in the direction of the restaurant.

"Good morning," he finally said. "Did you sleep well?"

"Very well, thanks," she responded, inserting a happy

lilt into her voice as if their final contact last night had meant nothing to her. "How about you?"

"Well enough," was all he said.

Which was a big, fat lie, Ryan thought as he slowed his pace to stay right beside Maya on the narrow but fortunately nearly empty sidewalk. So what else was new? He was used to lying for all sorts of reasons, especially to regular humans. Why should things be different now?

The thing was, his body told him for a long time into the night that he should have done more with Maya, since she seemed to be interested in him, too.

Yeah, your human body, he kept reminding himself—and also how she was likely to react if she ever learned who and what he really was.

They soon reached the restaurant. Once again there was a bit of a wait, and this morning eavesdropping was not likely to be especially productive. No strangers around here were likely to be discussing howls and wolves. Even so, they were soon seated.

They all ordered food similar to the prior morning's. And once they'd told their server what they wanted, Ryan made a few additional suggestions about how Maya should address her talk that afternoon. Strong suggestions. Dictated it a bit more, whether or not she liked that. Heck, it was for her own benefit.

Not to mention his—and the other wolves around town, natural or shifters.

Once they had coffee and their server had left, Ryan was amused when Maya looked him straight in the eye and said, "I know why you wanted to spend some time with me this morning."

Of course she would after that kiss last night…but that's not what she meant. Her expression was neutral—at least if he ignored what looked like a minor combo of heat and irritation in her lovely hazel eyes. Or was he just reading into them what he expected to see?

"Tell me why." He donned a mask of what he hoped looked like humor without much emotion—despite the inappropriate warmth he felt just being in her presence, especially here, at breakfast, with his aide and cover dog and a whole room full of diners around them.

"You want to try to figure out whether I intend to give the talk you want me to this afternoon. Well, it's my decision—and here's what I'm going to say."

Maya began expounding again on the thrill of having wolves in the area, and speculations about what might have happened the other night—not mentioning her own meet-up with canines, he noticed—and the reports on a person having been injured by a wolf after possibly trying to find the source of the howls.

"After that, I'll get into what WHaM is about again—keeping track of wildlife and appreciating it, and hopefully getting other people to appreciate it, too. Plus, maintaining as good a census as possible."

She paused as their server reappeared with food and more coffee. Beside Ryan, Rocky stood up and all but put his nose on the table, so both he and Piers gave the beggar a little of their own breakfasts.

As he did so, Ryan said to Maya, "Sounds exactly like what I'd suggest so far, but I assume there's more."

"Of course there's more," Maya asserted. A lot more, she thought—but she'd get into only part of it here. "That's when I'll again stress how wonderful our country is," she continued, "with its wildlife free in a lot of areas to exist and thrive and be there for us, sometimes, to see. But the threatened and endangered animals need to be kept safe.

And for that to happen, people who are interested in them have to use their supposedly more intelligent human brains and remember not to get too close. After all, we call them *wild*life for a reason." She gave a sharp nod as she stressed that first syllable. And then she opened her mouth to continue with her approach, what she wanted to say, how she wanted to convince people—

But Ryan interrupted. "I like it all. I know you'll do a great job." His eyes met hers, and despite her mouth still being open and her slight irritation at having been stopped, she felt warm inside. Appreciated.

"Thank you," she said softly, swallowing the rest of her ideas. "And—"

"And we'll be there, of course, to cheer you on," Piers added. Maya dragged her gaze away from Ryan to look at him.

"Thanks," she said again.

"Plus, we may contribute to what you say," Ryan added. "And help keep the audience under control as they cheer you."

Which made Maya feel even warmer. She hoped all would go well that afternoon.

Maybe with Ryan and Piers there, and Rocky, too, it would.

Breakfast was over soon, though the guys hadn't seemed to be in a particular hurry. Even so, after Maya had taken the time to let everyone in the restaurant know about her next upcoming talk, they all soon left. At least this time she didn't have to fight very hard to ensure she could pay her own bill, although they didn't allow her to treat them.

Well, maybe next time.

She felt rather sad when they said goodbye to her outside the door. "We'll see you at your talk this afternoon,"

Ryan said, and then the men and Rocky started down the sidewalk without asking where she was heading or inviting her to join them.

Oh, well. She had a goal of sorts in mind, although she wasn't sure how to fulfill it.

It wasn't enough just to let this morning's restaurant patrons know about her talk. She had to at least go visit the people in town who'd seemed interested in what she'd said before. Interested in wildlife protection.

Too bad she didn't know where that Trev was staying. She'd like to let him know, too. He'd at least stood up for her and WHaM before.

For the next half hour, she walked the streets of Fritts Corner, stopping in the Corner Grocery Store and other establishments, letting the owners know and inviting them to come to her talk.

When she figured it was almost time to head for the park, she saw Trev across the street, alone this time and not with the girl she'd seen him with the other day.

She waited till the street was empty of moving cars, then crossed.

"Hey, Trev," she called but didn't really have to since he had apparently seen her, too, and was waiting for her. Today his button-down shirt was blue, his light, short hair was messy, and he grinned geekily at her once more. "I hope you have some time this afternoon," she told him, and quickly explained why.

"Keeping the audience under control will be the big thing," Ryan said to Piers later as they stood beside the aging podium. Maya was already at it, getting her presentation together and preparing to show slides again on the screen behind her.

Right now, that part of the park was filling up with a lot of people, and Ryan recognized quite a few.

Any media folks? He wasn't sure but didn't think he saw any who'd admitted to it at Maya's last presentation, and no one appeared to be preparing to take notes and pictures.

Some of those present had been in the restaurant that morning, though. He'd been somewhat amused when, after they'd finished eating, Maya had insisted on circling the tables and inviting the patrons to come hear a talk this afternoon all about the wonders of wildlife—and how to protect oneself, too.

In fact, Piers and he had joined in, and Rocky's presence had garnered a lot of attention that indicated the people they spoke with actually had an interest in attending.

Some had mentioned coming back since they enjoyed Maya's last presentation.

But when they were done, Ryan had gotten Piers and Rocky headed back to their hotel. He'd have liked to stay with Maya but they had some Alpha Force business to attend to.

And he'd known he would see her soon. Here. In the park.

In fact, they'd already met up with her, right where they expected she would be.

"Wow!" she said. "There are a lot of people here already and I don't start for another ten minutes."

Ryan looked up at the podium to see that Maya had stopped fussing with the materials in front of her and began looking at the grounds. Her eyes looked huge, as if she was a bit nervous, but then she smiled.

"Guess I'd better do a good job," she added.

"Guess you'd better." Ryan made his tone sound stern, but when she caught his eye he grinned. "And I'm sure you will."

She seemed to relax a little as she got back to organizing her stuff. And Ryan looked around.

"She's right," Piers said. "And so are you." He stood near Ryan, with Rocky sitting on the lawn beside him looking interested and alert.

"Of course I am," Ryan responded. "You should know that."

He was teasing, of course, but that was a sort of reminder that, in their real life and job, Piers was his aide. Not that Piers ever needed a reminder. He had even taken charge of typing on his computer the list of to-do thoughts Ryan had dictated to him back at their hotel before—mundane stuff in addition to the way he assisted in Ryan's shifts. Now, he just raised his eyebrows at his superior officer, who smiled and looked down toward Rocky.

"Good boy," Ryan said soothingly to his cover dog, who remained still but tense as he sat there. Did Rocky capture the smell of shifters in this group? At least for now, Ryan didn't.

But as he had hoped, the whole Sharan family was there—Burt and Kathie and their son, Pete. At the moment, they all stood off toward the edge of the crowd, with some other folks Ryan recognized from the earlier presentation and otherwise, including bar owner Buck Lesterman. They were too far away from him to catch their scents unless he'd been in wolf form.

There were aromas around him, though: the freshness of the grass, some forest smells from the hills rising beyond them, too many perfumes and aftershaves worn by the growing crowd—and canine scents, since some of those people had also brought their dogs to the park for this talk.

A couple of the larger dogs—maybe a Great Dane mix and a Doberman—seemed interested in getting close to Rocky and tugged at their leashes, but their owners kept them well enough under control that they didn't approach. Rocky was aware of them, though, looking in their direction and keeping his nose working.

Good wolf-dog that he was, he didn't pull at his own leash and remained sitting between the two men who were his pack. Ryan kept his hand gently on Rocky's head to reward him.

As they stood there, Ryan noted that guy who'd been at Maya's last presentation and seemed too interested in her afterward now making his way through the crowd. What was his name? Oh, yeah, Trev. But Ryan didn't want to sound as if he cared if some other fellow flirted with her.

Even though, despite how dumb it was, he did care.

The September day was warm and a little humid but not particularly uncomfortable. It seemed a good day for an outdoor presentation.

And Ryan settled in to listen as Maya started to speak. The microphone worked well, and her voice resonated loudly enough so that Ryan believed everyone here could hear her. It seemed quite loud to his own enhanced hearing, and yet he welcomed it.

Welcomed her, and her attitude, and—

He forced himself to stop that train of thought and listen to the wonderful ideas emanating from her.

He'd already become attracted to her aroma, slightly floral and all woman...

"So who here heard the wolves the other night?" she was asking. Her arms seemed to hug the podium's stand as she leaned forward against it and scanned the crowd.

Ryan had a sudden recollection of her hugging him last night but shrugged it off as he, too, looked over the small sea of people. A lot had hands raised, including the Sharans and Lesterman and Trev, and a few called out replies like "Me!" and "I did."

"That's so great!" Maya said. She launched into some of the talk she had presented the other day, about how wolves had disappeared from this area ages ago and were only now reappearing in small numbers. They remained particularly rare in this part of Washington, and all were protected under the law.

The audience seemed interested, even though what Maya was saying now wasn't anything new. What she was showing on the screen behind her, though, included some shots of the area Ryan recognized as where she had gone in the middle of the night after hearing the wolves.

And showed first the two wolves that seemed ready to attack her, then joined by a third wolf.

Him.

Ryan attempted not to react. He should have anticipated that, since he'd seen her wielding her camera and knew she had taken video clips. If she knew what she was doing, it was easy enough to pull still shots out. And she clearly knew what she was doing.

As long as she didn't confront any more wolves…

And hopefully she wouldn't. She now began talking about how wonderful it was as an officer of WHaM to be able to potentially see and count wolves around here.

She didn't admit she'd already seen any or where she had gotten those pictures.

"But the thing is, even those of us who are real wildlife advocates have to understand, and remember, that wildlife is wild. I say that often, and I mean it. The animals, especially these wolves, are wonderful, and we all love seeing them, but we nevertheless have to be careful. If we get too close, they don't understand that we appreciate them, want to see them and get to know them better and all. They could get frightened, consider us enemies and attack. That means we should never get too near them. Appreciate them, yes. Approach them, no."

She had the grace to look away from the audience and down toward Ryan, as if looking for his reaction—and approval.

He smiled a bit grimly as a reminder to her that what she was saying worked for her, too, and nodded.

"Okay, then. I'm going to start describing a few scenarios that could happen under present circumstances, where potentially dangerous but oh, so wonderful wildlife is present in an area and what you should do to protect yourselves. First of all, did any of you see those wolves that were howling and barking the other night?"

No one raised their hands, not even the Sharans. Smart to lie about that, though, if they did happen to be shifters.

Or maybe he was all wrong and they weren't, in fact, shifters—although he doubted that. As a shifter himself, even before he had heard of Alpha Force and joined it and gotten access to the elixir, he and his family had been well aware of others, some who mixed with them in the remote area of Wyoming where he had grown up, and others who had stayed to themselves.

The old-timers knew who they were, in any case—even when they had just moved to the area. And Ryan's own parents and grandparents had given him pointers on how to figure that out, such as recognizing the special scents that shifters might give off even when in human form.

It didn't really matter what the Sharans admitted—or didn't. One way or another, whether he remained here or returned, Ryan would be here during the time of the next full moon and hang around them enough to see for himself if they were shifters.

Since sighting of wolves was fairly new to this area, any shifters were newcomers, too. They might already know how to protect themselves, but if Ryan, and Alpha Force, could help them, all the better.

But for now, he would hang around at least long enough to—

Hey. Maya was still talking, asking the audience to respond to various scenarios she was creating in which wolves might become too close to people, but the crowd was parting close to the podium.

Coming closer was someone who had apparently not just been in some fictional scenario, but had actually been attacked.

At the forefront was Morton Fritts, followed by his wife, Vinnie and by their wolf-hating friend, Carlo Silling.

They were stealing attention away from Maya, which wasn't surprising in this crowd that mostly consisted of locals who would know who Morton was—and what had happened to him. And Morton wasn't walking fast but appeared to be limping.

Rocky seemed to sense the tension in the crowd and stood. Piers had a good hold on his leash and looked at Ryan, who shook his head slightly to express his concern but tell his aide to stand down for now.

Maya finally saw what was happening and stopped talking. She seemed to hesitate for a minute, and Ryan quickly weighed whether he could help her better by joining her or staying where he was.

She sort of removed the choice from him when she began talking. "Oh, my goodness. I'm afraid we have an example of what can happen to people who meet a wolf under bad circumstances. Morton, I'm so glad to see you here and hope you're okay."

That was appropriate and sympathetic, yet it sounded sort of like an invitation for him to talk, Ryan figured. And apparently so did Morton.

He reached the far side of the podium from where Ryan stood, and Carlo helped him climb the couple of steps. Ryan got closer to the steps on the other side but didn't go up them—yet.

Morton wore a long-sleeved T-shirt and jeans that hid any of his injuries beneath. But his face was injured, too. The damage could have been bites or claw marks; Ryan wasn't certain.

Maya started talking again into her microphone but Morton grabbed it from her. "What the hell are you doing here again?" he shouted into it, glaring at Maya. "And saying things about how people should be welcoming wolves back to this area? I could have been killed by the one that attacked me. I was just trying to find it, see where one of the animals that was making noise that night was hiding out, and it leaped out at me. And there were more around, too. Wolves back here? That's dangerous. Horrible. And I'm going to do my damnedest to make sure the local laws are changed and we can kill them the way that one tried to kill me."

Chapter 12

"No!" Maya shouted, then took a deep breath as she scrambled to think of what to say next. "No," she repeated, still yelling since she no longer had the microphone. "I'm so sorry about what happened to you. But we need to find ways to get along with the wolves, stay away from them, not kill them. We—"

She was surprised to see a young man who looked familiar join them up on the podium and wrest the mic from Morton, who appeared equally surprised. Staring at Morton, he interrupted her. "Don't the laws of this country mean anything to you, like protection of endangered animals? Don't— Never mind. Why don't you tell everyone here exactly how you supposedly were attacked by that wolf the other night."

Supposedly? From what Maya could see, Morton did look injured. And even though she hated to admit it to herself, his injuries could have been inflicted by a wolf.

His middle-aged face had clearly been mauled, and he had been walking slowly enough to indicate that it wasn't only his face that had been hurt.

Even so...

Well, she could have shared a lot with Morton, maybe for the same reasons, if it hadn't been for chance—like that other wolf appearing and shooing the others away.

But she would never have complained about it if she'd survived. She would have realized she had brought it on herself.

And this man? Was he going to do as asked and tell what had happened?

Maya glanced past the others on the podium toward the crowd below. Some people she recognized from the restaurant were there, as were a few of the storekeepers. Trev was there, too. Unsurprisingly, they all seemed to stare toward the two men who now occupied the podium with her. But no one else said anything. Not yet, at least.

Then there were Ryan and Piers. Ryan watched what was going on with a grim but very interested expression.

Piers was working with Rocky who, for the first time since Maya had met the lovely wolf-dog, appeared almost out of control, as if he, too, wanted to join her up here with the quarreling men.

At the moment, the young man was trying to thrust the microphone back into Morton's hands. "Here," he kept saying. "Tell us."

"Yeah, I will," Morton said, finally grabbing the mic. He spoke into it. "I heard those howls and other sounds like everyone else in town. Like all of you, I was curious. Yeah, I'm not a tree hugger or animal freak but figured I should find out what was going on, so I drove as far as I could to where I thought I'd heard the wolves." He turned to point toward the nearby roadway that looped somewhat around the forested hillside behind them. "I parked, got out of my car and went to look for them." He turned to glare at Maya. "And before you ask, I brought a flashlight and a large stick to defend myself. That's all. No gun, which I regret now."

The rest of his story sounded both familiar and somewhat heartrending to Maya. He'd found a pathway, followed it up to a clearing—which could have been the one where they'd found the patch of possible blood just off it. Looked around, saw nothing, then decided to head back down.

"But before I did, I heard noise in the underbrush and suddenly a big, ugly wolf leaped out. Kind of like that thing." He pointed off the podium toward Rocky, who was standing now, and Maya saw that Piers had him restrained close beside him. Now, he hugged Rocky even closer as Morton continued to stare at the dog.

"So didn't you just walk away from him?" the young man asked. "Run away? Go back down the path and leave?"

"Hell, no. Not that I could have. He got close to me, too close, and then, before I could hit him with my stick, he leaped up on me and I wound up on the ground."

"That's not—"

"And then he bit me. My legs. My side. My face." Morton's voice shook and his eyes seemed to stare into the distance.

"But—"

Morton seemed to pull himself together and aim his rage at the other man. "You think it was fun? Or I should just suck it up and forget what happened? Well, no way. Forget that. I don't want it to happen to anyone else, and neither should you."

With that, he shoved the microphone back at the other

guy and headed toward the steps at the edge of the podium. Vinnie and Carlo helped him down the steps.

The young man looked at the mic in his hand, then spoke into it. "Er—look, everybody. I'm relatively new to town, and so's my family. I'm Pete Sharan, and my parents are right there." He pointed toward the edge of the crowd where the grocery store owners stood. "I just don't believe what that man said. I've studied wildlife for a long time, especially wolves. And unless they're in protective mode, to take care of themselves or their families, they mostly just run away when there are humans around. They don't trust humans."

"Right. They don't trust us? Well, we don't trust them, either." That was Carlo Silling shouting from where he now stood nearby with the Frittses. "Kill 'em all. That's what we need to do."

Pete Sharan looked as if he was about to leap down from the podium and attack the other man, so Maya drew closer. Arguing here, or, worse, getting into a physical altercation, wouldn't solve anything.

She reached out and gently pulled the mic from Pete's hand, at the same time touching his arm as if soothing him. Or at least easing his temper—hopefully.

"I agree with you," she said into the mic so that others could hear her despite how softly she spoke. "But we don't know all the circumstances. Despite what Mr. Fritts said, that wolf could have been in protection mode. Mr. Fritts might just not have seen what scared the poor animal. It's terrible that he was hurt, of course, but—"

"But the damn wolves have to go!" That came from someone else in the audience, a person Maya didn't think she'd met.

The call was echoed by others, and Maya felt as if she wanted to cry.

Pete Sharan did cry out. "No! You people just don't understand. They're not—"

Ryan was suddenly on the podium with them. He was the next to take control of the microphone.

"Please listen, everyone. I'm Ryan Blaiddinger of the US Fish and Wildlife Service. What happened to Mr. Fritts is, of course, terrible. I'll report it to my agency. But we need more information, as Mr. Sharan said. We want to prevent anything like this from happening again, and going after any kind of protected animal, like wolves, is not permitted except by obtaining an official exemption under the law. My colleague and I will conduct an investigation while we're here, but in the meantime everyone needs to listen to what Ms. Everton said before. No one is denying that there are wolves around. We all need to stay safe— and that means staying away from them. Now, let's all go to our homes or hotels and get out of here."

Maya wanted to hug Ryan not only for what he said, but also because he glared at the people who'd been arguing to kill the wolves, including Morton Fritts.

She could understand his rage, his desire to do something to the wolf that injured him.

But all wolves?

That man needed to be watched.

Something was going to happen.

Staring down at the crowd, Ryan could sense it—and not as a result of his enhanced natural senses.

But he saw the glares that the Fritts side leveled against the Sharans and other townsfolk who supported Maya and what she said and the return of the wolves.

He saw the equally hostile glares shot back in return.

He felt the anger. The emotions. He thought he understood why, at least from the Sharans' perspective—assuming he was correct in what and who they were.

He assumed that the Frittses' antagonism was partly because of the attack on Morton, yet he felt it was somehow more than that. That faction had been upset by the influx of wolves to the area even before.

Why?

"May I?" He heard Maya's whisper from beside him and looked down. She regarded him quizzically, her head cocked as one hand reached for the microphone. Before he could respond, tell her he had more to say—did he?—she added, "I just want to finish up here." How could he say no? He handed over the mic.

She thanked him with a nod, then said into the device, "Once again, I tell you all to be careful and stay away from any wolves you happen to see or hear—but please let me know about them, or let Ryan know, so WHaM and Fish and Wildlife can follow up. And now, I thank you all and say goodbye. Enjoy the sounds of the wolves—and stay safe."

Then she shut off the mic and placed it back on the stand.

"This is becoming even worse," she said to Ryan. "Dangerous. The two sides are getting even further apart, at least somewhat because of that attack on Fritts. I'm not sure how to handle this, how to protect the wolves. Can you feds do anything to make it better?"

"The wolves are protected here under the law," he said, staring right into her lovely, troubled eyes. "You know that. Under some circumstances we might capture and relocate them, but not now. And if we started searching for them, we would most likely have to look for the one that attacked Fritts and put it down if we found it. Maybe we should do that anyway, but for now I intend to let it go, as long as that's the end of it. But we all—you and us—want to see how things progress with the wolves now that they've returned to this area. We just need to try to ensure there are no further incidents."

At least the likelihood was that, if the wolf who'd attacked Fritts was a shifter, there'd be nothing else that could happen for a month.

But if it had been a feral wolf?

"I...I understand," Maya said hoarsely, and he wished he could sweep her into his arms and hold her tightly to comfort her. And maybe to comfort himself, as well.

This hadn't been what he had anticipated when Alpha Force had sent him here to investigate the slow influx of wolves and determine if any happened to be shifters. He had thought he would be here simply observing, in whichever form made sense at any particular time.

But now? Now he had an urge to protect. Who? Individuals of many kinds: wolves, and those who cared for them, and people who turned into them. And the wolf who had attacked Fritts? If it was feral and ferocious, was it legal not to put it down? He didn't know, didn't want to find out.

"Okay." He put a dose of strength and encouragement into his voice. "It's time for us to leave. Good presentation, by the way. You handled Morton's interruption well. Now, we'll wait and see what happens."

"Right." She clearly tried to shake off her anxiety, too. She started toward the steps.

And stopped. Ryan saw why immediately. The Fritts group was gathered at the bottom, facing one another and talking. They seemed to block any ability to get by them.

That didn't deter Maya for long. Ryan attempted to place himself in front of her but she walked down the few stairs and said, "Excuse me," edging her way around them.

"No, you are not excused," Vinnie Fritts asserted, planting herself in Maya's path. "Do you want more people hurt by those terrible creatures?"

"I am very sorry about what happened to your husband." Maya's voice sounded exasperated, as if she didn't like repeating what she had already said. "But really, I'm not sure we know the whole story. And even if we do—well, it was a regrettable incident but that doesn't mean anyone who does as I said, and stays far away if they happen to believe a wolf is nearby, will also get hurt."

"You bitch!" Vinnie shouted. "Are you calling my husband a liar?"

"I. Did. Not. Say. That." Ryan admired how Maya spoke slowly and with determination. "I'm sure the circumstances were very difficult for him and may have affected his memory of what happened. But—"

"You'd better watch out!" That was Morton, who'd come around his wife to confront Maya. "I told you what happened and that I was curious, yes, but didn't purposely get near a damned wolf." He was getting too near Maya, though, his fists clenched as if threatening her.

Ryan hurriedly put himself between Maya and the others. "I think we've gone as far with this as we're going to. We all know the situation. Everyone feels bad about what happened to Morton."

Although it couldn't have happened to a more appropriate person, Ryan thought. He deserved to be whipped by a wolf, shifter or not. But what had happened not only put the influx of wolves into the spotlight, but also potentially endangered them even more.

"But," he continued, "we're through here. Morton is unlikely to identify the wolf, and there's not going to be a change in their protected status because of this incident." Especially since Ryan wasn't convinced that Morton had explained it truthfully in the first place. "We are all sorry, but glad that Morton is recovering." He glared from husband to wife, then turned to Maya, grabbed her hand and began walking to the area at the far side of the podium where Piers stood with Rocky.

This afternoon's event had definitely come to an end. Or had it?

Piers asked Maya some questions about what she was planning to do next on WHaM's behalf, and as she began answering how she would keep her organization informed Ryan looked around. The Sharan group remained at the edge of the park area nearest where the forest began and rose up the hillside.

He focused his attention on them, wishing his hearing was as acute now as when he was shifted. Multiple conversations also made it harder to hear.

But Ryan believed he caught a few words—like *careful*. And *avoid*. And *protect*.

Interesting and appropriate, but inconclusive.

It was time to pay another visit to the Corner Grocery Store. He had more conversations to conduct with the Sharans, and a lot more to learn about them.

What was going to happen now? Maya wondered as she walked back toward the hotel with the two men and their dog.

She hadn't planned on staying in Fritts Corner for long. All she had intended was to visit on behalf of WHaM and try to rev up all the locals she could about the wonderful situation they had here, while she determined the best way to conduct a census.

Now, she wished she had a way to ensure the wolves' protection.

Could she count on Ryan and Piers and the Fish and Wildlife Service?

She wanted to. She liked Ryan, in particular. A lot.

But his being a sexually attractive guy who also cared about wildlife didn't mean he could work miracles. And ensuring the wolves' survival, their thriving, could wind up requiring a miracle.

"Will you join us for dinner again tonight?"

That was Piers, who walked on her right. The men had been kind enough to let her hold Rocky's leash again, and the dog was on her left.

They followed Ryan, who took the lead. Again. She had the sense the guy was always happy to be in charge.

This time it had been a good idea.

At Piers's invitation, she looked forward toward Ryan. Had he heard? Did he want her with them?

He kept walking at first. But when she hesitated and said, "Well, I'm not sure—" Ryan turned.

"Of course you're sure," he said. "You're joining us. We wolf-lovers need to stick together." The warmth in his gaze suggested that he wanted them to stay in each other's company for more reasons than because they were wildlife aficionados.

Or was she reading too much into it?

In any event, they made plans to meet at six o'clock in the hotel lobby, where they parted now after reaching their inn midafternoon.

Maya headed upstairs, exhausted and needing time devoted to something other than her beloved job. Or did she? She got on her computer a short while after reaching her room and found herself searching the internet for all she could find about the US Fish and Wildlife Service. And when she got onto the site, she tried searching for Ryan Blaiddinger.

She didn't find him, which wasn't a big surprise since

many directorships and positions were referenced but sel-dom those who held them.

But when she Googled him next, she learned something very interesting.

Not that it made any difference, but she decided not to mention it immediately. But it amused her…and made her wonder.

Maya decided she would at least attempt to rest be-fore dinner, but a while after she'd reached her room, as she tried to relax, the hotel room phone rang. She stood from the chair she had planted herself in and picked up the receiver from the small desk next to the TV monitor. "Hello?"

"Hi, Maya? This is Trev. I was at your talk before."

And he hadn't done or said anything helpful in favor of protecting the wolves.

"How did you find me here?" she asked.

"Well—" He sounded rather sheepish. "I…I wanted to talk to you so I kind of followed when you left the park."

She wasn't surprised. "Okay," she said, though she wasn't particularly pleased. "But why? And why are you calling?"

She half expected him to fumble around but ask her for a date. She felt half-sorry for him. Maybe the other woman he'd been talking to had shown no interest, or had dumped him.

But Maya wasn't about to make him think he had a chance with her.

"Would you mind coming down to the hotel lobby and grabbing some coffee with me? I really want to find out more about WHaM. Maybe I could even come up with some suggestions for dealing with that guy who was mauled by a wolf."

Really? She couldn't imagine how, but she didn't know

this guy's background. Maybe he actually could be of some use. After all, he'd said he had come to town to hear her speak about WHaM.

"All right," she said. "I'll be down in a minute."

"So what are your intentions regarding Ms. Everton?" Piers was in Ryan's room along with Rocky, waiting for a call back from Drew. "You seem to be watching and talking with her a lot. Any reason beside her love of wolves?" His eyebrows were raised, and Ryan's aide seemed amused.

"That's the main reason," Ryan said. "And don't start reading anything into it other than I want to make sure she remains safe. Sure, she's hot, but the thing that concerns me is that she's willing to stick her nonwolfen nose into anything that—"

His phone rang, relieving Ryan a bit. Piers was right. Ryan felt much too attracted to Maya, even though he hadn't acted on it. Not yet, at least.

The caller ID identified Drew Connell. "Hi, Drew," he said, pressing the button to turn his phone's speaker on. "Just called to give you an update."

And confirm with their commanding officer that they'd be hanging out there, under the circumstances, potentially a lot longer.

"So what did you think of what happened at my presentation?" Maya asked.

She sat across from Trev at a tiny table for two at a coffee shop attached to the hotel. A few of the tables around them were empty, but the shop was fairly busy for being this late in the afternoon.

"I didn't know what to think of it." Trev lifted his cup of frothy latte to his narrow lips and took a sip. His small brown eyes were trained on her face, though, making her feel uncomfortable.

She reached down for her cup of plain black coffee and just held it for now. "Well, I'd heard about Morton Fritts's injuries before," she said. "And I can understand his being upset by it. His family, too. But I gathered from what he said that he wished he had shot that wolf—and maybe that all wolves in this area should now be killed. That's definitely too much. Don't you think? Do you agree with that other guy, Pete, who came up on the podium, too? I do. Despite what Mr. Fritts asserted, we really don't know the full set of circumstances, and no one should rush to conclusions that the wolf was at fault."

Trev at least appeared to be pro-wildlife before. And if he wasn't, why would he have come here just because he had heard Maya was giving a talk on behalf of wildlife for WHaM?

"I sort of understand the Frittses' position," he said plaintively. "Pete's, too, and yours, and that Ryan's. But mostly—well, what is WHaM's position when someone, a person, is hurt by a protected wolf, or another wild animal that it is in favor of protecting? Or was in favor of protecting before the injury? Do you always assume the animal wasn't just a vicious and dangerous creature?"

"It depends on the circumstances," Maya stated. "As I've said since I got here, wildlife is wild. People should understand and respect that, and stay out of the animals' way. Allow them to flee if they're scared, rather than challenging them. I still don't completely understand how Morton and that wolf wound up confronting each other, but my assumption is that Morton should simply have recognized that a wolf is a wolf and backed off. Don't you think?"

"So that's WHaM's position?" Trev put down his latte and looked at Maya. His expression was almost accusatory.

Not that she knew the guy at all, but she was a little surprised. He'd seemed to be a wildlife advocate, or so she'd believed. And so far, he'd just seemed like a nice, nerdy guy.

On the other hand, it wouldn't be surprising if he liked people better than the animals and was torn by this kind of situation.

"Yes," she said, "although no one at WHaM is in favor of animals attacking people, or even attacking other animals except as prey for food. But the reality is that those kinds of things happen. Even animals recognize that others in or out of their species may be prone to attack or kill in some circumstances. People certainly should recognize it."

Trev leaned back a little, once more lifting his latte to his mouth. He appeared a bit pensive now. "So your position, and WHaM's, is that animals are just that—animals. And they can do what they want, without people having that right, too?"

"In a way, although like other animals, people have the right to protect themselves in dangerous situations. What we don't like is the idea of simply hunting down animals like wolves because they have a reputation of being dangerous sometimes."

Maya wondered what Ryan, as an employee of US Fish and Wildlife, would think of this conversation.

She suddenly wished he was here with her, helping her explain to this guy the best way to react to this kind of situation—or at least the best way from her, and the government department's, position.

She had no doubt that Ryan would back her position.

She also wondered why Trev was asking all this. She asked him. "So what's your position on this? Are you on WHaM's side?"

"Yeah. Sort of. I certainly understand what you're saying. Anyway, how long will you be in town? I'm really glad we got to meet this way."

"Me, too," Maya lied. "And I'm not sure how long I'll be here. I don't have any more talks planned, not now, at least. But I do want to be here long enough to make sure that nothing inappropriate is done to the wolves, despite the attack on Mr. Fritts."

"Me, too," Trev said.

And Maya determined that to be an appropriate end to their conversation.

She also hedged and lied a bit when Trev said how much he'd enjoyed talking with her and hoped they'd get a chance to do it again.

Chapter 13

That night, Ryan pondered whether to go right to bed, or return to the forest and shift and…well, just explore. Wait. Look to see what feral wolves might be hanging out there.

No shifters should be, at least.

He'd said good-night to Maya right after dinner, then done the same with Piers a short while ago. His aide had taken Rocky and headed to his room. Now, Ryan was alone, which should be good for letting him relax and fall asleep.

He was, in fact, in bed, looking up some things about the area on his tablet computer, mostly stuff he had already read. But he hoped to find more on the history of wolves around here.

Also, out of curiosity, he tried looking up that guy he'd met and Maya had mentioned, Trev Garlona.

Maya had said Trev had invited her downstairs for coffee that afternoon, after her talk. They'd discussed what had occurred in the park, she told Ryan—what Morton Fritts had said and how he'd wanted to kill all wolves, and how Pete Sharan had confronted him about it.

Maya indicated that Trev seemed a bit confused, even though he was a wildlife lover and claimed to have come to Fritts Corner mainly because he'd heard that she, as a representative of WHaM, was coming here to talk about the influx of wolves and how wonderful that was.

Was, perhaps, being the operative word now.

Well, Ryan hadn't been able to find anything about a Trev Garlona, his background, where he'd come from, whether he'd ever done anything to help protected wildlife.

And Ryan realized that he'd looked mainly because he felt irritated that someone, even a wildlife aficionado, would invite Maya out for coffee. A dumb irritation. She was here to talk about wildlife protection, particularly wolves. And of course she'd be thrilled to talk to anyone else who felt the same way. It was her job. It was her passion.

Although…well, no, it was totally wrong to even consider her thinking of Ryan as her passion…

He gave up soon on Garlona, figuring he'd check the name in the morning. Instead, he did some more research to locate any additional posts about wolves in this part of Washington State. He did find a couple of social media posts about the apparent attack on Morton, some anger by people who weren't on the side of protected wildlife, but nothing indicating they intended to do anything about it—a good thing.

Starting to nod off, he shut down the computer, turned out the lights and settled in.

Until—a howl! It interrupted and ended his twilight sleep status. Was it real? Or had he dreamed it?

Another one. He jumped up and reached for his phone to call Piers. They needed to find out where this wolf was.

What it was. It had to be feral since the moon wasn't full. And Ryan would need to chase it away before its life was endangered...any more than it already may be.

That meant he had to shift.

But before he pressed in his aide's number, his phone rang. He looked at it.

Maya.

"You heard that howl, right?" he said immediately after pushing the button to answer. "I did, too. Piers and I are going to check it out so you can just stay safely in your room. Got it?"

"But—I want to come with you."

"You'll only slow us down." And no way was he going to allow her to see him shift. "You're slowing me down right now. Promise you'll stay in your room. Now. So I can leave."

"But—"

"Promise."

A silence for a beat, and then she said, "Okay, I promise, if that's the only way—"

"It is. Bye. I'll call you later and let you know what we find. Now, stay in your room. You've promised."

With that he hung up—hoping that the woman would actually do as she'd said.

Then he called Piers—who turned out to be in the hallway outside his room.

And when Ryan opened the door he wasn't surprised to see that Piers was without Rocky—and wearing his heavy backpack.

"Great," he said to his aide. "Let's go."

Maya stayed in her room for all of a minute, staring at the walls. The windows.

The door.

Sure, she had promised…but had crossed her fingers to take some of the sting out of her lie. She'd had to promise, and she knew that Ryan's heart was in the right place.

He wanted to protect her.

Well, she wanted to protect him, too—but at the moment that wolf was on her mind. If they'd heard the howls, the likelihood was that a lot of other people in this town had, too.

Possibly including the Frittses and their cohorts who wanted to get rid of the newest visitors to Fritts Corner.

The wolf's life was undoubtedly in danger. Also undoubtedly, Ryan, of US Fish and Wildlife, would do all he could to protect and save it.

Well, so would she.

With a sigh, she dressed quickly in dark clothes and athletic shoes, issued a silent apology to Ryan and sneaked her way into the hotel parking lot, which was filled with cars but no other people. She didn't see the rental car Ryan and Piers used. They were undoubtedly already on their way.

Thanks to the direction from which the howls had emanated, she would assume that this latest wolf incursion was around the same location as the last—on the forested slopes beyond the park. The two of them—Ryan and Piers—couldn't cover the entire area, although they had one advantage: Rocky, whose nose could help them find the wolf more easily than people could.

But her advantage was that she thought she knew where the guys would at least start out: the location where they believed Morton Fritts had been attacked, where she'd spotted the stain on the ground that they'd assumed to be blood.

She would head there.

Sure enough, their rental car was parked in the nearest lot to that location. She exited her car and looked around.

She didn't see anyone else, though there were a few more cars in the lot. That could be the situation every night, as far as she knew.

She headed toward the path she had taken before in daylight. She hadn't heard any more howls. Did that bode badly for the wolf?

She wished she could run toward her target area, but that would be foolish. First, despite the beam from her flashlight, it was too dark. She might trip and hurt herself—and make herself more vulnerable in the event that wolf truly was ready to chew up some more people.

Second—and probably more critical—she'd most likely make enough noise that not only wolves would be able to hear her. She didn't want Ryan or Piers, or anyone who might be hunting that wolf, to know she was around, even though she might prefer being somewhere near them in case she got into trouble.

And so she moved slowly, frustrated, sure, but this was the safest way to go. She hoped.

Notwithstanding the light she carried, darkness enveloped her among all the tall trees as she trod slowly along the underbrush. She tried to stay alert to all sounds around her, since she would probably hear any wolf before she spotted it in the dark forest.

Any people, too.

The forest at night smelled lightly of pine trees and other plants. Her breathing was heavy, and she thought she smelled a light skunky odor—but nothing nearby.

She'd gone a significant distance, believing the clearing she aimed for was fairly close, without hearing or otherwise getting the sense that any wolf was nearby—and then she heard a sound.

Voices. Soft, yes, but it sounded like one man's voice, followed by another. Off to her right.

Could that be Ryan and Piers?

Or someone out to get the wolf?

Remaining as quiet as she could, she maneuvered in that direction. If it was them, should she let them know she'd lied and come out here this night anyway?

She'd observe them for a while and decide.

A ray of light seemed to emanate off to her left and she headed that way, shutting off her own flashlight.

There. This was a different, smaller clearing. The two men she assumed would be there were, in fact, there.

But what were they doing?

Ryan stood there in the nude. In the nude! Under other circumstances Maya would be more than impressed with his amazing muscular physique. Her gaze was drawn below to his even more amazing man parts, large and taut and the sexiest she'd ever seen.

But why was he undressed?

The light she had seen emanated from a large battery-operated lantern that Piers held, aiming it toward Ryan.

Ryan suddenly let out a sound that resembled a cross between a groan and a growl—and then he began to change.

What was going on? This couldn't be real!

The man writhed as his limbs shortened. The rest of his body shortened, too, even as fur began to emerge from his skin.

And his head. His face. It elongated into…

Oh, heavens! Maya had never even considered that the old myths could be true.

In moments, a creature resembling Rocky, whom Maya had not seen here this night, crouched on all fours on the ground.

Even with the information Maya had seen, and laughed about, online, she'd never considered this as a possibility.

Ryan Blaiddinger was a werewolf!

The discomfort and pain of a shift never became easier. And this time there was the additional distraction.

He had drunk the elixir. Piers aimed the light toward him. And then he had heard and scented and become fully aware that they weren't alone.

They had checked the area before. No indication of wolves or those who wished to harm them, or even other humans.

But she had somehow located them. Maya.

She had seen him shift.

He needed to protect her—and himself and Piers. He quickly motioned his head toward his aide, who had shut off the light. He then turned to indicate the direction he would now be going.

In moments, he was in the woods. He slunk toward her as if in submission, hoping she would not feel threatened or scream.

"What are you?" she demanded. She sounded hoarse, incredulous, frightened, but fortunately kept her voice low.

He made a noise deep in his throat that was not a growl, then nudged her side with his muzzle. At the same time, Piers joined them.

"What are you doing here?" his aide demanded, keeping his voice low.

"I—I wanted to help protect the wolf. I hoped to find you but didn't know you were here. And—" She turned and faced Ryan. "What is going on?" Her voice had risen and Ryan nudged her again.

"Come with me." Piers took her arm. "We'll stay together and talk. This wolf has work to do."

Good. His aide had things under control as much as possible. Ryan loped into the woods.

He listened with his enhanced, wolfen hearing. Yes. He heard human voices in the distance and ran that way.

Then he scented something off to his side. Another scent similar to his and to other wolves'.

He changed his course, heading in that direction.

He spotted the other wolf soon. Heard the sound of his paws on the underbrush.

He was heading in the direction from which the voices had come.

He had to be stopped, and so Ryan accelerated his pace, aiming to place himself in front of the other canine, soon succeeding.

The wolf growled, showed his fangs, acted altogether threatening.

So did Ryan—for the protection of this fellow wolf. This fellow shifter, for his scent seemed somewhat familiar.

Yet another shifter on this night with no full moon? He would need to learn answers...later.

For now, the only language they shared was that of their wolfen sides. And so Ryan growled as well, crouching as if ready to leap, to attack.

He showed his own fangs first, then nodded his head. Closed his mouth as if in submission. Moved forward to bump his counterpart, urge him to run off in the opposite direction.

He sensed confusion in the other wolf. Stubbornness at first, until Ryan pushed him again with his head against the other wolf's side. And again.

The communication worked. With a look toward him first that looked puzzled yet belligerent, the other wolf stopped. Stood still. Then ran off into the woods—going the way Ryan had urged him.

Away from the sound of the voices.

For minutes, Ryan stayed still, listening in an attempt to be sure the other wolf wasn't simply skirting around to return to where he wasn't welcome.

Then Ryan headed stealthily in the direction of those voices.

In the same clearing where blood had been found stood several humans. One was the male Fritts who had allegedly been attacked here. The others were his female, and that Silling human.

They were listening. Talking about wolves and how they would make sure all were disposed of—properly.

Properly in their point of view.

Ryan had an urge to leap into the clearing and dispose of them properly from a wolf's point of view, but that was his wild and wolfen side.

His human side took charge and he listened some more. Smelled the air.

No other wolves were nearby.

Even if these humans had weapons, no other wolf would be harmed that night.

After a while, they began laughing. Said that seeing no wolf here, despite the howls, was fine.

They began walking farther up into the forest.

He walked back toward where he had left the other humans.

When he reached that clearing, he found the two he had left there remained.

But he also caught the scent of the wolf he had chased off from the other location.

He moved around the clearing until he found the other canine, who also simply stood there in the shadow of the nearby trees, staying at the periphery and appearing to listen.

Not seeming in attack mode.
This shifter outside the full moon. Like him.
They looked deeply into each other's eyes, but only for a moment.
And then the other wolf ran off down the hill.

Chapter 14

Maya's stress level rose, making her feel like shouting. After Ryan, the wolf, disappeared into the woods, she had joined Piers in this remote clearing lit only by the dimmed lantern—where that frightening yet amazing event had occurred—and stayed there with him for a couple of reasons. First, because her legs were so shaky that she couldn't have made her way down the pathway to the park without falling, let alone following the wolf that had previously been Ryan, which was what she craved doing.

Second, because she wanted more information. A lot more. A full and credible explanation, if there could be such a thing.

But when she had asked Piers, who'd seemed shocked and unhappy to see her, he had kept dissembling, hinting he was under orders to stay quiet. From whom? Ryan? Not him? Not *only* him? Then who? And wasn't Maya supposed to have stayed in the hotel? Hey, wouldn't she like an energy bar or a bottle of water? As if that would distract her.

So now, she sat on the ground on a towel Piers had removed from his backpack and laid down there for her.

"How long do you plan to stay here?" she asked for the umpteenth time.

Piers, who'd remained standing, repositioned his stocky frame yet again, scanning the trees blocking the view to everywhere rather than meeting Maya's stare. His arms were crossed, and his expression appeared grumpy—or was that anxiety?

If only Maya could read his mind. Hey, she'd assumed mind reading to be a myth, a legend, wholly untrue. But after seeing what Ryan had done, she wondered if there was truth in all the old supernatural fairy tales of the world.

"I take it you're waiting for Ryan to return," she tried again. "Did you both somehow hypnotize me from a distance? Will he come back here looking like he usually does—" handsome, sexy and wholly human "—or is he really some kind of werewolf right now?"

"Don't know for sure," Piers said, this time glancing at her.

But which didn't he know—whether Ryan was a kind of werewolf, or if, when he got back here, he'd still look like a wolf instead of a person?

He clearly wasn't saying.

So Maya continued to sit there and fume and worry—both about Ryan and about her own sanity.

She listened for the howl of a wolf. The one she'd heard back at the hotel couldn't have been Ryan, so at least one more had to be out and about, possibly in this area.

She hoped Ryan would return soon. Maybe he'd actually explain what had happened. Or would he be able to?

Could he talk as a human if he was still a wolf?

Was she insane?

This all seemed so bizarre. As much as she adored wild-life, as much as she loved wolves and learning about them and conducting censuses where they now resided, she had never even considered what had happened here as a possibility.

And now—well, were there more beings like Ryan?

Should she plan on taking a census of them?

Ryan would have preferred doing his shift back to human form in Piers's company so his aide could help with the necessary details, like bringing his clothes over and making sure there were no harmful obstacles in the area that could hurt Ryan during the uncomfortable change.

But, once he'd sensed that Maya was now with Piers, he'd done it while he was alone in the forest. Thanks to the elixir he was able to choose the time as well as the place, and he'd done it not far from this area, yet far enough for them not to know he was there.

He even had some ability to choose the time of shifting back under a full moon, thanks to the elixir. But he, and all other shifters, changed under the full moon, though with more control with the elixir.

And now—well, he stood behind a tree just outside the clearing. Nude. He kind of liked that idea, considered strutting through the coolness right into that area to show it all off to Maya. Bad idea.

He hadn't wanted her there when he'd shifted before. Now, to keep control of the situation this night, he didn't want to be naked in front of her again. Though the idea wasn't exactly displeasing. But this wasn't the time or the place.

Some other time, maybe—one of his choosing. And hers. For more than a shifting.

As if that would ever happen…but he recalled again that kiss he'd backed away from, and a critical part of him that had been pretty much at rest started rising to attention.

Damn. He shouldn't react that way. After all, he was angry with her. She had broken her promise to stay at the hotel.

He glanced around again. He didn't see his clothes, and figured that Piers had tucked them away in his bag as usual till they were needed again.

He considered strutting out there once more, just as he was. Ignoring any stare she leveled on him—or staring right back in challenge.

Yeah, he liked that, but figured there were better challenges to be met that night, like convincing Maya that what she had seen needed to be kept to herself.

He did see a towel on the ground—the one Maya sat on. Hell. Enough of this.

"Piers," he called loudly and was pleased to see Maya's eyes widen, her body spasm because he'd startled her. "I'm here. Bring me that towel."

He half expected an argument from Maya, but she merely stood up, still staring in the direction of his voice—though he felt certain she couldn't see him behind this tree.

"Yes, sir—er, be there in a second," Piers shot back. Damn. The "yes, sir" might give away their military status, although maybe they should tell her anyway. Ryan would have to determine whether to obtain permission to do that as they talked—for he felt certain they would be talking about what she'd seen and who he was, and he'd have to be as discreet about Alpha Force as necessary.

Although, with her love of wildlife, maybe honesty would work with her.

Maybe.

Well, he'd rather have his superior officer's okay before revealing anything about their special military unit.

Piers had grabbed the towel and was now at the other side of the tree. "You all right?" he asked Ryan—no "sir" this time.

"Fine. I'll tell you about it." He took the towel and wrapped it around his middle so it hid everything critical. "She handling this okay?"

"She's one nosy woman." Ryan had stepped away from the tree and saw, in the dim light, that Piers's round head was shaking back and forth, as if he was in total bemusement by Maya.

That somehow made Ryan smile. "Not surprising. Now, whatever I decide to tell her, you back me up, okay."

"Yeah," Piers said. "Although I've got a feeling that no matter what you say she's going to dissect it, and you, till she feels comfortable she knows everything."

"That," Ryan said, "is what I'm afraid of. Well, here goes." He walked around Piers and approached Maya, who stood where she'd been seated before, watching them. "Hi," he called to her. "I'm sure you're having an interesting night. I hope it's a good one, too."

Even though nothing personal was showing at the moment, she looked down toward the critical area hidden by the towel and that made him stiffen there even more. "It could be better," she said, her gaze returning to his face. "As soon as you explain to me what's going on, and what I saw."

"Sure," he said, although he didn't mention there were parts of the situation he'd need to keep to himself—and Piers. "Just let me get dressed and we'll talk." Piers had already retrieved his clothes from the backpack and handed them to him. "Excuse me a minute."

"I'm not sure I'll ever excuse you," he heard Maya mut-

ter as he returned behind the tree where he'd been standing before.

This time, Piers stayed with him, handing him items of
clothing to put on and taking the towel.

"You doing okay with all this?" Ryan asked his aide.

"Not really. I didn't tell her a damned thing but even
when she wasn't pressing me for information I felt pressure flowing from her. She's determined."

"We already knew that about her feeling toward
wolves," Ryan reminded him with a smile. "And now we'll
just have to find out how she feels about shifting wolves.
You ready?"

Piers nodded. "Sure, I'm ready. Are you?"

"Of course," Ryan lied.

He had a feeling that the remainder of this night—and
maybe even way beyond that—was going to be made extremely interesting by Maya Everton.

They all started walking down the hillside, along the
same path that Maya had scaled to get there, their way lit
only by the flashlights they held.

It wasn't always easy, but she stood right beside Ryan,
her athletic shoes allowing her some traction on the
crunchy dry leaf-covered slope. Piers followed, and she
had the sense the guy was relieved that she wasn't urging
him to talk any longer.

"So when are you going to explain everything to me?"
she asked after Ryan said nothing for a long minute, although he did take her arm to help balance her. A real
gentleman.

A wolf in man's clothing—casual, ordinary-looking
clothing, right down to his own athletic shoes.

A wolf…

"There's not much to explain," he said. "You saw me. I'm a shapeshifter who changes into a wolf sometimes."

"Then it was real, not some kind of hypnosis or mind control?" Although even if it had been, she'd have no idea why he'd have done it to her.

"No, it was real."

She slipped a little on some leaves beneath her feet, possibly because of the distraction and unease his words caused within her. He caught her, and she was very aware of his touch.

A human's touch.

But still... "So when does it happen? All the old legends say that shifting occurs under a full moon, right? Like the other night. But the moon tonight wasn't full. It's waning." A thought hit her. "If any of that is real, does that mean the wolves I saw a couple of nights ago were shifters, too?"

"At least one of them was," he told her, and she thought she heard some humor in his tone.

The crunching of dried leaves beneath their feet stopped as she stood still for a few seconds and turned to stare at him. "You? You were that third wolf who ran the others off?"

"That's right." She couldn't see him well in the darkness lit only by the flashlights all three of them held, but she knew he was grinning at her. He found this fun.

She found it...well, actually she was fascinated by it. She'd always been a number cruncher and a scientist, too, with degrees both in statistics and biology. She particularly loved wildlife.

Could she learn to accept the reality of people who changed into wild animals?

Somehow, she thought she could. How weird!

How fun.

"Then why—" she began, but he interrupted.

"Look, this is neither the time nor place for me to answer your questions."

"Why not? We have a few minutes before we—"

"I'm tired. What I do takes energy."

More likely, he simply didn't want to discuss his shifting.

But she wasn't about to give up. Not completely, at least. "Okay, then. Go back to your room and get some sleep. But let's set a time to meet tomorrow to talk about all this."

He didn't respond right away. Was he trying to come up with some excuse why they shouldn't ever talk about it?

Somehow, that possibility nearly made her eyes tear up. Why was she so emotional about this?

About him?

Because she now associated him even more with wolves, the animals she particularly loved?

"Okay," he finally said, and instead of tears she felt a smile on her face. "It'll have to be someplace with total privacy. And not first thing tomorrow. We can meet for breakfast, if you'd like, but I have some things I need to take care of in the morning right afterward so that won't give us enough time. Let's meet in the park later, find an area with just one bench where we can be alone and talk privately. That okay with you?"

They'd reached the bottom of the trail, and the street was nearby, the parking lot just at its other side.

"That sounds fine." At least assuming he meant it.

They walked together to her car, and she pushed the button to unlock it. There were a few lights hanging on poles in the parking lot so she could now actually see him.

Ryan, the man. The handsome, attractive…and strange and mysterious man.

Piers now stood behind him, clearly waiting.

"See you back at the hotel," she told the two men. "Although if you take much time to get there I'll head up to my room."

"In that case," Ryan said, "we'll see you tomorrow."

As she opened her car door, she looked at him again, recalling how she had kissed him the other night—and how he'd seemed uncomfortable because of it.

Well, heck, he'd certainly made her uncomfortable by more than a kiss that night. And though she had no idea at the moment what she thought of this man, and who and what he was, she leaned toward him, grabbed him again and kissed him once more on those sexy lips.

He seemed to react this time as well, but before he could kiss her harder—or pull away—she was the one to back off and hurriedly plant herself in her car.

"See ya," she said, and pulled the door shut.

"I can't wait till later," Maya shot at Ryan first thing the next morning, when he reached the lobby with Piers and Rocky and found her standing not far from the registration desk. "Please—can we talk now?"

"We figured that out last night," he said calmly, hoping to soothe the clearly upset woman. He led her away from the busy area of the hotel where lots of people were in line to check out or check in. There was an empty corner nearby, not far from the single elevator. When Maya was situated there, he looked down again into her huge-eyed face. "Like we discussed, we'll have breakfast now, then meet up again later at—"

"At the park," she finished, keeping her voice low as she shook her head. "I know. But I have so many questions and couldn't sleep for the few hours I had left last night, and—"

He needed to calm and quiet her. This wasn't the right

place or right time, but they were at least temporarily out of the main stream of people.

He glanced toward where he had left Piers and Rocky and didn't see them, so he figured his aide had taken his cover dog out for his morning walk while waiting for Maya and him. Good.

"—and the thing is I'm not sure if—"

Ryan bent down and placed his mouth over Maya's. That shut her up.

It also got him possibly as stirred up as she was, for different reasons.

He had a sudden urge, while their kiss deepened and grew even hotter, to forget about breakfast and what else he had to do this morning and lead Maya back upstairs to his room.

But what else he had to do this morning was critical. It might help him fulfill the mission he had been sent here to Fritts Corner to accomplish.

And so, just as he'd been the one to start this encounter, he was the one to regretfully pull away.

As he did, he looked down and saw that Maya's hazel eyes regarded him with what appeared to be both lust... and suspicion.

"Are you trying to distract me?" she asked in a normal tone, as if what they had done meant nothing to her. Except that, as he watched, she took a deep breath, clearly trying to calm herself.

"Yeah," he said. "Am I succeeding?"

She let out a brief snort of laughter. "I guess so. Maybe it's time for breakfast, after all."

She turned and preceded him out of the lobby.

Chapter 15

Surprisingly, their breakfast had worked out well.

They again ate at the popular local restaurant Andy and Family's. They sat in an area of the patio where Rocky was welcome.

They ordered pretty much the same meals as they had before.

And Ryan was relieved that Maya had gotten the message, that he wasn't about to have the conversation she wanted until later that morning.

So, instead of quizzing him about what she had seen, she instead got into a long discussion and Q&A session about wolves and where they were endangered in the United States, and what Fish and Wildlife was doing about it.

Which suggested to him that she'd guessed he actually wasn't employed by that federal department. But she didn't press him—then—to explain what his connection was, or wasn't, to it. Or to anything else.

He felt certain she didn't know about Alpha Force.

When they were done eating, he had insisted on paying the bill, claiming once more that it was on Uncle Sam. In a way it was, though not via US Fish and Wildlife. Alpha Force was, after all, a US military unit—albeit a covert one.

They had parted ways outside the restaurant. He hadn't told Maya where he intended to go, but he'd already requested that Piers and Rocky accompany her back to the hotel.

He didn't know what she might do to occupy her time until their planned eleven-thirty meeting in the park, but being with him was definitely not on the agenda.

He'd walked the other direction—and was just approaching the Corner Grocery Store. He had called in advance, so the Sharans were expecting him.

Whether they wanted to talk with him was another matter. But he would definitely talk to them—and he had also told them he wanted their son, Pete, to be present.

And in fact he was present—in the store. As Ryan walked in, he noticed Pete taking cash at one of the registers, the line extending quite a ways in the busy establishment. Hopefully, someone else would take his place soon.

Otherwise, Ryan would need to insist on it, and he believed that what he was going to approach Pete's parents with would cause them to ensure their son joined their private conversation.

Scanning the crowd, he soon saw Kathie Sharan talking to someone in the produce aisle. She might have been watching for him, since she immediately caught his gaze, then smiled at the customer she'd been talking to and walked in Ryan's direction.

Her smile disappeared. She soon joined him at the front of the place and looked up at him. "Come into our office.

I'll get Burt and Pete." Her voice was cool, but her expression appeared troubled.

Kathie was short and wore a lacy white top that extended over the waist of her jeans. Her multishade brown hair appeared rumpled, giving her the appearance of an anxious woman, and perhaps hinting about the possibility of her shifting background.

She easily led Ryan between patrons to a door near the rear corner of the store, opened it and said, "Go on in. We'll be right there." She left the door open as she hurried into the crowd they had just left.

The office was a small, enclosed square with a plain wooden desk in the middle, a few chairs and a file cabinet. A laptop computer sat on the desk, and nothing else. There were no pictures on the pale yellow walls, no other decoration in the room. It was functional, Ryan supposed, and maybe it hadn't had time yet to accumulate extra paperwork or memorabilia since the Sharans were relative newcomers to town and new owners of this store.

In any event, nothing there stood out to prove or disprove Ryan's suspicions of who the Sharans were.

But he knew.

He walked over to look out the small window near the rear corner. It fronted on the building next door—an ice cream shop, Ryan believed, though from the back portion he couldn't view any signage.

He heard a noise and turned back toward the door. All three Sharans had just entered, and Burt closed the door behind him.

"So why are you here?" Burt's voice was sharp and clearly uninviting. His arms were at his sides, hands fisted, and his expression belligerent—not merely a kindly local grocery seller.

Without responding at first, Ryan walked over to the

desk chair and sat, assuming they would recognize that he was the alpha at this meeting. Maybe beyond it, as well.

"Why don't you all sit down, too?" he asked, his tone congenial for the moment.

"Why don't you answer me?" Burt countered.

"Tell you what. I'd like you all to sit down first, then take a very deep breath. I'm going to, right now." And he did. In doing so, he inhaled a lot of scents, some emanating from food in the store outside the office, aromas he had smelled here before. But the strongest were right in here, with him.

He'd smelled them before, at different times and each in two different incarnations—as they were here, and otherwise.

They hinted of shifters. True? Ryan believed so, and he hoped to confirm it right now.

And get some of his questions answered…

Maya's face popped into his mind. He'd be meeting with her later, too, and it would be her questions they'd discuss. Would he let her in on anything he learned here?

Meanwhile, he watched the others crammed into this small office with him. Burt just eyed him warily, but he did sit on one of the chairs, and his wife and son took seats, as well. They all tilted their chins upward then, and Ryan watched their heads move and their chests expand as they obeyed and also took deep breaths.

Pete wasn't as beefy as his father, but his nose was as long, and Ryan allowed his mind to imagine them as wolves right now.

All three stared at him, suspicion on their faces.

"Good," he said. "Now, tell me what you smell."

"Tell me what you think we should smell," countered Pete. His parents looked at him and nodded.

"Here's where this conversation will get interesting,"

Ryan said. "I could continue to dissemble, address what I'm driving at only tangentially and keep up the mystery. But let me try this another way. I'm going to get all woo-woo as a human here—or maybe not."

"A human?" That was Kathie, whose deep brown eyes were huge.

"That's right. As we all are at this moment. But otherwise?"

"Otherwise what?" That was Pete, and although his tone was sharp, the younger man appeared both wary and nervous.

Good. He was the one on whom Ryan had intended to levy the brunt of his initial inquisition, focusing on last night.

And Ryan's own plentiful questions.

"Otherwise—well, first of all, consider what you smelled as you took that deep breath. Some would be familiar, since you're always around together. But then there's me."

Pete nodded. "Then you're—"

"Wait a second," his father broke in, and Pete grew silent again though the look on his face was pensive.

"Okay," Ryan continued, "let's do a bit of pretending but also make some promises. I'm going to approach some pretty offbeat things, or at least they'd seem offbeat to a regular...human."

"What are you talking about?" Pete demanded. He looked anxious and curious, and glanced at his father for approval.

Burt nodded, and Pete appeared to relax, but only for a moment—till Ryan began speaking again.

"Oh, let's go back to last night, shall we? Did you happen to be in the woods up behind the park? If so, I saw you there—and I'm going to assume that neither of us looked…human."

Pete's eyes grew huge, and he looked away from Ryan to his father's face once more, then his mother's.

"Don't let him goad you, son," Burt said. "This conversation is weird. Stupid." He turned from Pete to stare at Ryan, and his expression appeared as if he was trying to look skeptical and scornful.

"Maybe so," Ryan said. "But if you show me yours, I'll show you mine." A little, at least. He wasn't about to reveal all. "I happened to see a wolf up in that area last night, and communicated with him. And that wolf also saw me and responded." His wry smile was levied now on Pete. "Right?"

Instead of appearing frantic now, Pete appeared thoughtful. "Right. Then that was you? I mean—well, tell me what you know."

And Ryan did…somewhat.

The rest of the conversation in that office went pretty much as Ryan hoped. The Sharans did admit they had come to Fritts Corner about ten months earlier with some other people like them when things in the part of Idaho where they'd lived became stressful, and they'd heard that wolves were being seen in the area around here. Wild wolves.

And they had something in common with them. They were obviously reluctant, but when Ryan asked again about what they had smelled, and gestured toward himself, they mentioned that what they had in common with those wolves was that they were like them, a bit. Shifters.

When they admitted it, Burt appeared challenging, as if expecting Ryan to back off the position he had taken before and tell them what fools they were.

But he didn't. And when appropriate, he admitted he was a shifter, too.

"Most shifters only change under a full moon, though," he said to Pete. "You were shifted last night. How?"

"I'm a scientist," he asserted defensively, as if expecting an argument. "I've always been interested in what we are and all its angles. I came up with a formula that allows us to shift outside a full moon. It's pretty new and raw right now and I hope to perfect it soon. But what about you?"

"Oh, I have access to a formula that I think is a lot more perfected than yours. I'm not going to get into detail now, but my bosses—not Fish and Wildlife, by the way—are going to want to hear about this conversation and probably want to hold more talks with you. If all goes as I think it might, you at least, Pete, might get access to that formula one of these days."

After all, part of Ryan's assignment was to see not only if there were shifters around here, but also if any could be recruited into Alpha Force. This young, smart, eager shifter might be one excellent addition to the unit.

"Now tell me," Ryan said. "Why did you shift last night? And why weren't you more quiet about it?"

Pete appeared a little sheepish. "I made a small modification to my formula and, with all that's been going on around here lately, I wanted to try it. It didn't really make much difference, though, and I shifted back right after you and I saw each other. But you're right. I shouldn't have been howling—especially since those admitted wolf-haters are around. But I still can't always control myself... Believe me, I'm glad you're the one who showed up—and I'll be more careful next time."

"Good," Ryan said. "Okay now, I think our conversation today is over—but we'll talk again. And just like you'll deny admitting to anything that came out here if things

go wrong or the wrong people ask questions, so will I—
and one thing I can assure you of is that I do have some
pretty official backing, though it's premature to get into
any detail now."

"Really?" Pete sounded impressed. "Like, the government? Someone there actually believes in shifters?"

"Like I said, I can't get into detail now, so believe what
you want." But Ryan grinned in partial assurance to the
young man. "Anyway, I'll let you know when it's time to
talk again, but I can tell you it'll be soon."

Their goodbyes, though somewhat wary, were a lot
more congenial than when Ryan first came into the office this day.

He felt good that things had gone as well as they had.

He just hoped they would continue to get better.

Maya sat in her room fuming. Hanging around. Playing with her computer.

Looking up shapeshifters.

But it all appeared unreal, legendary, part of the lore
from which fiction books and movies were created.

Somehow the reality had escaped general notice. Or
real shapeshifters had been able to hide it, make it all appear like fiction.

Real shapeshifters like Ryan.

She wanted the truth. She wanted more. But how could
she just wait here—

Her room phone rang. It was unlikely to be Ryan, who
now had her cell phone number. Trev?

"Hi, Maya," said that geeky male voice that she recognized. "Could we get coffee together again now? I'd really
like to talk to you."

About shapeshifters? Did he know?

"What about?" she asked.

"Did you hear those wolves howling last night?"

"Yes," she said, "I did." But what did he think about them? "Sure," she told him. "I have a few minutes. I'll meet you downstairs right away."

Which she did. His button-down shirt that day was beige, and his small, dark eyes seemed hidden in shadows.

Had he been awake last night? Had he been on the hillside, too?

She shouldn't want, shouldn't need, to protect Ryan—and yet, she felt compelled to learn what Trev knew. Or maybe she simply wasn't ready to talk about it, let alone accept it.

"So how are you doing this morning?" she asked as they exited the Washington Inn lobby into the adjoining coffee shop.

"Okay," he said. "But tired."

They placed their orders— basically the same as last time, a frothy latte for Trev and plain, ordinary coffee for Maya. The place was a bit less crowded than before, and this time they chose a different small table, near one of the front windows.

As soon as they sat down, Maya prompted, "So you heard those wolf howls last night, too?" She watched his face for any indication that he'd not only heard them, but he knew what kind of wolves they came from.

She saw nothing but some wryness there.

"Yes, I heard them. There really are a lot of wolves in this area. A good thing for WHaM, I guess."

WHaM and not werewolf hunters. She supposed that was an indication that he knew nothing. "Yes," she said enthusiastically. "I'm really delighted." She paused. She wasn't sure what she thought about shifters, but she actually was delighted about real wolves. And surely the wolves near Fritts Corner weren't all shifters…right? "Aren't you?"

"Well…it's a good sign that the wildlife protection around here is working."

She wondered at his waffling. "You didn't go out and try to find any wolves, did you?"

"Heck, no," he said immediately. He smiled right into her eyes. "I listened to you. Wildlife is wild, right? I don't want to go find it. I didn't want to go and get attacked like that Morton did."

"That's good."

"You didn't go try to find them, either, did you?" he asked, the expression on his face now anxious.

"No," she lied. If he wasn't out on the hillside, he wouldn't know the truth about what she'd done, where she'd been.

What she'd seen.

"But do you think it's even safe to be in this town with all the wolves we've been hearing and all?"

"I think so," she said. "As long as no one is confronting them." She assumed the same rules would apply to shapeshifters.

At least she hoped to find out in a little while, when she got to talk to Ryan privately.

"Do you know of any other dangerous forms of wildlife that are close by?" he asked, still appearing worried. "And would WHaM try to protect them?"

"I'm only aware of the newest wolves, and I haven't yet conducted any kind of survey, as I'd like to. But I need to be careful like everyone else, no matter what I'd like to accomplish for WHaM."

"Okay," he said, still sounding worried. "We all have to be careful."

"Exactly. And now, I'm afraid, I'd better get moving. I've got some WHaM stuff going on soon."

And more.

It was eleven thirty. She'd ended her coffee with Trev when she'd said she was busy, then Maya had come to the park as Ryan and she agreed.

Though she had kind of liked the distraction of sounding Trev out about his apparently minimal knowledge, what he had heard and assumed, it was time. She wanted to talk to Ryan.

There, in the distance, apparently holding a remote bench for them near where the hillside forest began, sat Piers with Rocky sitting at his feet.

Where was Ryan? Piers had refused to answer any of her questions before and she didn't expect more from him now.

But Ryan had promised they would talk.

She strode over a gravel path along the rolling lawn till she reached that bench, not far from her favorite spot here, the podium.

She was glad she wasn't scheduled to give another talk now. What would she say? That she was having hallucinations about werewolves?

That she couldn't get the view of one of them, especially before he had shifted, out of her mind?

Or what the sight, and memory, of that naked body was doing to her psyche?

She'd reached the bench. Rocky stood up and wagged his tail.

The dog looked so much like Ryan appeared when he was in his wolf form.

Undoubtedly by design. Ryan might have chosen his

twin to be his pet, although she figured there was a more strategic reason for it, whatever it was.

Patting Rocky on the head, Maya said, "Hi, Piers. How's your day going?" What she wanted to demand was where Ryan was, and whether he'd sent his friend here to try to divert Maya and her questions.

"Fine." But the stocky guy appeared uneasy. Even so he said, "In case you're wondering, Ryan's on his way."

"Yeah, I was wondering." She paused to sit down, and he joined her on the bench, still holding Rocky's leash. "I don't suppose you have anything to tell me today that you didn't last night."

"No, although I think Ryan will answer at least some of your questions."

"He'd better." Maya scowled, then asked, "And you? You're friends, so I've been wondering if you have the ability to—what's that called? Shapeshift?"

"That's the right name but, no, I'm not a shifter."

"How about Rocky? He looks like Ryan when…when he's—"

"Oh, there he is." The expression on Piers's round face suddenly looked relieved. Maya turned to look in the direction he was facing and saw Ryan striding across the lawn toward them.

Good. Piers was off the hook to talk to her, at least for now.

And, hopefully, she'd get her answers.

She tried to settle down better on the bench, relax so she would appear more in control. She did have some control over the situation, after all. Whatever a shifter was or wasn't, she doubted Ryan would want word to get out about his strange ability.

She could make things difficult for him if she chose—

like revealing the truth, as she'd considered, then cast aside, while talking with Trev.

But she also realized Ryan could make things difficult for her. How could she effectively represent her organization and support the existence of wolves if people thought she was insane? Not that she intended to go public. Ryan would undoubtedly deny what she saw, maybe tell the world she was nuts—

Well, she needed to see how things went here, while at the same time thinking about how to protect her reputation and her work with WHaM.

"Hi," Ryan said with a huge smile on his face as he reached them. He looked so ordinary—well, if one considered a guy as sexy and gorgeous as him ordinary. "Sorry I'm a little late. Interesting morning." That comment was leveled at Piers, not her.

She noted in her mind that she needed to find out what that was about. But not right away.

"That's fine," she said. "But now's the time for truth. What did I see last night?"

She noted that, before Ryan sat down, both he and Piers scanned the area where they were as if checking to see if anyone else was around.

There weren't any kids running around or playing ball as there usually were on weekends. A few people in the distance walked their dogs or stared at their cell phones or both, but no one was nearby.

No excuses for Ryan not to talk—unless he believed someone was aiming some kind of super recording device toward them.

Not likely.

"You saw what you saw," he finally said. Great. What was that supposed to tell her? But he continued, "Things are a little muddled regarding my purpose being here, although that appears to be improving. Because of your background and support of wildlife, I'd like to tell you all and hope to soon. But for now...well, you saw me last night and I do owe you an explanation. Yes, some of the old myths that people look at as sci-fi in movies and all—well, they're true. Or at least there are such things as shape-shifters. And I'm one of them."

"Wow." Maya didn't mean to act all awed and amazed, but one word, wow, probably expressed best how she felt.

Of course she'd had hours to think about it and hadn't concluded that she'd been drugged or turned into a nut-case or anything like that, but still...

"Wow," she repeated. "I want to learn all about it. Were you born that way? And the myth says werewolves shift from people form into wolf form under a full moon—unlike last night. Is any of the mythology real? And—I'd better shut up. I don't want to just keep asking questions and not let you answer anything."

He laughed, and she was amazed when he reached over and took her hand and held it on his leg as he looked straight into her eyes.

His deep brown eyes looked so amused, so intense, so sexy. She couldn't help smiling—and trying to hide the shiver that rushed through her body.

How could she feel so turned on by this man who wasn't exactly a man?

"Look, the main reason I wanted to meet you here was so I could tell you what I'm able—although there are reasons I can't tell you everything, at least not right now. But I'll tell you about me, and a bit about shifters in general, and why I'm here, okay?"

"Great," she said, then added, "Oh, and one more thing before you start. I should have known—kind of. Not that I'd have believed it. But I looked you up on the internet.

Didn't find anything specifically about you, but I did learn something interesting."

"What's that?" Ryan asked.

"That *blaidd* is the Welsh word for wolf."

Chapter 16

Of course he had to be judicious in what he said, but Ryan didn't hide his pride in who he was as he talked to Maya.

She sat beside him on the bench. Close beside him, which he liked a lot. Her hands were in her lap, and her attention clearly was on him.

Piers and Rocky were on his other side, so he couldn't observe his aide's expression, which was a shame. Piers, as a nonshifting member of Alpha Force, had nevertheless been given the standard instructions of what to reveal to whom, and when. Ryan had no intention of overstepping his boundaries here—not till he had received at least Drew's okay, and perhaps other commanding officers', which he intended to seek considering Maya's background and dedication to wolves. But not yet.

He watched her face, though—lovely, with lips slightly pursed as if she was ready to say something yet held back. Her hazel eyes were huge and appeared skeptical yet fascinated. Or was he simply reading what he wanted to there?

He wanted Maya to believe and accept him and…well, like him.

Maybe more, no matter how inappropriate that might be.

He'd started way back, about where legends of shape-shifters originated in ancient times because there really were such beings. "But except for families and some rare and remote communities, they were disjointed, no matter where they existed in the world. At least that's how our legends go, since such isolated individuals didn't share a lot, mostly because they couldn't. And they needed to stay quiet about it since superstitious and fearful humans killed any shifters they came to know about. Plus, shifters not only become wolves, but other animals, too—lynxes, hawks and more, which remains the same today. But you're right about the somewhat ironic meaning of my name. Someone way back in the family must have chosen it."

He went on to talk about the first shifters in the United States, arriving also in small groups during the days of early settlers and finding areas to settle, often where wild creatures of the same kind they changed into lived to make it easier to hide in plain sight.

Today, he told her, there were enclaves of shifters all over the country, all over the world, but they mostly kept to themselves without even letting others know they existed or where they lived.

Mostly.

He felt Piers move behind him on the bench and realized his aide was getting a bit concerned about how much Ryan intended to tell Maya.

He needn't have. Ryan was about done with his talk—and he hadn't even hinted at the existence of Alpha Force.

But he hadn't counted on the intelligence of Maya, who

deemed herself a statistician and more, to attempt to push him into a further discussion.

"So how do shifters shift?" she asked. "I guess the old legends are wrong about there having to be a full moon."

Ryan hesitated. She had seen him shifted, so this question was logical. He considered how to respond, but he had to be careful. Maya was too smart just to buy into some stupid explanation.

"The old legends were spot-on during their times," he finally said, looking beyond Maya, not wanting to meet her eyes as he continued to ponder the best way to handle this. "Shifters had no control over when they would shift, and it always happened during a full moon." He didn't bother to mention that they had no human cognition then, either.

Only shifters with access to the Alpha Force elixir or some other kind of chemical modification could choose, at least to some extent, when to change—and be able to think like their human counterpart then, too.

"But now?" Maya pushed.

"Oh, there've been experiments over the years and a few shifters—not all of them—have been able to work things out to have a little more control."

"How?" she insisted. "I assume you're one of those with control. And I saw that Piers took some kind of bottle from your hands and shone a light on you when you started to change."

Of course she had noticed. She was too intelligent not to equate what she had seen with what he had done. What could he tell her now?

The barest minimum.

"That's right. I'm among the lucky few with access to a formulated drink that gives us some control."

"That's how you did it last night. Was it the same under the full moon the other night?"

He wanted to grab this woman and shut her up—by kissing those full lips beneath her light, furrowed, puzzled brows.

He also had an urge to tell her the truth, but he couldn't. Not yet at least.

"It was similar," he said. "Because I like the degree of control it provides, I take one of those drinks then, too."

"And the light is supposed to resemble the full moon?"

Damn, but she was intuitive. And if he didn't watch out, she'd ask about the origin of the drink he took, and why Piers, a nonshifter, helped him, and more that he couldn't respond to.

"Kind of. Now, I've pretty much told you what I can. Would you like to join us? I'd like to go get a cup of coffee."

"So werewolves drink coffee like anyone else when they're not shifted. And you seem to eat pretty standard stuff, too. But why can't you tell me anything else?"

Piers was suddenly standing beside them. "Hey, guys, my coffee addiction's calling. Let's go find the nearest coffeehouse and get a quick cup, okay?"

Maya looked toward Ryan and laughed. "Whatever is going on, I think you have your buddy Piers well educated in when to intrude to protect you. That tells me something, although I don't know what. But you can be sure, Mr. Ryan *Blaidd*inger—" she stressed the "blaidd" part "—that I won't rest until I know it all."

Which was exactly as he'd feared—but expected.

"Then you won't rest for a long time," he countered, but he smiled at her, and she smiled back.

"Oh, we'll see about that. We'll talk again, very soon, here or someplace else. I don't mind us being away from everyone else, but I intend to hear everything from you. Count on it."

Which meant he needed to talk to Drew and others within Alpha Force today. He'd already intended to, since he also wanted the okay to reveal the covert unit's existence to the Sharans after getting their promise of secrecy.

Mostly because he wanted to start recruiting Pete.

"Okay," Maya said, standing to face Piers. "I assume you know what's going on even if you can't change into a wolf. But I also assume you're not about to answer all my questions that Ryan hasn't."

"You assume right," Piers said, nodding and grinning.

"How about you?" Maya bent down to look right into Rocky's face, but the dog just leaned forward and licked her cheek. "Sweet, but not what I was after. Okay, guess I won't get it all today." She turned to face Ryan, who'd also stood up. "But I will get it one of these days. And you can be sure I appreciate the bit that you did tell me."

She looked ready to lean forward as Rocky had done, and Ryan assumed it wouldn't be to lick his cheek. He just smiled and said, "I like your challenge, Maya. And just to be clear, I intend to keep as many secrets as I want. Got it?"

"Just wait and see," she said, standing with her hands on her hips as if challenging him even more.

This was amazing!

Well, the explanation wasn't as amazing as what she had seen, Maya thought as she strode alongside Ryan beneath the sunshine—no full moon now—back through the park toward the street. They talked about the town again, how they had each decided to come here to check out the wolves, what the weather was like, what other parts of Washington State they had each visited, all kinds of neutral stuff.

But all the while, Maya's mind was churning.

As she'd told him, she wanted to know more. A lot more than she'd even suggested to that man. That shifter.

How did it feel to be a human one moment and a wolf the next? What did he do as a wolf—the same thing as real wolves did as far as hunting and prowling or whatever?

Was it possible for a person who wasn't a shifter to become one? If so, how?

And…well, she probably shouldn't even be thinking of this, but if they happened to have sex what would it be like? Not that she'd want to get that near him while he was in wolf form. But in his current, all-man form, would it be different from sex with other men?

She believed it would be, no matter what. This part man, part wolf, was one very sexy human male, and she'd seen the sexiest parts of him. Been briefly in his arms and kissed him.

Oh, yeah, what would it be like? And could she get pregnant by him? She certainly wouldn't want to, but if she happened to, what would their offspring be like—her, or him?

This man, or whatever he was, was making her nuts!

She nearly stumbled on the uneven path along the lawn, and, as if she'd planned it that way, Ryan reached over to steady her and held on.

They followed Piers and Rocky, so there was no embarrassment involved in her reaching over to clutch Ryan's hand as he still held her arm. They walked that way for a while, until they reached the sidewalk at the edge of the park. The street nearby wasn't crowded, but cars passed by frequently. Maya quickly released Ryan, and he did the same with her.

She felt suddenly bereft and alone—and maybe even wanting to see this guy shift again. How odd was that?

"So," Ryan said, "it's lunchtime. I know we had breakfast together, but are you interested in joining us again, and not just for coffee?"

Piers, who now stood facing them with Rocky at his feet as usual, moved a little, and Maya had a sense that he was silently conveying his wish that Ryan hadn't asked—and that she wouldn't agree.

Which might mean he'd hurry them through the meal, and she wouldn't want that.

"You know what?" she said. "I think I'd rather get a dinner commitment tonight. Is that okay with you two?" A nice, long dinner, but she didn't say that. At least if that worked out she'd get to see Ryan again—and maybe come up with a new approach to get him talking more. Too bad they were staying in a hotel. If she had her own place here she could cook him dinner...and seduce him with food. To talk, at least.

"Sure," he said quickly, turning back to her. His expression now seemed somewhat relieved, and that made her feel a bit gloomy. He was jumping at a chance to get out of her company more quickly, at least for a little while. Piers must have reminded him of something.

Oh, well. They'd see each other that evening.

And might she be able to convince him to consume whatever he ate or drank and change into a wolf that night? She smiled at the idea.

But her smile immediately evaporated as she saw a crowd of people heading down the sidewalk toward them. They were still a distance away, but the man in front looked like Morton Fritts.

That identity was confirmed as the people got closer. How many were there? They didn't move fast, but Maya thought that the people bringing up the rear were photographing the area and the Frittses.

Why? As they drew closer, Maya saw Trev among them.

Some of the others fanned out and seemed to take photos, and maybe videos, of Maya and the people and dog she was with, too.

What was going on?

Piers asked the same thing. "What are those damned animal-haters up to?" he whispered to Ryan.

"I'm afraid we're about to learn."

"Shouldn't we just get out of here?" Piers pulled slightly on Rocky's leash as if preparing the dog to run.

"No. We need to find out...in case we need to deal with it."

Maya wondered if the group was about to say they'd started killing wolves or something horrendous that they wanted photographed so the world would know about it.

But a minute later, Maya wished she had just fled the area.

Things were never simple.

For as soon as the group reached them, Morton Fritts, his face still covered by healing wounds, bellowed, "So we found you back here again, you wolf-lovers. Bad enough that your damned vicious creatures attacked me the other night. But look at this. Look what they did to my Vinnie."

He moved off to the side, and Maya saw that, behind him, his wife was being wheeled in a chair pushed by Carlo Silling.

She was dressed in shorts that revealed bandages up and down both legs.

And her neck was bandaged as if she'd been bitten, her face even more mangled by scratches, or worse, than Morton's had been.

Maya's mood immediately shot from excited and happy and curious to—well, she still was curious. But she was also scared. Not for herself, but for all wolves around, regular and shifters.

Ryan and others.

Surely he hadn't hurt Vinnie. But who had? A truly wild wolf?

Were there other shifters around besides Ryan? She thought he'd hinted at it, but that was one of the things she'd have to somehow wrestle from him.

For now, she stepped forward around Ryan and made herself ask Vinnie, "What happened? I know you're hurt, but will you be okay?"

As she anticipated, the first thing the injured woman did was say, "What do you think happened? Just like my poor, dear husband, I was attacked by one of your damned wolves." She glared at Maya the entire time she talked, and winced a lot between words.

"I'm very sorry." And she was. For Vinnie, yes, although for her to have gotten hurt by a wolf she had to have ignored Maya's talk yesterday and put herself in that wolf's presence.

It was one thing for Maya to ignore herself, knowing the possible dangers and deciding to do what she wanted anyway.

But Vinnie should definitely have known better, especially after her husband had been hurt, too.

"Of course you're sorry," Vinnie hissed, wincing some more and placing her hand on first one cheek, then the other. "Because you know this can't go on. Something has to be done about your horrible wolves."

"And we're going to do it." That was Morton, who'd maneuvered to stand beside his wife. "You can tell your damned WHaM group. And you—" he looked around Maya toward where Ryan still stood "—can let your damned Fish and Wildlife tree huggers know that keeping wolves on a federal protection list anywhere is not acceptable—never mind that this is the western part of Washington. If anything, our state fish and wildlife group should be in charge here, too, not just in the eastern part, but it really doesn't matter. You won't see which, if any of us, disposes of the wolves so you won't be able to arrest us. But you can be sure they're going to disappear."

"Oh, we'll know," Maya spat back. "You're threatening them. We'll protect them." She certainly would do her darnedest and figured that Ryan, who had even more reason to do so, would do all he could, as well. "And if anything happens to them, just guess where we'll start looking for the perpetrator."

But the very idea of anything happening to those wonderful, wild animals made her quiver inside.

They had to do something to make sure they stayed safe. Immediately.

But what?

She turned toward Ryan, knowing she looked hopeless.

He, on the other hand, stood there straight and tall and strong-looking.

"I don't know what your problem is with wolves," he said, "or why you apparently put yourselves into situations where they attack you. But Maya is right. If it's just one wolf and it's particularly dangerous, maybe we can do something about it. But if you're doing this purposely, for some reason of your own—"

"We just want things to go back to the way they were before more damned wolves started showing up here!" Vinnie stood up from her wheelchair and hobbled toward Ryan to face him. "And if the government won't do something about it, we will."

Chapter 17

What provoked Ryan most at the moment were the members of the media who had followed the Frittses here and were taking videos. They started hollering out questions.

"Why are there wolves around here now?"

"What is the government going to do about capturing dangerous animals like that?"

"What is US Fish and Wildlife doing here now? Are you already involved in locating and euthanizing the dangerous wolves?"

Ryan, who now stood beside Maya on the crowded sidewalk to attempt to protect her from this mess, bit his tongue to avoid yelling at this group of humans who didn't have a clue.

The problem was, he didn't, either. Which wolf—which type of wolf—was doing this?

He'd considered the possibility it could have been Pete Sharan, since he had been shifted last night. Ryan would ask Pete some questions but didn't believe it was that young shifter. The aspects of their meeting, and Ryan's brief viewing of the Frittses, made that very unlikely.

And why had both Frittses been hurt that way? Sure, they'd apparently put themselves into a dangerous situation, confronting agitated wolves of whichever type. But why?

And why were so many media representatives here, in this remote town? There were more than had shown up for Maya's first presentation. Had the Frittses called them, piqued their interest by mentioning the attacks? Maybe they'd have had no interest in just one, but now it was becoming an epidemic, even though both of those who'd been hurt were in the same family.

"Sorry, everyone," Ryan finally said after tamping down his temper. "No comment. But I will be looking into this situation further. We don't want any more incidents in which people are hurt. We don't want any wolves to be hurt, either. Please remember that they are still listed as an endangered species, especially in this part of Washington, and cannot be hunted." And be sure to put that in any articles you write, he thought but didn't say.

Questions still bombarded him as he turned and started walking toward Piers and Rocky, glad that Maya remained beside him. There was more he could have said about what constituted an endangered species—but in fact he didn't have all the answers.

He was a shapeshifter in the military, not really an employee of the Fish and Wildlife Service. He knew a little, but not enough.

That gave him an internal excuse not to answer any questions, but he was hardly going to admit that rationale.

"What are you going to do?" Maya asked as they hurried away. "I think we need more information about where the Frittses have found the wolves and gotten so close and—well, do you think they're endangering themselves on purpose?"

"I wouldn't be surprised," Ryan said. "I'd like to know why, though."

"Because they're obviously interested in wolves." Piers kept up with them along the sidewalk, with Rocky leading the pack. "And dislike them. But it doesn't make sense that they endanger themselves unless they have some other motive to cause the wolves to look bad. Getting rid of them in this area, sure—but why is it that important to them?"

"Yeah, we need to find out their motive, and also which wolf or wolves are involved."

"Which, as in whether they're shifters?" Maya fortunately kept her voice low. She looked between Ryan and Piers as if unsure which would answer.

"That's right," Ryan responded even more softly. "But we don't talk about that here."

Not that anyone was close enough to hear, certainly not the media behind them. But Maya needed to understand that there'd been a reason he had only spoken with her in a remote area of the park.

Secrecy. It was extremely important, especially to Alpha Force. The world wasn't to learn about the covert military unit. Especially not on his watch.

"I get it," she said. "But—look, I want to stress that I need more information, too. I want WHaM to help protect the wolves around here. *All* the wolves, even if the rest of my group isn't…well, aware."

He could have hugged her. She was willing to do what she could to help shifters as well as feral wolves, and was listening to him, not being specific in what she said.

He had even more of an urge now to explain his

own background and reason for being here. Piers's and Rocky's, too.

That meant he had to leave her presence for a while, right now, to make sure he followed all necessary protocols.

"We really appreciate that," he said, looking at her. "And—well, we're going to walk you back to the hotel, then Piers and I need to go find a place to make a phone call."

Her expression turned wry. "A private call, I take it. That's fine. I know you're full of secrets." She grinned, then grew solemn again. "But just don't forget that we're on the same side. I just want to help."

He had an urge to grab and kiss her right there, despite Piers being beside them and a whole slew of locals and media still following them. He hadn't turned to check out how many were there, but he could hear the footsteps—some that sounded uneven, so they were probably the Frittses keeping up despite their limps—and irritated comments. It might be hard to get away to find a quiet and private location. But hopefully his group's heading into the hotel for a while would get the others bored enough to leave.

In addition, some cars on the road beside them slowed as drivers gawked at the parade behind them. Some shouted questions, too, and a few got responses from the gang— explaining they were trying to get more information about dangerous wolves.

Ryan was relieved when they finally reached the hotel. He turned to face their pursuers. Carlo Silling still pushed the wheelchair, but Vinnie was no longer in it. "Thank you all for caring about wolves," Ryan said. "Now, we're heading to our rooms for a little privacy." There was some grumbling, and the Frittses appeared ready to limp inside and confront them, but Ryan turned away.

The lobby wasn't extremely busy, fortunately. Though Maya said she'd be fine here, Ryan insisted on accompanying her upstairs to her room. Piers led Rocky to the rear of the first floor, where their rooms were.

The stairway was empty except for them as they walked to the third floor. No one followed, not even the Frittses.

After Maya used her key to unlock the door, Ryan pushed it open, then followed her inside, instinctively wanting to make sure no one waited for her there—like another anti-wolf protester.

Was that really his reason? After checking the place out, he returned to her side near the door.

"What's that about?" she asked. "Do all Fish and Wildlife people act like police or security people and look for intruders—wolf or human?"

"Maybe not all," he said with a laugh, and then, knowing he had to leave, he grew serious. "Just be careful. And I don't only mean keep away from wolves in the woods."

"I promise that—"

She didn't finish, since he took her in his arms and gave her a quick—yet hot—kiss. It felt better than he wanted to think about to have her curvaceous body snugged up against him—making parts of him stand at attention. He quickly let go.

"See you later, for dinner," he said.

"Yeah, see you later," she responded with a grin so sexy he considered staying for a while.

But he didn't. He left the room, closing the door behind him—and looked forward to seeing her again in a few hours.

Maya had an urge to dash right back out the door.

To kiss Ryan again? Yeah, right. But she didn't think

she'd be able to just hang out here for the few hours until they met up for dinner.

One of these days, she'd head to places like the local animal shelter or, better yet, city hall, to discuss the wolves and their reception by citizens other than those like the Frittses, or people who showed up at her talks. How about the rest of the locals? What did they think?

How had Trev learned about what happened to Vinnie? Or had he simply seen, and joined, the crowd and found out about it then? She might ask him next time she saw him, but she wasn't about to try to contact him now. Despite his initial appearance of being a wildlife lover interested in WHaM, he'd seemed to vacillate a bit when they'd spoken. She wanted him, and the other wolf fanciers in town, to stay that way no matter what had been going on with the Frittses.

Yes, she'd have to start mingling again soon. Asking questions phrased to encourage people to recognize that wolves were wonderful representations of wildlife— stressing the *wild*.

But not now. She was too keyed up, plus she wanted to at least pretend to obey Ryan this time. And since today was Sunday, no one would be at city hall anyway.

Heading into the woods at night after hearing a wolf howl was an entirely different matter.

She sat down on the edge of the lacy coverlet on her bed, crossing her jeans-clad legs and holding her cell phone, which she'd extracted from the small purse she'd been carrying. She pushed a button to call a person whose voice might help calm her: Cheryl Jaker, a fellow WHaM member who also lived in Colorado.

Cheryl answered right away. "Maya! Good to hear from you. How are things in the state of Washington?"

Maya stared at a picture on the hotel room's wall, a representation of a train with an old-fashioned engine at the base of a mountain. She had wondered, on seeing it for the first time, where that area was located—and whether there were wolves around at the time.

"Not great," she said. She proceeded to give her friend a rundown on her talks here and the people she'd met, the existence of wolves—some of which she'd seen—and the apparent attacks on people by them.

Her only reference to Ryan, Piers and Rocky was a mention that some US Fish and Wildlife folks happened to be there, too. She didn't say anything about shapeshifters.

Even if she hadn't promised to stay quiet about them, she wouldn't want her good friend and colleague at WHaM to think she'd gone crazy.

"That's terrible!" Cheryl exclaimed when she was done. "What are you going to do to help protect the wolves?"

"I'm fortunate to have the Fish and Wildlife guys around. They're aware of the situation and seem to be taking charge. Fortunately, with the protected status of wolves in this area, they're not just giving a license to the people who've been hurt, or anyone else, to kill the animals."

A license like that under the circumstances could be an even bigger mistake than usual, if the attacking animal happened to be a shifted human...

"Well, that part's good, at least. Keep me informed. And you take good care of yourself, understand? I know how you love to go meet the animals you're just supposed to view from a distance and count for our census. If some around there are particularly likely to harm people..."

"I get it. And as I said, I've been telling everyone to avoid the wildlife to be safe."

"Are you heeding your own warnings?" Cheryl knew her too well.

"I will from now on," she said—crossing her fingers

as she had before when making promises to Ryan. She would take care of herself—but she would do what she needed to do.

"You have a better idea?" Ryan asked Piers. They were in the rental car, with Rocky lying on the backseat, still in the hotel parking lot. There was no particular place they needed to go, but this was certainly a private location.

A good place, Ryan thought, for them to make their phone call.

"No, but I thought we were getting into the car to drive somewhere to call HQ. I'd have brought a cup of coffee or something."

This guy certainly liked his java. "We could drive to a coffee shop, if you'd like."

"Why not?" Piers was in the driver's seat and immediately backed out of the parking spot. The hotel had an adjoining coffee shop, but a big-name chain was only a block away, and had a nice-sized parking lot, too.

About ten minutes later, they were back in the same positions in the car, this time with hot drinks in the cup holders between them.

A few patrons got into their cars nearby, and others exited a vehicle parked in the row facing them. None looked interested in a couple of guys sitting in a car sipping coffee. The air outside was cool enough that the inside of their car felt pleasant, so no problem about the windows remaining closed.

"Ready?" Ryan asked his aide.

"Go for it."

Ryan immediately pulled his phone from his pocket and pushed the button to call Drew. He also put the phone's speaker on since they weren't hooked up to any Bluetooth in this vehicle.

Drew answered immediately. "I've been waiting for your update. What's going on there?"

"A lot of interesting stuff." Ryan began by informing their commanding officer that there were indeed other shifters around. Then he got into the apparent attacks on humans by wolves. "I don't know yet if they're shifters or not."

"I've heard something about that in the news," Drew said.

"I'm still trying to figure it out," Ryan said. "In the meantime I'm also getting to know members of one family of shifters—both parents and their son, who's in his early twenties. I met the parents in shifted form on the night of the full moon." He quickly summarized how he had shooed them away when they had started harassing the representative of WHaM who was out trying to find the source of some howls that night. "And guess what?"

"I have a feeling you're going to tell me that there are other shifters around besides you who're changing on nights when the moon isn't full."

"You got it." Ryan told Drew more about the Sharans, and how their son, Pete, who focused on science in school and apparently did a good job of it, had come up with some kind of formula that allowed shifting on other nights, as well. "We haven't talked about it in any detail since, though I've told them I know about shifters and hinted I might be one, too, I wanted to get your okay before I mentioned Alpha Force under these circumstances. And I'm hoping, when things settle down here—and I figure they will— that I can convince Pete to come visit our Alpha Force headquarters. He might make a good addition to our unit."

"Maybe so. And, yes, consider this your okay to mention it to them as long as you get their promise of secrecy— and you reasonably believe they'll comply with it."

Piers chimed in then. "If he hints at what could be in store for Pete based on the family agreeing to confidentiality, I'm sure this group will keep things quiet for their own sakes. Ryan'll have to figure out who else around here are shifters, though, and determine whether it's good for Alpha Force for information about us to go any further."

"Good point," Drew said.

Ryan looked at his aide and nodded. "I was going to mention that, too, but glad you beat me to it. I got a sense from the Sharans that they weren't the only ones who came to town because the situation wherever they'd been living was getting tense, and I have an idea who some might be. I don't see any as potential recruits yet, but who knows?"

"We'll see," Drew said, "but I at least like the idea of the Sharans' son."

Some people got into the car nearest Ryan's side, and for a minute he talked about the weather around this part of Washington, taking a sip of his cooling coffee.

Drew's laugh echoed through the car, thanks to the speaker on the phone. "I take it you have company."

"Not sure if they could hear anything outside our closed car," Ryan said, "but just in case…"

"Got it."

In another minute, that car drove off. "Okay, back to our subject," Ryan said. "Telling other people about Alpha Force."

"Other people—as in shifters or nonshifters?" Drew asked.

"You guessed what I'm about to get into." Ryan had been a member of Alpha Force for less than a year but he had come to not only like their commanding officer a lot, but to highly respect his intelligence.

Not to mention who he really was. The guy was married to a nonshifter, a veterinarian, and they had a couple of kids who were too young for a determination of whether they, too, would be shifters, but Drew, and even his wife, Melanie, often expressed their hope that they'd have that in common with their dad.

Drew obviously trusted some nonshifters, *some* being the operative word. And could Ryan be certain that Maya was as trustworthy as Melanie Connell?

He had a sense she would be. After all, she already knew what he was, had seen him shift and hadn't gone crying to the world or even hinting at it to the media. She seemed to be willing to protect him the way she protected nonshifting wolves.

He said to Drew, "There's someone else here I want to tell about Alpha Force."

"That WHaM representative?" his CO immediately guessed.

"That's right. She's seen me shift—accidentally—and fortunately she has been discreet about it. Her appreciation of wildlife, especially wolves, seems to be what drives her." Not necessarily any appreciation of him, he told himself—notwithstanding the kisses they had shared, the way they sometimes looked at each other...

"Well...under those circumstances I guess you have to trust her some anyway. Just lead into it like you did with those Sharans, getting promises of secrecy before saying more. But I don't really think it's as critical that she learn about Alpha Force. You're not going to recruit her or anything like that."

"No, but someone else who gives a damn and looks at the situation of those attacks from another angle might be helpful." He described in greater detail how Morton Fritts had been attacked on the night of the full moon, and his nosy and careless wife had done as he had, apparently chased after whatever wolf was howling in the dis-

tance last night and had also been injured. He just hoped
it wasn't Pete Sharan.

He had continued to ponder that possibility, often re-
playing in his mind his meet-ups with Pete that night, and
still didn't believe the attacking wolf had been Pete. He
had seen the Frittses on the hillside around that time, but
not close to either instance when he had been with the wolf
that was Pete. The wolf he'd seen had run off in a different direction from those humans, and Pete had said he'd
shifted back right after Ryan and he had met up.

Therefore, it was more likely a feral wolf—or another
shifter with some way to shift outside the full moon. He'd
keep the possibility in mind but for now wouldn't let it
deter him from possibly recruiting the smart young shifter.

"We need to prevent that from happening with anyone
else," he finished.

"Yeah," Drew said. "You do. Okay, I'll trust your judg-
ment about the WHaM lady. I just hope you're thinking
with your head and not any other part of you."

Ryan felt his eyes widen. He looked over at Piers. Had
his aide mentioned anything about the apparent attraction
between Maya and him to Drew? But Piers just shrugged.

This could just be another example of their commanding officer's intelligence and intuition.

"Well, I can admit that the woman is attractive in ways
beyond just her appreciation of wolves," Ryan said. "But
I'm not giving in to any impulse—or I won't unless I think
it'll help me protect shifters or other wolves, and that would
be a stretch."

"Yeah, it would," Piers agreed, grinning at his superior officer.

"Well, okay. You've got your orders. Revealing a bit to
shifters, and this one particular nonshifter, as long as you

receive believable promises of secrecy, is okay, but only if you really think they'll keep things to themselves."

"Yes, sir," Ryan said, still looking at Piers. "We'll report in again soon, let you know how things are going."

"No need to send any other representatives of Alpha Force there now, right?" Drew asked.

"Right," Ryan replied, and Piers expressed his agreement. They hung up a minute later.

Ryan didn't say anything to Piers at first. His mind was churning.

Could he trust the Sharans? He still felt fairly certain that Pete hadn't been the attacking wolf. The Sharans had an agenda of their own, and all three of them would want not only to protect the idea of shifting, but also potentially help Pete find a new and highly appropriate career. The answer, therefore—as long as he was right about Pete's innocence that night—was yes.

And Maya? Was Ryan thinking with body parts other than just his brain, as Drew had suggested?

"What do you think?" Ryan asked Piers. "You've been with Maya when I've been shifted. Can we—should we—trust her with more?"

"I've got a feeling that she is one smart and trustworthy woman—but it's up to you, sir."

"I'll sound her out when I get her alone, soon, and decide then," Ryan said.

But he was fairly certain he knew what the answer would be.

Chapter 18

Dinnertime. Maya felt more antsy than hungry, but she was ready to eat—or at least meet Ryan and Piers for dinner.

Walking down the stairway to the lobby, she thought once more that it was a shame they were staying in a hotel like this. She enjoyed cooking and wouldn't mind putting a meal together for them.

Only—what did people like Ryan really enjoy? She'd seen him eat steak as well as breakfast food. Red meat might be his favorite kind of meal, but maybe not.

Maybe it was just as well that they were eating out and he could order whatever he wanted.

They were waiting in the nearly empty lobby for her. Rocky the wolf-dog was with them and made Maya smile.

Would she smile as broadly if that was Ryan sitting there on the floor in his own wolf form?

To her own surprise, she thought the answer was yes.

But she remained a bit confused. Not that she expected a bunch of detailed websites on the reality of shapeshifters and how they lived and shifted and all, but she had spent an hour or so that afternoon online after her conversation with Cheryl researching as much as she could about what Ryan truly was.

All the sites referred to the whole idea as myth or legend, or horror movies—nothing with any truth to it. But she knew full well that shifters were real. She'd seen it, more than once.

Kind of admired it…

She also admired how shifters had apparently been able to keep who and what they were as secret as they did. For surely Ryan wasn't the only one, and he had hinted at others.

"Hi," she said immediately as she reached them. Ryan and Piers sat on chairs in the center of the lobby with Rocky lying on the floor between them. "You guys hungry?" She looked directly at Ryan as if to ask if he was ready for some meaty food—and found herself flushing. He did appear hungry—but the kind of hunger she thought she saw in his hot glance toward her didn't suggest he was ready to eat a meal.

Instead, she had an urge to invite him to her room. Into her bed.

Which was ridiculous. She wouldn't do that with any guy she was interested in without knowing him better. And getting more involved with someone with—well, secrets—like Ryan made no sense at all.

"I'm definitely hungry," Piers replied. "We thought we might try another restaurant tonight, if that's okay with you."

Not the steak house? "Where did you have in mind?" Maya asked.

"The local pancake house, Griddle Junction. It's just a few blocks from here."

Pancake house? For dinner? Well, the ones Maya was familiar with served other meals besides breakfast. There might even be steaks there, if that was what Ryan—and Rocky—wanted.

"Fine with me." Maya wondered why they had chosen that place. From what she had gathered, these two didn't do anything without a reason. Was there something there they could learn about wolves? Or shifters like Ryan? She might never find out, and she knew better than to ask questions here, in the hotel lobby. Or there, at the restaurant.

Well, maybe as they walked there. But when they got on their way and she started asking questions, Ryan, who strode beside her, said, "Look, there's a lot I want to talk to you about. But it'll have to wait for now. We need to find a place with no one else around again."

Back at the park? Maybe. But that wasn't going to happen tonight.

Just be patient, she ordered herself, though that wasn't in her character. Yet if she wanted answers to her questions, she needed to wait.

And, yes, be patient.

Ryan let himself enjoy walking with Maya to the restaurant despite the frustration she apparently felt, too, though for different reasons. She didn't talk much on this stroll, just appeared to look around and take in the sights, such as they were, of the downtown area of this small city.

He'd already told her he wanted to talk with her but hadn't said when or where. Yet despite his receipt of permission to tell her more, this wasn't the time. Not that everyone on downtown Fritts Corner sidewalks was a shifter with hearing acute enough to eavesdrop on what he said, but he didn't want to take any chances with the few regular people who were also out there, shifters or not.

Not when it came to talking about his covert military unit, Alpha Force.

For one thing, Piers, now walking behind them with Rocky, had done additional research online about the Sharans, such as when they had arrived in Fritts Corner—about ten months ago—and who else had moved here around the same time.

He had learned that Buck Lesterman, owner of Berry's Bar, had arrived around the same time. Plus, the owners of Griddle Junction had bought a home here, as well as the restaurant, at nearly the same time as the Sharans. Their names were John and Georgia Maheus, and there had been no indication they had lived here prior to that time. Ryan hoped to meet them this evening.

Had they and Lesterman come with the Sharans? For similar reasons? He would try to find that out, and hopefully learn if they, or anyone else in the area, were shifters, though he might not get all that information tonight.

And if they were, could they shift the way Pete did? Had he shared his formula?

Had any of them shifted—and attacked the Frittses?

For now, it would be a bonus to share another dinner with Maya. He certainly wouldn't be able to talk with her in private at the restaurant, but he'd find a way to do so as soon as possible since he now had permission to tell her more. Maybe they could walk Rocky together after they ate, not around the park but someplace a lot more private than the sidewalks of downtown Fritts Corner.

He already had plans in mind for tomorrow. He'd decided he'd remain hungry after breakfast, a good time to visit the Corner Grocery, buy some snacks and find a way to speak with the Sharans again, especially Pete. They, at least, had a private office.

But for now—well, he'd find a way to talk with Maya, if not tonight then tomorrow.

After passing Berry's Bar, some clothing stores and a couple of gas stations, they soon reached Griddle Junction, a single-story restaurant with lots of windows that occupied nearly half a block. He listened as they headed inside and heard a lot of conversations, as with a typical restaurant. He also inhaled scents typical of a pancake house at dinnertime—including sweet syrup and eggs, as well as hearty red meat. And that wasn't all.

"Cute place," Maya said. "I even see a couple of other dogs here."

Ryan had smelled them, too. Both were small and lying on the floor inside the place, perhaps not permitted by law here but no one was complaining, which made Ryan like the place immediately.

"Hi," said a fortysomething woman carrying menus and smiling her welcome. Her graying hair was caught up in a clip on top of her head. Ryan caught another scent as she approached.

One that suggested she could be a shifter.

"Hi," he returned. "Are you one of the owners of this place?"

He wasn't surprised when she said she was Georgia Maheus. "Have you eaten here before?" she asked.

"I haven't," Maya said, "but I'm sure I'll enjoy it tonight." She looked toward Ryan for his response, her expression somewhat quizzical as if she realized he had an ulterior motive for coming here.

"We're just visiting town," he replied, "but we've heard good things about this place."

Georgia showed them to a table in the middle of the

moderately busy restaurant, notwithstanding the fact they had a large dog with them. That emphasized Ryan's belief that they might have good reason to welcome canines here.

So did their hostess's scent.

It wouldn't hurt to meet her mate, too. "Is the rest of your family involved with this restaurant?" he asked. "I travel a lot and enjoy seeing how families work together running businesses in so many locations. I'm with the US Fish and Wildlife Service, by the way."

The woman's brown eyes widened as she regarded him. "I'll bet you have an interesting job," she said, then added, "Are you here because people around this area have been seeing wolves?"

"That's right." He continued to watch her reaction, which she clearly attempted to keep blasé.

"And I'm with WHaM," Maya added. "That's Wildlife Habitat Monitoring. I'm interested in learning more about the wolves, too. What do you think about them?"

Ryan was both amused and pleased that Maya seemed to work as a team with him, and with Piers, too, who was watching them all.

"Oh, we like wild animals," Georgia said. "But I've heard some people were hurt by the wolves. That's truly sad, from both the people's and the wolves' perspectives, I'm afraid."

"Do you know of anyone who's going after the wolves?" Piers asked, his tone just as Ryan hoped to hear it—interested, but not too interested.

"No—but if I do, do you gentlemen have a card so I can let you know? I assume Fish and Wildlife would be interested."

Ryan nodded at Piers, who took a card out of his pocket. Fortunately, as part of their cover, they'd gotten phony identification for just this kind of situation.

He noticed Georgia motion to someone behind a nearby table. A man approached, tall and thin, with a wary expression on his face.

"John, these people are with US Fish and Wildlife, and with WHaM." She turned back toward Ryan and said, "I've got to get busy now, but I wanted to introduce you to my husband."

"Good to meet you," John said. "Sorry I don't have time to talk to you, but welcome to Griddle Junction." He reached his wife's side and they walked away together quickly.

"So what was that about?" Maya asked immediately.

"I think you can guess," Ryan responded.

"Something else we'll talk about some other time?" Her tone was sweet, her expression irritated.

"You got it. Now, are you in the mood for breakfast food for dinner, or what do you have in mind to eat?"

"I saw someone eating a really huge and great-looking omelet," Piers said. "That's what I'm getting."

"I need to look at the menu," Maya said. "I might go for an omelet, too. And I assume you'll at least consider the steak." She smiled and batted her eyes at Ryan.

"I'll consider it," he confirmed.

Dinner was over. Maya had enjoyed her omelet.

She'd enjoyed the company even more. But now they were walking back to the hotel. There was no indication they were going to do anything when they arrived except to all head for their beds.

She didn't want that. She wanted to chat with Ryan. He'd already said he had things to talk to her about, too.

Why not tonight?

They reached the door to the lobby. They'd taken their time somewhat to make sure Rocky was able to accomplish all the sniffing and relieving himself that he wanted, and now the dog seemed quite happy to come inside.

Maya was, too—maybe. "I'm not really tired," she said to her two male companions as they entered. "And we discussed the possibility of talking about some of the stuff that's going on around here. Why not here and now?"

She anticipated Ryan's reaction. He'd only talk to her when he felt comfortable no one else would be able to listen in.

Then, as she'd said, why not here and now? The hotel lobby was empty except for the senior guy at the registration desk. He most likely wouldn't be able to hear what they said as long as they kept their voices low.

"Not here," Ryan said. "But just a minute."

He motioned for Piers to join him off to the side of the empty room. Maya didn't know what they were talking about but she had an idea. She approached the guy at the registration desk and asked some questions. Then she hurried back across the lobby to where the men stood. Apparently their quick conversation was over since they both just looked at her.

"Okay," Ryan said as she reached them. "Here's what we can do. Piers will take Rocky to his room to bed, but you and I will go for a ride to talk."

"Sure," she said, her mood lightening. She'd been concerned they would just tell her they were tired and no one really wanted to talk to her, after all. "Or, we can go to my room." She told them she'd seen the people on either side of her leave with luggage earlier, and she'd just confirmed that they had checked out—and that no one else had checked in. "No one'll be close enough to hear anything if we talk there."

"So we've got two good possibilities." Ryan's smile looked relieved. Good! He must really be serious about wanting to tell her…something. What? She already knew what he was.

Still…

"So which will it be?" Maya asked.

"Let's look at your room first," Ryan said, "and if all seems as quiet and private as you indicated, it'll be fine not to run around anymore tonight."

"Great." Maya felt her heart rate accelerating.

She shouldn't feel at all excited that she might be alone with Ryan in her bedroom for an unknown length of time.

They were going there to talk, for him to tell her even more, she believed, about the kind of person he was, and how he melded into the regular world of regular people.

If nothing else, that should be a huge turnoff. In fact, she had a sudden urge to change her mind and say they should go for a drive to talk.

But she didn't. And in another minute Piers and Rocky were heading down the hall toward their room…and Maya was leading Ryan up the stairs toward hers.

Chapter 19

She'd invited him into her room—to talk, Ryan reminded himself. She had confirmed that the nearest rooms were unoccupied, and as they reached her doorway and she opened the door with her key, he listened carefully.

Sure, he'd have felt even more comfortable that no one was around if he'd been in his wolfen form listening with his superior sense of hearing. But his hearing in human form wasn't bad—and the only things he heard on this floor were a couple of television sets turned on down the hall, a conversation between a man and woman nearby but not in the closest rooms, and apparently the sound of a mother reading a book to a kid who giggled and talked about the doggy in the story.

If he only knew what other kind of doggy stood nearby...

But Ryan had the answer he wanted. Even so, as they entered the old but well-maintained room and Maya put her purse down on a chair near the door, he listened once more.

Then he said, "Okay with you if I put the television on? I'll keep the volume low but it should help drown out our conversation in the unlikely event that someone is listening."

Of course if that other person happened to be a shifter, too, then drowning out what they said would be unlikely. But it was better than nothing.

"That's fine. Sorry I don't have anything here I can offer you to drink unless you'd like a bottle of water."

Like his room and Piers's, hers had a small refrigerator.

"No thanks. I'm fine." He looked around. The only chair in the room was the wooden one with a woven cane seat where Maya had put her bag.

The most inviting place for him to sit was her bed, with its attractive lacy coverlet. But...the bed?

Heck, he was here to talk. Nothing else.

He could tamp down the sexual attraction he felt for Maya. It was totally inappropriate. And he really did want to talk with her.

That was all.

He planted his denim-clad butt on the bed and patted the area near him—but not right beside him. Maya gave a silly smile that he wanted to kiss right off her face but didn't.

He'd need to see if she was still smiling after he'd told her what he wanted to...

"Okay, here's the thing," he said, looking straight into her face. She was really beautiful, and her hazel eyes looked intense, interested—and maybe a bit turned on. But he was probably just imagining that. "Piers and I don't actually work for the US Fish and Wildlife Service."

Her grin as she laughed only made her look sexier. "Tell me something I don't know—like who you really do work for."

He'd already figured she was smart, and it wasn't much

of a stretch for her to determine, from the way he'd been acting, that he'd told a few lies for expediency's sake. And for the secrets he needed to keep.

"That's exactly what I intend to do, but I only got permission based on securing from you a credible promise that anything I tell you will be kept utterly confidential. That you won't repeat it, or even hint at it, to anyone else—except in the highly unlikely event that I give my consent."

"Whoa," she said, still smiling. "Sounds pretty hush-hush…and important."

"It is. Part of the reason is national security, and you'll see why." He reached over and took her hands from where they'd been propping her on the bed. She remained seated there but allowed him to hold on to her hands. They were warm, and her grip, as she turned her arms so she could hold his hands as well, was as tight as his.

And sexy. Very sexy.

He continued looking at her eyes, not touching her anywhere else, and said, "So, Ms. Maya Everton, do you agree that everything we discuss tonight will be kept utterly secret by you, that I can rely on you not to disclose anything to anyone?"

"That sounds pretty restricted and important," she said. "And hopefully at least partly in protection of animals, not just national security?" She made the last a question, and he couldn't help just a hint of a smile as he nodded.

"I think you and I will make a pretty good team as things continue," he said. "And, yes, some of what I'm about to tell you involves protection of animals. And people."

"And people who are also animals, like you." She made that a statement, as if she was already reading his mind.

"You got it. So…?"

"Of course I promise. Do we need to do a pinkie swear to prove it?"

"No. But as I indicated, national security is involved. If you breach your promise, there could be some pretty nasty consequences."

"What, you'll have me thrown in federal prison?" Her tone sounded scornful—but her expression was troubled, as if she understood completely that what she said could in fact be true.

"Let's hope it doesn't come to that," he said. "And if it helps you to agree, we can pinkie swear if you'd like."

That should at least take some of the pressure off this conversation, though it could seem to minimize its importance.

He had a sense that she knew better.

"All right, I swear I won't tell anyone what you're about to tell me, not without your approval. Pinkie swear. Okay?" She pulled her hands away from his only long enough to extend her right hand so her pinkie finger pointed toward his.

With a laugh, he wrapped his finger around hers. "Okay," he said. "So here it is. I happen to belong to a highly classified, totally covert military unit called Alpha Force."

Her eyes widened, but she didn't pull her finger away from his. He had an urge to use it to pull her closer, but didn't.

"Are all members of your Alpha Force like you?" Her tone suggested awe, which only made him want to hug her even more.

"Some are," he said. "Piers is a member who isn't a shifter, though. He's my aide. The shifters all have aides and cover animals who look like them while shifted."

"Then Rocky's your cover dog. I thought he looked

like the way you were when I saw you in werewolf form."
She looked delighted now. "Are all your shifters wolves?"

He started giving her more of a rundown on the shifters comprising Alpha Force, who were mostly wolves but also included other kinds of animals, as well.

"Wow!" she said when he was done and had released her finger. "What kinds of military assignments do you get involved with? And why are you here? Is this area in danger?"

"This was more of a hunting expedition on my part," he said. "With the sudden influx of wolves to this area, I was given the assignment of checking whether any were shifters—both for their protection and, possibly, recruitment into Alpha Force."

"And you have found shifters, right? Are any of them going to join your force?"

"Still looking into who around here might be a shifter, though I know a few for certain. So far I haven't tried to recruit anyone, though I hope to."

"Wow," she said again. "Wow, this is just so amazing. Werewolves, more like you and part of our military. Wow!" Suddenly, she launched herself along the bed toward him.

In moments, she'd wrapped her arms around him and pulled him down onto the coverlet. Her mouth suddenly captured his.

And he was engaged in one amazingly hot and sexy human kiss that he wanted never to end.

This wasn't what she'd had in mind...was it?

How could she know, even ponder that, now that she was in Ryan's arms and he lay on top of her with his amazing, hard body, kissing her like he was? While she was kissing him back. Enjoying every moment.

Yet a shapeshifter. Many shapeshifters. A military—

Oh, my, he was running his hand under her shirt, reaching toward her breasts. Her bra miraculously seemed to disappear—or was it simply pushed up and out of the way by his searching fingers?

In fact...he moved a bit and suddenly her shirt and bra were missing. Was that a special act of a shapeshifter?

Heck, no, for she used the opportunity of his no longer keeping her in place with his body to yank off his T-shirt, as well.

But he moved back on top of her once more, holding her more tightly so she could feel the warmth of his skin against her now-naked breasts, the hardness of his ripped muscles, as he again sought her mouth, surrounding it with his for an incredible new kiss.

She wasn't about to let things stop there, though. Or should she? She wasn't exactly thinking things through with all her logic as a human being when she moved her hands around to his back, first squeezing his butt through his jeans, then reaching around to the front—still outside his pants, but, oh, how his erection grew to fill her grasp and then some.

He moaned her name. "Maya. Do you know what you're doing?"

"Hell, yes," she said. And then she stopped still. "Don't I? I mean, can you do what...what people do when you're in the shape of a man?"

His laugh sounded so damned sexy she felt the moistness that had started to gather below increasing. But had he meant he couldn't do what regular men do? Or—

"I'm not about to take the time to give you a rundown on what could happen if we continue," he whispered against her mouth.

And then he pulled away.

Maya felt lost suddenly. Well, not entirely, since this

way, as he stood, she could see him—the hard muscles of his bared chest rippling as he first reached into his jeans pocket. He pulled out his wallet. What? There'd be no money involved if they—

No. She heard the crinkling of plastic as he pulled out a condom.

The guy wasn't only sexy, he was considerate. And smart. But she knew that.

She used the time to grab the remote on the nearby nightstand to turn off the TV.

"But I damned well want to continue," he said. "As long as you do. And what I can tell you briefly is that this'll give the kind of protection we need to ensure that there'll be no other result if we go on with our lovemaking."

"Then let's do it." She gasped as, smiling, he pulled his pants down till they crumpled onto the floor.

His erection was every bit as large and thick as she'd anticipated, and it was pointing toward her.

"Wow," she whispered, even as she reached down to remove the rest of her own clothes and remained lying on the bed. Enticingly, she hoped.

Must be, since in a moment, after he'd sheathed himself, he was back beside her. He reached over, first stroking her breasts once again and then reaching lower. Touching her moistness, reaching a finger inside her and pumping it slowly as if informing her what else he would be doing in a moment.

"Please," she whispered.

In moments, he was on top of her. Inside her. Moving slowly at first, then more heatedly and faster and—

She swallowed her cry, knowing he didn't want anyone to hear them. Sure, no one was in nearby rooms, but—

He groaned at the same time, then dropped quickly back

on top of her, gently enough not to hurt her. His breathing was erratic.

Well, so was hers.

Neither said anything for a long moment. Then Maya heard herself say "wow" again.

"Oh, yeah," Ryan added. "Wow."

"So that's how shapeshifters do it?" Maya asked a long moment later when her own breathing was somewhat tamed.

"That's how shapeshifters do it," he confirmed, once more sort of repeating what she'd said.

"Then shapeshifters are amazing," Maya whispered hoarsely into his ear. "And I wonder. Would this shapeshifter " she reached around and hugged him closely again "—like to stay the night?"

His laugh was husky and sounded amused. "Yeah, this shapeshifter accepts that very welcome invitation."

He did stay. And he had brought more condoms. Maya lost count of the number of times they made love, possibly because what they did sometimes resulted in fulfillment and sometimes just tantalized her enough to touch him even more. Taste him even more. Enjoy his tasting her...

It didn't all result in consummation, but it did make her feel absolutely wonderful.

Then there were those fantastic times when they did it all...

In between, well, she did sleep some. Snuggled up against his hot body beneath the soft sheets, feeling his flesh touch hers, his arm often around her, as he slept, too—or at least seemed to.

She wasn't sure how long she had slept the last time when she was awakened by Ryan's movement beside her. She smiled and turned toward him, to find his head on the pillow, his gaze on her, his sexy lips that she had felt on her—how many times and places?—now smiling in a way that suggested satisfaction.

Satisfaction? Not total. Not yet. Not if she could help it. And so she smiled back, and moved her hands, then her mouth, until they once more experienced the kind of sex she had only dreamed about.

Even that drew to an end eventually. She was out of breath when he started to get out of bed after kissing her once more.

"It's still early," she whispered teasingly.

"Yeah, and that's why I'm leaving now, so hopefully no one will know I was here. This has been one hell of a night, but I don't want it to end with your being embarrassed about it."

"I won't be," she responded quickly. But how would she feel if the people she needed to impress, so they'd be supportive of the local wolves, knew what else she was up to?

Probably fine…since none would know who and what Ryan really was. Right?

Well, Piers knew. And he was part of Ryan's strange and secret military force. What would it mean to Ryan if it got back to his commanding officers that he was having sex with a normal human female?

"I hope not," Ryan said, "but let's make certain of it." He'd already pulled on his undershorts and had his jeans and shirt in his hand. He bent down and kissed her on the cheek before heading toward the bathroom.

Well, fine. She'd had a simply amazing night. One she could—and would—remember for a long time. And those memories would include not only that she'd made love with one amazingly sexy man. Emphasis on *man*. She might know what he really was, but nothing she'd experienced that night was different from how it would have been with a regular human.

Except how astoundingly wonderful it was…

She heard the sound of the shower and lay back with her head on her pillow, eyes closed for the moment as she inhaled and still smelled the aroma of their lovemaking.

Someone like him would smell it even more intensely, she imagined.

Someone—something—like him…

Would she want to repeat this sometime? Sure. It had been wonderful.

And they had agendas that were at least somewhat similar, in learning about the wolves around here and making sure they remained safe. Ryan and she could work together, and play together.

For now.

But that was all. They couldn't possibly stay together. He had to go back to wherever his strange military unit was headquartered—outside Washington, DC, he'd previously indicated. She would return to her WHaM headquarters.

And that would be that.

So…could she, would she, ever make love with him again knowing their time together was, and needed to be, quite limited?

She hoped so.

He popped out of the bathroom then and bent over her. He was dressed, and now he smelled of the soap supplied by the hotel. His hair was wet.

And once more he gave her one amazing kiss.

"Let's get together for breakfast in a while," he suggested, "after I get back to my room and change clothes and hook up with Piers and Rocky. Okay?"

"Okay," she said, and as he left she felt both a slight bit of relief and a lot of regret.

No matter what or who he was, she'd had a fantastic experience.

But would it be the only time?

She would think about it long and hard—and just have to see how things worked out.

Chapter 20

What a way to end one day and start another, Ryan thought once he had returned to his room. Now, he was standing by his bed—with a lacy coverlet like Maya's—getting dressed. And thinking.

And remembering what an amazing night he'd just had.

Well, this day promised to have some very interesting aspects, too. But nothing would compare with what he and Maya had shared.

As he enjoyed the memory, he pulled his neutral navy T-shirt on over his jeans. He liked his ability to dress casually most of the time here, even while claiming to be an employee of the federal government.

He hoped Maya had found last night as good as it had felt to him, and that it would be the first of many such nights—as long as she remained receptive not only to who he was, but also to keeping secret his identity and the existence of Alpha Force.

And as long as they shared an affinity to wolves—
although clearly for different reasons.

Shirt on and wallet in his pocket, he got ready to leave.
He'd already called Piers, and now he hurried from his
room and out through the hotel's lobby to catch up with
his aide and dog. He needed to share with Piers that he
had informed Maya about Alpha Force and what her reaction had been.

Everything else could remain private between Maya
and him.

He spotted them on the next block, Piers on the sidewalk and Rocky sniffing nearby grass.

All three were about to meet Maya for breakfast—
again. And when they had finished, Piers and he absolutely needed something from the grocery store.

It was time to let the Sharans in on their little secret,
too—as long as they also promised to keep what he revealed to themselves.

"Hey," Ryan said as he caught up with Piers. Rocky had
spotted him first and pulled on his leash in his direction.
Ryan strode toward his wonderful wolf-dog and ruffled
the thick fur on his head, scratching behind his erect ears.

And thinking about how it would feel if someone patted him the same way when he was shifted…

"Morning, boss." Piers joined Ryan at Rocky's side. He
looked quizzically toward Ryan as if he sensed something
was different, but he was tactful enough not to ask. Even
so, Ryan wondered if his pleasure was evident on his face.

Instead Piers asked, "What's on our agenda today?"

"I've already followed through on letting Maya know
our background," Ryan said, starting to walk toward Andy
and Family's restaurant. He purposely didn't look at Piers
as he spoke, not wanting to see any amusement there if his
aide knew what that had led to. "Since we've got Drew's

okay, next thing I want to do is approach the Sharans and see how that comes out."

What he hadn't done with Maya, though, was to invite her to walk to breakfast with them. He'd wanted to bring Piers up-to-date about his revelation to Maya and plans for the Sharans.

He felt certain that telling Maya had been the right thing. In fact, he hoped he would find ways to utilize her knowledge and assistance.

They reached the restaurant. Ryan squared his shoulders before proceeding inside after Piers and Rocky. Heck, he was a professional, as well as a shifter. He would do what was right for his military unit, fellow shifters and even wild wolves.

If that permitted more interaction with Maya, all the better. But if it didn't, he would do what he had to.

Breakfast at Andy and Family's was becoming a pleasant habit, Maya thought as she saw Ryan, Piers and Rocky enter and head for the table she'd saved for all of them just outside on the patio.

Interesting that she had arrived before the others did this time. But, though Ryan and she had talked about when they'd meet for breakfast, she hadn't tried contacting him to see if they should all walk together once more. In fact, after the night they had shared, she needed a little space.

To think more about it? That hadn't been her intent, but it was what she'd done nonetheless.

To fixate on it as she walked alone in this direction.

To recall the most delightful moments, with Ryan's hands on her, with her hands on him. And more. Much more...

Enough. She could certainly move her mind off it now, out in public, while they ate. She had to.

Plus—well, she'd have to follow Ryan's lead in how to act with Piers. She now knew Piers was Ryan's aide in his odd but appropriate military unit. Presumably, Piers wouldn't criticize his superior officer. Or could he in these circumstances?

"Good morning." Ryan smiled down at her as he pulled his chair from beneath the table.

"Hi." She leveled a neutral grin first on him, then Piers and finally Rocky. She reached over to scratch the wolf-dog behind his ears, watching him and not the men who accompanied him. But she looked again toward Ryan as he sat down. "Hope you slept well last night."

Was that a stupid thing to say? Had he already revealed to Piers what they'd been up to? She managed a sideways glance at the other man. His pleasant expression gave away nothing.

"Well enough." Ryan raised his dark eyebrows for an instant as he regarded her. Even that fairly neutral expression was enough to heat her insides once more, but she ignored it. "I'm pretty hungry this morning. Hotcakes and sausage sounds good to me. How about you?"

Their conversation glommed on to food possibilities. Nice and nonchalant, Maya thought. A server came over to bring drinks nearly immediately. Maya chose coffee, since she needed caffeine to keep her going after her lack of sleep.

They soon placed their food order, as well. Everything seemed nice and calm and not much different from their prior breakfasts together.

How could that be? Maya had an urge to stand and dash toward Ryan and take him into her arms, covering his face with kisses. Touching as subtly as possible those parts of his body that had given her such pleasure last night.

But she of course stayed still.

"So what are your plans today?" she asked Ryan, as neutrally as she could manage.

"We have some official business to take care of first thing," he said. His slight smile had some kind of message behind it. She probably wasn't supposed to ask questions.

Even so, she would ask anyway, though she would maintain the cover story.

"Then Fish and Wildlife has you out and about today?" She opened her eyes wide as if fascinated by whatever answer they'd give. And she truly would be interested.

She would be even more interested in having them tell her the truth. If they had an official assignment today, it wouldn't be something US Fish and Wildlife ordered them to do.

But that fascinating Alpha Force Ryan had told her about? It was another story. She felt certain that whatever they were up to, it would result from the covert military unit he had described. And she wanted to know more about it. A lot more.

"That's right," he responded.

"This is a great area to deal with wildlife issues," Piers said, backing Ryan up. "We've got more ideas about looking into the wolves around here before we go back to our headquarters."

Piers looked at her with an expression that appeared to give her orders, maybe even more than his commanding officer did.

"Well, if there's anything I, or WHaM, can do to help you protect those wolves, just let me know," Maya said.

They seemed to agree, but she doubted they'd follow through. Bringing her closer, giving her more knowledge, wasn't something either was likely to do. She'd need to figure out a way to do it herself.

But for the moment, she would just play along—first enjoying her breakfast and, later, determining on her own just what they were up to.

Maya apparently had administrative work to do for WHaM that held some urgency but could be accomplished online, or so she told them as they finished their breakfasts. That sounded fine to Ryan, especially since she said goodbye at the restaurant door and headed back to their hotel after insisting on paying for breakfast for all of them. He'd let her—this time. She now knew he wasn't being funded by Fish and Wildlife, but he was still an employee of the federal government.

Even so, he appreciated her insistence on taking care of things herself. She was independent. She loved wolves.

She was the sexiest woman he had ever met...but he couldn't keep thinking about that.

As they separated, he, Piers and Rocky headed toward the Corner Grocery Store. They had a meeting to conduct.

Ryan wasn't especially pleased that Maya was joined on the next block by that guy Trev, but he trusted her not to say anything.

He just didn't trust that guy, geek though he appeared to be, to avoid coming on to Maya. Hopefully, they would just discuss wolves—nonshifting ones—and WHaM.

It was around 10:00 a.m. by then, but the store wasn't particularly busy when they arrived. There were a few patrons in all the aisles but no big crowd, and only a couple of people waited in line to check out. Someone who wasn't a Sharan, presumably an employee, was helping them.

A strong aroma of hazelnut coffee permeated the place, and Ryan assumed that some beans had just been ground somewhere in the back to brew a large urn for patrons. Other aromas he inhaled included fruit muffins—sweet and tart and sugary. Good thing he'd already eaten breakfast, but his mouth watered anyway. There were a lot more scents around here in the morning than later in the day.

The Sharans might not think having so few patrons was a good thing, but Ryan was glad. He hoped he'd get all three of them to invite his group into their office to talk.

Burt was nearest the door, refreshing some shelves with pastries including the ones Ryan had smelled. Ryan approached him first. "Good morning." He smiled as if all was well between them. Hopefully, it was.

"Hello. What can I help you with today?" Burt's skeptical expression suggested he didn't want to hear, whatever it was.

Ryan kept his voice low. "Are Kathie and Pete around? I'd like us to get together in your office. I've gotten approval to let you in on something I think you'll want to hear about."

Burt lifted his chin, staring at Ryan down his long nose, his apparent skepticism building. "Why would we want to hear about it?" he asked, keeping his voice muted as well, his eyes darting around as if to make sure no one was close by. "We already know too much about each other."

"But there's something I can reveal to you soon that I think you'll want to hear. Something good. Something that might make Pete especially happy."

As they'd been talking, Ryan had spotted Pete approaching along the nearest aisle. He'd raised his voice slightly—not that someone like Pete wouldn't have been able to hear him anyway.

"Why is that?" the younger man asked as he reached them. He appeared somewhat interested, his shaggy brows raised but his dark eyes not radiating the same skepticism and mistrust as his father's.

"Why don't we go into your office and talk?" Ryan

countered. "Then you can be the one to judge whether what I have to say can change your life the way I think it potentially will."

That clearly got Pete's attention. He first obtained his dad's reluctant okay for the meeting Ryan suggested, then went off to get his mother.

Soon, after Burt talked to their few employees on duty, the Sharans headed to the office at the back of the store with Ryan's group. Ryan had scoped it out before for its privacy, and the walls were thick enough to contain some insulation. Perfect soundproofing? Unlikely, but with the store patrons talking outside only shifters were apt to be able to hear anything from the office, and Ryan would make sure they kept their voices low.

"Okay," Ryan said as they all settled into the small room. Burt Sharan had the main seat behind the desk this time, with Kathie on a chair beside him and Pete standing behind him.

Ryan took another chair, and Piers sat at his side with his hand on Rocky's head. The wolf-dog soon lay down on the floor, obviously not stressing about what the people around him were up to.

"So what the hell are you talking about?" demanded Burt right away. "You've got our attention. We all know that most of us except a couple—" he looked toward Piers, then at Rocky lying on the floor "—have something in common. Is that what this is about? We've already discussed it."

"Let's keep our voices down," Ryan directed him, muting his own voice. "And, yes, we've discussed some aspects of it." He looked beyond Burt and up toward Pete, staring him straight in the eye. "But Piers, Rocky and I are here for some very special reasons. We have been sent by a particularly special organization to learn about local shifters as well as feral wolves—but primarily the former."

He stood, maneuvered around the desk and placed himself directly in front of Pete.

"First things first, though," Ryan said, still speaking softly. He turned to Pete. "I don't know whether you've heard, but Vinnie Fritts was attacked by a wolf the way her husband was—the night you and I ran into each other in shifted form. Did you have anything to do with that?" He hoped he knew the answer.

"Really? No!" Pete exclaimed. "Like I told you, I shifted back right after you and I saw each other. And—in case you're wondering—I do remember images of what I see while shifted so I'd know if I attacked a human. Which I'd never do."

"How dare you—" Kathie began, but at least she also kept her tone low. She'd started to stand up at Ryan's question.

"I hoped, and believed, that would be the answer," he said. He looked Kathie in the eye, and although she still looked troubled she sat down again. Her husband, too, regarded Ryan suspiciously but said nothing—for now. "And I accept it," Ryan continued, "although if any of you happen to hear of other shifters in town who might have been involved, or any rumors of wild wolves who could have attacked, please let me know." He wanted answers, actual answers, but intended to do what he could to protect whatever wolf was involved. One of the other Sharans? He doubted it.

And could he really believe Pete? He wanted to. *Did* believe him. Could he be wrong? Sure, but he didn't think so.

Besides, Vinnie Fritts should have known better than to confront any canine, especially after what had happened to her husband.

"Okay, now," Ryan said next. "Let's get to what I really wanted to talk about. Pete, I recognize that this is now your home and respect that. And before this goes any further, I need to get a promise from each of you that what I'm about to reveal will be kept utterly secret by you, that you'll talk about it only among yourselves and even then in circumstances when no one will be able to hear you— not even other shifters, so you'll have to be particularly careful that you're not within their hearing distance while shifted or human."

"What is this all about?" This time Kathie stood up completely, facing Ryan and her son. Her voice was somewhat raised now. Her usually fluffy light hair was now styled close to her face, and her deep brown eyes were even wider than usual beneath brows that gave her a particularly troubled look. "Are you playing games with us? With Pete?"

The movement stirred Rocky's attention, and the dog now rose, looking from one human to another. "It's okay, boy," Piers told him, scratching behind his ears. Though the dog sat back down again, he remained alert—and looked even more like Ryan's cover dog, taking on a more concerned expression than the smart canine usually did. Ryan couldn't help smiling at him before responding to Kathie's questions.

"Not at all," he finally said, once more acting as an example by lowering his voice. "And this is what I actually came here for today. I might be wrong about Pete's ambitions, but I think he'll appreciate the choice of whether to remain here helping to run your store for the next years, or giving something else that could be part of who he is a try."

"What's that?" Pete's expression remained neutral, but something flashed in his eyes that suggested to Ryan that his interest had been piqued.

"Like I said," Ryan continued, "do I have promises of secrecy from all of you?"

He saw the parents exchange glances first with each other, then with their son.

Even if they agreed, could he trust them? Probably, since they, too, were shifters. But somehow he felt that the promise he had obtained from Maya would be worth even more.

Was that just because of what they'd shared? He didn't think so. He trusted her and her love of wildlife—of all kinds.

But these people, if they agreed to stay quiet, would have more at stake if they didn't.

"Yes," Pete finally said first. "I promise to keep it secret."

"Me, too," said Kathie.

"I will, too," Burt finally added.

Ryan traded glances with Piers, whose smile looked wry yet genuine. "Go ahead," his aide said.

"Okay." Ryan grinned broadly at each of them, then continued, "We, my friends, are members of a very special covert US military unit, Alpha Force."

For the next few minutes, Ryan explained a bit of what Alpha Force was about—how it had been started, how it continued with shifters and cover animals and aides, and some of the amazing and productive goals it had achieved to help the United States. All was done undercover and achieving only the kudos of the few members of the government trusted with knowing what they were about.

"We're always checking into the potential existence of other shifters," Ryan said, "and looking to recruit additional qualified members." They'd all regained their earlier positions by then, but he rose once more to face Pete directly. "That," he said, "might include you."

"Really?" Pete sounded like an excited child told he was about to meet Santa Claus.

Swallowing a chuckle, Ryan said quite seriously, "Really. I'll want to talk to you more about your qualifications. And I'd also like you to interview and audition for us, starting tonight if possible."

The young man had the decency to look once more at his parents, although his excitement remained written on his face. "I don't want to do anything to make things harder for you, Mom and Dad," he said to them.

"And we want the best for you," Kathie said. "Keep us in the loop, okay? But go ahead and do your interview and all, if it's what you want."

"Thanks!" He bent to give each of his parents a kiss, then he looked back up, first at Rocky and Piers, then at Ryan. "And is Alpha Force the best?"

"The absolute best," Ryan said with a smile of his own.

Chapter 21

Ryan could almost hear what Kathie and Burt Sharan weren't saying as their brief meeting closed and they all shook hands and headed back into the store. Pete's parents kept looking at each other, and at their son, and back again.

Were they concerned about how the store would do with just them around to run it? Maybe, but they had already taken on help. Ryan was curious whether any of the clerks were also shifters. He hoped to find that out.

In any event, he figured the Sharans were worried about how their son would potentially do far from here, in a military unit no one was permitted to talk about much. Would he be in danger? Possibly, but he might be in danger here as well, where some people were pleased to have wolves around…and others weren't.

Perhaps the unknown aspects of the situation were also worrying them. He could understand that. But if Pete's testing went well, and if the young man remained interested, Ryan would invite them to come along when he took Pete to introduce him to the other unit members. If Pete was then recruited, Ryan himself would reassure the Sharans about how wonderful that was and make sure they had his contact information. After that, they, as shifters, could come visit the Alpha Force headquarters in Mary Glen, Maryland, as often as they wanted to talk to others in the unit, as well.

Yet they were parents—apparently caring ones. He had wondered now and then how his parents had coped, living in a remote part of Wyoming that nevertheless contained not only shifters but regular humans, as well. He still had a loving family, and Ryan knew his mom and dad and grandparents worried about him, but they clearly were proud of what he now was doing.

Would he ever marry and have kids—presumably shifters? How would he feel if they integrated into partially nonshifter society, as he had?

And who would he marry? Maya's face popped into his mind even as he placed himself in the main grocery store aisle to say goodbye. He immediately erased the image. Sure, they'd shared wonderful sex, but that was all.

That had to be all, considering the many differences between them.

"So," he said softly to Pete, who had stayed beside him. The store was more crowded now, filled with an undercurrent of voices though fewer tempting aromas. "I'll come by around nine tonight and we'll go have a…drink. And I'll interview you." He got even closer so he could whisper into the young man's ear. "The formula you've developed to…well, you know. Please bring it for a demo, okay?"

"Fine." Pete smiled, even as Ryan turned to leave—and stopped.

Just entering the store were the Frittses, both of them.

Morton and Vinnie had come through the door and were now side by side, looking around.

Vinnie's eyes lit on Ryan first. He could still see the healing scratches on her face, and she was bent over as if it remained difficult to walk.

For Morton, too, although his healing scabs were now turning into scars.

Both glowered at Ryan, then at Piers, who was now beside him—and, of course, at Rocky, who resembled a wolf. Then they started walking toward Ryan.

"Hello," he said, painting a big, caring smile on his face. "You look better, both of you. I assume you're healing well, or at least I hope so." He gestured around the store. "I just came in for some snacks. You?"

"Yeah. Snacks. And more." Morton looked as if someone had attempted to shove crispy graham crackers down his throat. "I don't suppose you feds have come to see the light and have decided to round up the wolves?"

"I don't suppose so." Ryan kept his voice as friendly as possible. He wanted to shout out, ask these injured people again just how they'd both happened upon wolves in the middle of the night—shifters or not—and put themselves into positions to be attacked.

He still suspected they'd somehow done it on purpose so they could wind up looking this damaged and pitiful. But if so, why did they hate wolves that much?

If it truly had been two separate and unfortunate confrontations...well, again, how and why?

And surely Pete Sharan hadn't been involved either time...

"Well, we really just need some stuff for dinner tonight, that's why we're here." Turning so his gaze no longer met Ryan's, Morton maneuvered his way around him in the aisle, still coming close enough to bump into him as if asserting nonverbally who was in charge.

Which might have made Ryan laugh if the circumstances here weren't so challenging. He wouldn't be surprised if the Frittses knew, or suspected, that there were shifters around.

Either way, they clearly weren't thrilled. Or at least there was no indication they'd be more accepting if the wolves were genuine wildlife. Or if, perhaps, they preferred shifters, after all.

As both Frittses meandered farther from him, Ryan looked at Piers and nodded toward the door, essentially telling his aide it was time for Rocky and him to leave.

And Ryan? He decided he was in desperate need of some supplies to bring back to the hotel. At least he wanted it to appear that way. He hurried to the entry, got a plastic basket to drape over his arm, then began wandering after picking up a loaf of bread so it appeared he actually was shopping.

But what he really was doing was attempting to subtly observe the Frittses.

What kind of game were they playing? He knew what kind of game *he* was playing: watching this unfathomable couple and how they appeared to interact with others who were shifters, the Sharans.

Did they know or suspect that, or was their visit to this store completely innocent?

Ryan was interested when the Frittses both approached Pete, who appeared to be restocking a refrigerator case with red meats. Ryan inhaled the enticing aroma and figured that Pete was doing so, too.

"Is there any fresh meat in this store?" Vinnie asked, her expression sardonic. "Like, anything we should carry so we can throw it far from us if a wolf approaches to get it away from us?" She didn't move her gaze from Pete's face, and the young man appeared amused—though not without some effort.

"I'd suggest you just stay inside at night, far away from where any wolves might be. You were attacked at night, both of you, right?"

"That's right. And do you have any other advice?" That was Morton talking, and both the Frittses took further steps toward Pete as if attempting to back him into a corner.

Which Ryan didn't like at all. He maneuvered toward them and pushed between the two Frittses, bending over the refrigerated counter. "Hey, this stuff looks good. I think I'll buy some for tonight." He turned slightly to face Vinnie. "Maybe that's what you should do, too. Cook at home to let yourself heal better, go to bed early and all that. And so far everything I've bought here is good, so load up now." Ryan picked up a package of raw T-bone steak figuring he wouldn't have anyplace to cook it at the hotel, but its cost, even if he just left it in his room's refrigerator, would be worth it to calm this situation.

"Mind your own business, Mr. Fish and Wildlife," Morton growled.

"Oh," said Ryan, "I am." He slipped the steak into the basket he held and continued to stand there, moving his gaze from one of the Frittses to the other until they apparently grew uncomfortable enough to move.

"Here." Vinnie shoved the basket she held at Pete. "Put this stuff away. I've changed my mind. I don't want to buy anything in this filthy, nasty store." She grabbed Morton's hand, and they both stomped out of the place.

"Thanks, I think," Pete said softly. "I already wondered if they thought…knew…you know."

"They clearly aren't fans of wildlife," Ryan agreed.

"And I think it would be best if all of us who are wolf aficionados stayed out of their way."

He soon paid for his steak and other stuff, then, bags
in hand, once more sought out Pete. "We're on for tonight
still, right?"

"Can't wait," Pete replied.

Why was it, Maya wondered, that she felt certain Ryan
and Piers, and maybe even Rocky, had a very different
agenda from hers that day?

She'd been a bit surprised when Trev had caught up
with her during her walk back to her hotel, but fortunately
he had mostly just said hi, asked how she—and WHaM—
were doing that day and mentioned not hearing any wolves
last night.

Not a surprise to Maya. She hadn't heard any, either.

But she had certainly had a wonderful time with one
of those entities who could have been on the hillside
howling…in a different form and under different circumstances.

Trev had seemed a bit pushier about the wolves, giving
her his phone number and asking her to call if she heard
them again. But then, fortunately, he had left her, crossing the street as she reached the hotel.

Now, sitting on her hotel room bed with her computer
open on the coverlet in front of her, she'd started to work
practically the instant she had returned after breakfast.
It was all essential stuff, and she was glad to work on it.

Even as her mind floated off now and then to wonder
where Ryan and his gang were, and what they were doing.

Oh, she knew she had a unique assignment, speaking with her fellow WHaM executive Cheryl Jaker on the
phone, then working with her on the group's remote as-
sessment of the origin of the wolves now in Fritts Corner

and where she might be able to observe some more. She was the only WHaM representative in the area, sure, but her organization had developed a computer program that helped to predict where wolves that had been seen and listed in their census had come from and where they might roam in the next weeks.

Always accurate? No. And Maya figured that its accuracy would be even less when it came to predicting where shifters might go.

On the other hand, shapeshifters would most likely remain in the areas where their human selves had set up their homes.

While talking on the phone with Cheryl, Maya thought that, if nothing else, demonstrating what she was seeing online might be a good reason to approach Ryan and all, in case they were interested.

It at least gave her a good excuse to contact Ryan.

But first, she had additional administrative items to attend to despite her distance from headquarters, and so she dug into that. And eventually realized it was midafternoon.

She had pretty well finished all she needed to do—for WHaM. But what about for herself? Or the local wolves?

She made a few other small entries into the computer, placed another brief call to Cheryl to substantiate some items she had seen and wanted to confirm, then decided to call it a day, at least with reference to her professional association.

It was nearly four o'clock, late enough to consider plans for the evening.

Not that tonight would be anything like last night—although she could dream, couldn't she?

No. Last night's experience with Ryan was a once-in-a-lifetime event. Now, she had to get back to being totally professional with him.

Work with him in preserving the wolves that had shown up around here.

Maybe even get him to reveal which were like him. If so—well, she'd have to work with him, and maybe his Alpha Force to some extent—to determine the best way for WHaM to ensure the wildlife's ongoing existence without violating her promise of secrecy.

Alpha Force. What an amazing-sounding military unit. She hoped to learn more about them. A lot more.

But not right now.

Closing her computer, she got off the bed. She'd sat there most of the time during the last few hours, so she was stiff. She walked around for a minute or two, then hurried back to the bed where she had left her phone.

She called Ryan, and he answered right away—a good sign. "Hey," she said, "I've been working all day and need a break this evening. Are you free for dinner? All of you, if you'd like."

He didn't answer immediately, which troubled her. If he was as enthusiastic as she was, surely he'd jump right on her invitation and agree. But his answer, only a few seconds later, was positive. "Sure," he said. "But we'll need to eat early. And, just so you know, we've got some other plans later tonight so it'll have to be a relatively quick meal."

"That's fine," she said, maybe a little too brightly. He was trying to be kind while pulling away from her.

Or maybe they really did have other plans for that night. If so, what were they?

Hopefully she would find out at dinner.

But dinner turned out to be a lot earlier, and a lot quicker, than Maya had hoped for. Plus, Piers and Rocky were with them. That was no surprise. She had included them in her invitation.

Even so—well, she felt irrationally, or perhaps rationally, disappointed when all three of them met up in the hotel lobby not long after she'd spoken with Ryan and walked to the House of Steak together. It didn't help that she got to walk Rocky there. Not that she didn't enjoy holding the wolf-dog's leash and teasing him, and the men, as they hurried along. After all, they all had their own relationships with wolves, whether or not they could talk about it.

But right or wrong, she really wanted to be with Ryan.

It was early enough that the restaurant wasn't overly crowded. "I'll bet you're in the mood for a nice, big, rare steak," Maya gibed at Ryan after they'd been seated inside but near the patio door.

"Maybe I'll have a chicken sandwich tonight," he countered, his raised brows suggesting the picture of innocence on his utterly handsome face. But then he smiled. "Or not."

They ordered. Maya decided on a steak, though a smaller one than either of the men. None of them asked for wine or any other drink.

Maya again wondered what they were up to this evening, and whether that had anything to do with the guys choosing not to have alcohol.

Her curiosity led her to avoid any, too. Could she get them to reveal what was going on?

Could she find out some other way? Maybe she was reading things all wrong, but her curiosity was stoked.

She couldn't help wondering whether whatever it was involved Ryan shifting that night...

"Don't know what you three did today, but here's what I was up to." Maya began describing the wolf-tracking and prediction program used by WHaM.

"Really? Does it actually work?" Piers in particular looked impressed.

"Somewhat, though it's not perfect." Maya told them how well it had appeared to work in another location, in Alaska, when it was being tested, and in some Colorado locations, as well. "And there are some factors about... well, certain wolf characteristics that haven't yet been programmed in, and probably will never be."

She caught Ryan's eye as if to assure him she was talking about shifters, and that she'd never reveal anything, as promised.

Soon, dinner was served, and they all enjoyed their meals, even Rocky—or at least the dog received samples from each of the humans.

And eventually it was over. As always, Maya attempted to pay her share, which seldom worked, and she was almost never permitted to treat the others. This time, Piers insisted, and Ryan backed him up.

They walked back to the hotel together. Maya was able to maneuver things so that Ryan and she followed Piers, who had Rocky on his leash.

"This was a very pleasant evening," she told Ryan, smiling at him with just a hint of suggestion in her smile to see his reaction.

"It was. Sorry it has to end this early, but as I said we have some plans that can't be changed."

"Oh." Maya hesitated, then said, "Don't suppose I could tag along, could I?"

"Sorry. Not tonight." He actually did appear somewhat sorry, as his mouth curved into a grimace. "Hopefully we'll get more time together soon—to talk more about that program, for one thing."

Then he wasn't suggesting another night of passion, or even hinting there could be one. Oh, well. It was better that way.

But Maya remained curious. What were they really up to that evening?

Could she figure out a way to find out?

She was definitely going to try.

Chapter 22

Any regret Ryan had about shrugging Maya off that night had disappeared—well, mostly—as he and Piers drove to the lot at the far side from the park, at the base of the hillside. They'd brought Rocky along, too, in case Ryan needed extra cover, though they considered that unlikely.

Ryan intended to shift. But he particularly wanted Pete Sharan to shift first, using his own formula so Piers and Ryan could observe what occurred. They were also meeting his parents there because the senior Sharans wanted to be kept in the loop as much as possible, and they already knew about the existence of Alpha Force.

Their rental car, which Piers had driven, was the only vehicle there, a good thing even though it was expected. They had arrived earlier than they'd told the Sharans to meet them, and their meeting place was the clearing partway up the hillside. That family could approach it other ways.

"So, you ready?" Piers asked as he removed the key from the ignition switch.

"I'm always ready." Ryan tried to sound as if he meant it. But Piers knew him well enough to recognize when he was acting fine but had a few qualms inside.

They opened their car doors simultaneously, and while Ryan got Rocky out of the backseat Piers used the key to pop the trunk. He extracted the large backpack he used to carry his Alpha Force supplies, including light and elixir.

Ryan wondered what kind of concoction Pete had put together to aide him in shifting, if it contained any ingredients also within the Alpha Force elixir. He might never learn that with certainty, but if he was able to recruit Pete the guys with the scientific backgrounds in their military unit who kept improving the elixir would undoubtedly figure it out.

The few lights on poles in the parking lot emitted only a dim glow, as if it was nearly a given that no one would really park here after dark. Well, in his short time in Fritts Corner, Ryan had learned otherwise. They'd parked in a darker area where the car would not be beneath the glow of any light. If anyone else happened to come by, they might even think the car had been abandoned here, at least overnight. After all, who in his right mind would be hiking up the thickly forested hillside after dark?

Never mind that it had been done before.

"You ready?" he asked Piers once the trunk was shut and he'd helped his aide fasten the bag over his shoulders.

"Yeah. Let's move."

Piers made it look easy to carry all that heavy stuff. They'd both donned black athletic clothes to allow them agility while keeping their visibility at a minimum. In seconds, all three of them were on the worn path up the hillside, and only then did Piers remove a light from his pocket to illuminate their way.

Though Ryan would have preferred moving more briskly, they kept their pace slow, mostly to minimize how much they could be heard by regular human ears if anyone, as unlikely as it was, happened also to be hiking in the dark.

If they were heard by shifters, in either form, that was most likely okay.

They maneuvered around trees and bushes, and Ryan listened for sounds of any life around them. He heard rustles of creatures of the night and confirmed by their scents that they included raccoons, possums and skunks, and other nocturnal beings that were longtime natives to this area. Then there were the owls and other birds he anticipated, as well. Rocky put his nose into the air often but didn't slow them down.

No wolves. Not yet.

"Almost there," Piers whispered. In addition to holding the flashlight, he'd been peering at his phone's GPS. The area was somewhat familiar to Ryan since they'd been there before, but even someone with his enhanced senses needed some assistance in finding places in the dark that were hidden by canopies of trees.

In another minute, the trees gave way to an opening, and Piers shone his light around. The clearing was vast, and they stayed along its periphery—but only for a moment.

Three people stepped out of the darkness off to their right and approached. It was the Sharans.

"What kept you?" The broad smile on Pete's face told Ryan he was just joking. "Hey, we just got here, too. So— what magic are we going to create tonight?"

He looked directly at Ryan, and his parents were right behind him. All of them, too, were dressed in dark clothes, right down to their athletic shoes. Kathie Sharan appeared concerned, or at least Ryan saw a big frown on her face in the glow now emanating not only from Piers's flashlight but hers and Burt's, too.

Pete held a large brown duffel bag in his right hand. Was that where he stowed his equivalent of an elixir? Ryan figured they'd find out soon.

"Magic?" Ryan repeated. "I don't think any of this is magic, but it's certainly stuff that regular people might consider, well, supernatural, or at least different."

"I'll say." Pete put his bag on the dirt ground around them. "So where do we start?"

"Okay, as I first said before we decided on this meeting, you've already made a promise of secrecy. Do you confirm that promise?"

"Of course," Pete said, and his parents agreed. But then Pete added, "Can you tell us more now about Alpha Force?"

Good request. If he really was a potential candidate for recruitment, he would want to hear a lot more about the highly specialized military unit.

"Sure," Ryan said. "Hey, let's sit down here first for just a few minutes and get as comfortable as we can." The others followed his suggestion, and when they were all seated on the hard ground in a circle, he stopped to listen to make sure they remained alone. He again heard the sounds of some nocturnal animals but nothing stood out as presenting any danger, so he continued. "Okay, here it is—the short version. We do whatever is required of us by the military, going undercover a lot in various circumstances and, yes, getting involved in some combat, too. I'll tell you about some of our successes. And no, there haven't been any failures at all that I'm aware of."

For the next twenty minutes or so Ryan revealed some

of the missions Alpha Force had been involved in, even going up against anarchists and training a similar unit of shifters in Canada.

"There's more," he said when he was done. "And as I indicated before, we're always eager to recruit other shifters who can jump in and help our unit—possibly including you, Pete."

"Heck, yes!" The young man jumped up. "I'd love to join Alpha Force. What do I have to do?"

"First thing, that formula that helps you shift—tell us more about it."

"Our son was always great at science in school," Burt said proudly.

"I was interested in science because I started shifting when I was a young kid and wanted to learn more about it, even though I couldn't talk about it to many of my school friends—only those who were also shifters. But I wanted to do more than be forced to shift, like it or not, under full moons. It took me a long time and a whole lot of experimentation, but I finally came up with something that lets me shift whenever I want to even outside a full moon."

"How does it work, and how long do you stay shifted?"

"It's far from perfect," Pete grumped. "But I shift about five minutes after I take a spoonful and stay shifted for about half an hour for every dose I take. Do you want to hear the ingredients?"

"If all goes well, I'll need for you to tell some of the unit members who get all the technical stuff better than me. But I want to observe you now, and then, when you're done, I'll give you a brief look at how Alpha Force's very special elixir works."

"That's how you changed the other night—an elixir?" Again, Pete sounded utterly excited. Ryan explained that the elixir was the basis of the unit, that it allowed shifting outside a full moon as Pete's medicine did—which he already knew after seeing Ryan shifted since he apparently recognized and recalled it from when he had been shifted, too—and that it permitted shifters while in shifted form to maintain their human cognition.

"Really?" Now even Burt sounded excited. "And can shifters outside the unit use that stuff?"

"Unfortunately, no—though we might be able to make occasional exceptions for family members."

"Okay, son, we're with you," Burt said to Pete. "Go for it." He glanced toward Kathie, who nodded.

Pete reached into his duffel and pulled out a plastic bag. His parents helped him place a dose of his liquid onto a spoon from a small bottle. He removed his clothes, then Kathie held him as, in a few minutes, Pete's shift began. He groaned and was clearly in pain as it went on, but it didn't take long despite there not being a full moon.

Soon, she was hugging a wolf. It was a larger wolf than Rocky. It backed off some, knocking at her with his muzzle and acting somewhat like a tame dog like Rocky, now sitting calmly beside Piers, who held his leash.

Rocky was definitely used to seeing people shift, though not exactly this way.

"May I?" Piers asked and at Burt's nod drew closer. "Okay, Pete, sit."

The wolf just looked at him without obeying.

"Do you understand what I'm saying?" Piers continued, but again, though he didn't run, the wolf stayed standing where he was.

Piers and Ryan took turns talking to him for the next ten minutes, but Ryan was certain that the wolf had no more human cognition than Rocky and most likely remained around only because he recognized his tie to his parents on some level.

Pete had said before, though, that he recalled what he saw while shifted, even if he couldn't use his human thinking abilities then.

Soon after that, his shift back began and then Pete lay naked on the ground, panting as he withdrew from his discomfort.

"Very impressive," Ryan said when he figured Pete could understand him. "Do you let other shifters use it?"

"Burt and I do, a little," Kathie said, "and some of our friends do, too, just for the fun of it—if you can call it fun."

"I can," Ryan said, "when I use the Alpha Force elixir. Do you want to see?"

"Sure," Pete gasped.

It was Ryan's turn to strip. He took a vial of the elixir Piers handed him and drank it, then waited in the light his aide shone on him that resembled that of the full moon.

Soon his own discomfort began, and in minutes he was wolfen in form.

He looked at the others, nodding his head. Then Piers, who had told an obedient Rocky to stay where he was, began talking to Ryan.

Sit. Piers had said that, and so Ryan sat.

Shake hands. He held out his paw.

When Piers told him to touch the ground as many days as they had been in Fritts Corner, he scraped it six times. The others looked somewhat impressed—although that could have been some of his training.

But then Piers told him to use his paw to scrape the loose dirt in the form of the moon that night, only a few nights after the full moon, he did that, too.

He heard all of those around him, shifters, too, gasp their amazement.

"I want that!" Pete exclaimed.

And Ryan believed he would soon introduce a new re-cruit to Alpha Force.

Maya hurried onto the tree-shrouded upward path before turning on her flashlight.

She had parked her car on the opposite side of the lot from Ryan's, in a corner as dark as possible at the foot of the hillside. She had left her purse in the trunk, although she'd stuck her cell phone into her pocket. She could use it to take pictures, but she hadn't brought her camera.

Before, certain Ryan and Piers were up to something that night—something important, she figured, since Ryan had let her know they had plans without revealing what—she had sat in her car in the shadows at the hotel parking lot for almost an hour, waiting.

Was Ryan shifting again? Maya felt certain of it. But why couldn't she watch this time?

She might just watch without their consent, if all went as she hoped.

Maybe they were walking to wherever their *plans* took them, but she somehow hadn't believed so. And her conjecture was proved correct when they arrived at their car around 9:00 p.m. and headed out.

She'd followed at a distance, not surprised at all when she saw they were heading toward the far side of the park and its forested slopes.

Where she knew full well that Ryan had shifted before.

She drove by the entry then, turning around and returning a while later when she figured they'd had time to leave their car and head up the hillside. Sure, they could be heading toward a different clearing for this night's shift, and in any event she'd have to be as careful as possible not to be heard by Ryan in either form or allow him to see a glow from her flashlight.

If she was lucky, she could pretend to be a creature of the night and make only the sounds an animal might create while hunting prey this late—the lightest footsteps possible. Her work at WHaM, and her prior visits to this hillside, gave her at least a little hope of achieving that.

She finally returned, and had again parked her car in those shadows, this time as far from the other car as she could in the extended but empty lot, got out of her car and secured her purse in the back. She did it all quickly and carefully to minimize the possibility that the lights, or sound of the car door or trunk closing, would capture Ryan's attention. In moments, she'd reached the threshold of the path up the hillside to the clearing.

Sure, she'd had to turn on her flashlight then, but hoped that the cover of the trees and other flora here would keep her from being spotted by Ryan or Piers. Ryan's extra senses were more focused on scents and sounds anyway.

She took a few steps, listening. Yes, she did hear some distant noises like animals stepping on the forest's dried leaves, and she attempted to imitate them with her own steps.

She hoped she remembered all the turns on the upsloping path. There were branches away from it, after all, but the main path was the one she wanted.

She hoped it was the one Ryan and Piers wanted, too.

She hated going so slowly, but would hate it worse if she was discovered.

But she would hate it worst of all if she didn't arrive at the clearing in time to see Ryan shifted. She figured that, if he was already there, he would have changed into wolf form by now, but even if he ran into the woods he would return there, where he was likely to have left Piers, before shifting back—right?

Well, she'd just have to see.

For now, she attempted to curb her impatience and continued upward—also hoping she recalled enough to avoid getting lost up here in the dark. At least she wasn't cold, since she wore a hoodie—charcoal in color, and her pants and athletic shoes were dark, as well. She'd learned from Ryan that keeping a low profile at night included wearing drab and unexciting clothes that wouldn't grab the attention of any person who happened to be around, let alone any animals.

She figured she was about halfway there by now. Just a little farther and—

A moan sounded off to her left. A *human* moan.

And then a gasp, and a "Sshh."

What was going on? Was this Ryan's important task of the night, something to hurt a person? Had he attacked someone while shifted?

Which made her wonder again if it had been a shifter who'd attacked the Frittses—and whether that shifter was, indeed, Ryan.

Okay. She didn't want to get lost, but she had to check. Still attempting to sound like a stalking wild creature, she moved off the path and in the direction of the sounds.

Which were followed by more sounds, like hisses and a "damn," which was also shushed.

What was going on?

Still trying to go slowly enough not to attract the attention of a person or creature, she continued forward. The aromas of blossoming trees and other plants seemed mushed together, and she didn't actually sense by smell or hearing any creatures like those she tried to emulate.

But were there wolves around? Shifters?

Suddenly, she saw a light ahead of her—and stopped walking. She moved behind a tree, though, to gaze forward into the small clearing that was ahead.

There, in the middle, beneath a light on what appeared to be a portable pole, sat Carlo Silling. His friend Morton Fritts knelt in front of him with some kind of gadget in his hand that appeared to resemble a claw of some kind. No, not a claw. It was like scissors with curved teeth—and Morton leaned forward and raked the thing against Carlo's face, which was already torn and bloody.

And resembled how Morton's, and Vinnie's, had looked after their apparent wolf attacks.

Apparent was now the operative word. They must have done this themselves, setting it up to look as if wolves had hurt them to garner sympathy—and more.

They undoubtedly wanted someone to go find the wolves, perhaps themselves, and kill them, using the attacks as an excuse.

And now they were performing a third one to help make their point.

Maya wished she could confront them. Better yet, call the authorities to confront them.

But for now she could do neither.

Except…she reached very slowly into her pocket, where she'd stuck her silenced phone. She needed to take a picture of this—and then get away. Far away.

She pulled it out and checked to make sure the flash wasn't on—a shame, since the picture wasn't likely to turn out well. But she didn't dare do anything to call attention to herself.

She aimed it toward her view of the supposed attack and pushed the button, moving the camera as she took several shots, glad the sound was off so there'd be no clicks to indicate photos were being taken.

She stuck her phone back into her pocket, took a few breaths, then turned to leave.

And felt her arm and neck being grabbed as she was thrown to the ground.

"What are you doing here, bitch?" yelled Vinnie Fritts's shrill voice.

"Hey, let her go," said a voice from behind Maya.

But it wasn't Ryan's voice, or even Piers's.

No, it was Trev. What the heck was he doing here?

And how, Maya wondered, was she going to get out of this?

Chapter 23

Still lying on the ground, Maya managed to look up toward Trev. He had a gun, and he stood there aiming it not toward Vinnie, but at her.

What was going on?

"Trev?" she said, hating the quaver in her voice. "Have you come up here looking for wolves? I haven't seen any. Or heard any. But I'd certainly like to see them." And please don't shoot me, she thought. Or any wolves. What was going on? Was he somehow a worse threat than the Frittses and Carlo?

"Yeah, I want to see them, too," Trev said. "I want to get rid of them—as many as I can." His face was an ugly sneer now, his voice angry.

"Really?" Vinnie, who'd been standing near Maya, now edged closer to Trev. "Who are you?"

The nearby illumination grew brighter suddenly, and Morton and Carlo joined them. Morton held the pole with a light attached, probably battery powered.

"Yeah," Morton said, facing Trev. "Who the hell are you, and what are you doing here?" He didn't look nervous about the gun that Trev whipped around to aim on him.

Maybe that was because Carlo also had a gun—a larger one, and he had it pointed toward Trev.

"Hey," Trev said, holding up his hand so his gun was aimed toward the sky. "I'm on your side. You want to get rid of the wolves, don't you?"

"Yeah, we do," Morton said. "But you're not from around here. Why do you care if there are wolves in this area? Tell you what. You sit down right there and explain to us." He motioned to the ground below where Trev stood. It was covered with dead leaves like the rest of this woodland. Above, the tall trees obliterated any view of the moon or stars in the otherwise clear nighttime sky.

Vinnie knelt now beside Maya, binding her hands together. "This is getting more interesting all the time," she muttered.

Interesting, yes. And also frightening. Maya's wrists hurt beneath the ropes. The rest of her, lying on the ground, was uncomfortable, too. But she wasn't about to complain. She just wished she understood what was happening, and why.

And who, really, was Trev?

"Okay, okay," Trev said, still holding his gun but not pointing it at anything. He obeyed and sat on the ground— too near Maya, she believed.

What was this supposed wildlife aficionado doing here, threatening wolves?

Threatening people, too. Only now, he was being threatened.

And so was she.

"Here's my story," Trev said. "And why I'm determined to get rid of wolves, or other protected wildlife, wherever it happens to be. And yeah." He glared toward Maya. "I'm against your wonderful WHaM. Like I told you, I came here because I heard someone from that damned organization was going to give a talk. I wanted to hear you, learn all about you. Figure out a way to turn you, and your group, into an example. Put an end to your organization and do the opposite of what you're saying. All those damned beasts out there, they should be killed by anyone who wants to."

"Then you're a hunter?" Maya ventured. Was that what this was about? He just wanted to kill animals for the fun of it?

She wished then that she was in a better position to rise, to run away from here.

To hopefully find Ryan, and get Piers and him and maybe their military organization to grab this guy, take down this entire group.

And make sure that wildlife remained protected from horrible people like him.

But...

Oh, Ryan, she thought. Would she even see him again?

Would she survive what was happening to her here?

"Yeah, I'm a hunter—now," Trev said. She saw him look toward Morton, then Carlo. "You guys, too?"

"In a way," Morton answered. "But we've got reason. Do you?"

"Of course." He looked back at Maya. "Did you by any chance think enough about me to try to find me on the internet?"

She had but didn't want to admit it. Besides, she hadn't located anyone with his name.

"Not at all," she said, shooting him a disdaining grin.

"Well, it wouldn't have mattered if you had," he said. "See, my name's not Trevor Garlona. It's Tim Grant—so even if you knew that and tried looking me up, you'd find a lot of guys with my name."

"Why'd you do that?" Vinnie asked. She was now sitting on the ground beside Maya, no longer touching her.

"I needed a new name for what I intend to do," he said.

"Kill wolves?" Carlo asked scornfully. He was still standing, beside Morton.

He was still holding his gun.

"Exactly. And more wildlife, too. Anything I can—especially grizzly bears. But with all the publicity that's now being given to wolves coming back to Washington in large numbers, and mostly getting protection, especially in this part of the state—well, I just figured I could make a statement by killing a bunch of them, then explaining why. But I needed to do it under another name, another appearance, before going public."

"Why is that?" Maya asked. Keeping these people talking might give her time to figure out what to do. She couldn't get her phone out of her pocket with her hands bound, even if she had a way to call Ryan. But if he was up here on the hillside, his special wolflike abilities would let him hear human voices.

Assuming he was close enough.

"What do you care?" He sneered toward her. "You like those damned animals more than you like people, right?"

"No," she said quietly. Then, more defiantly, "Of course it depends on the people."

His laugh sounded bitter. "I'll bet it does. Well, what about if a person is the brother of a really cool, smart guy who was studying to be a doctor, who loved people and taking care of them—and even liked animals enough to go hunt them, not to shoot them but to take pictures? You might like that cool, smart guy with the camera, but what about his brother?"

"You're the brother?" Maya ventured. She shifted slightly on the dirt, trying to see him better—and get more comfortable. She succeeded a bit in the former, but not the latter.

"Yeah, the brother of that poor, smart, *dead* guy named Jerry Grant who was up on a mountain like this in another part of the state and happened to run into a grizzly bear. A damned *protected* grizzly bear, in that area."

Oh. This was starting to make at least a little sense now. Horrible sense. But Maya still didn't know what to do.

"That's why I came here to learn more about WHaM, to figure out how to put an end to it and its damned animal-loving members at least as an example to other groups who'd rather see vicious creatures live than people."

"I'm very sorry," she said quietly. Then, to all of them, she said, "Look, I know we have some major differences of opinion. Could we all just go back to town? I can leave tomorrow, not give any more talks favoring wildlife. I can even go public with something in addition to my advice to remember that wildlife is wild, something sympathetic to those who have been hurt by wild animals. Because I certainly am sympathetic."

She moved slightly to look toward Vinnie—and then realized she had seen, upon arriving here, the most likely way that Vinnie and Morton had been "attacked" by wolves.

The same way they had been goring Carlo with a fake claw.

No, she wasn't sympathetic toward them. But she didn't mention that.

"Sorry," Morton said. "That's not going to happen. But Trevor, or Tim, or whoever you are, we're really sorry for your loss, too. I can't even tell you how sorry we are, and with good reason. But I'm especially glad to hear that you

hate lots of wild animals. Since you're here, you're going
to get your wish to help bring down wild animals, to help
us make our case against wolves. You see, I just had a
damned good idea. You're going to be attacked by wolves,
too. Like your brother was with a grizzly. And when people see one—or better yet two—people have been killed
by them, then their protection is bound to end."

What was he talking about? Maya tried not to panic,
but her breathing sped up. People being killed? Trev—or
Tim—being killed?

Her being killed as number two?

"Now wait a minute," she began, but it was too late.
Morton leaped down to where Trev sat on the ground,
yanking the gun from him and throwing it to the side.
He then pulled out that same gadget he had been using to
wound Carlo, thrust the sharp claws hard into Trev's neck
and yanked it sideways, as Trev gagged and coughed, till
blood spewed from his throat.

*"Then you really can think like a person while shifted?
That's so cool! I love that you can count, and make shapes
on the ground, and all of it!" Pete, who had also shifted before but remained in human form now, pranced all around
Ryan as he responded to Piers, eyeing him, clapping his
hands.*

*"No hand clapping," Piers whispered sharply to Pete.
"There aren't likely to be other people around but we
don't need to make noise that could draw attention to us,
just in case."*

"Sorry." Pete dropped his hands to his sides.

*Piers looked deeply into Ryan's eyes, his expression a
question. Ryan nodded his head. Then Piers again faced
Pete and said, "He wants you to come with him through*

the forest. He'll show you more of who he is, what he can do. Are you interested?"

"Am I!" Pete nodded vigorously, but then he turned to his parents as if seeking their consent.

Both nodded, too.

"Then go ahead. Follow Ryan. But be careful, and obey whatever he conveys to you. He'll give you instructions even without talking. You okay with that?"

"For sure."

"Here's a flashlight. Ryan's unlikely to need it since there is some brightness to tonight's moon, but you can use it. We don't want you tripping and hurting yourself."

"Thanks." Pete took the flashlight and turned it on. Good guy. He aimed it toward the ground and not into the trees.

And then Ryan slowly began stalking into the woods.

He could not go very fast with a human at his side, though he liked to bound through the brush in areas like this. But his current mission was to show this young man that not only was he a shifter, but that the Alpha Force elixir gave him powers and insights that only members of his unit had.

After a short while, he stopped and put his nose into the air. He captured the scent of a squirrel. He stalked carefully in that direction, then stood on his back legs with his front paws on that tree, looking toward the large knothole where he knew the small rodent resided, and most likely nested with young ones in the spring. He looked at Pete, barely visible in the light, and nodded.

Pete got the message. He examined the ground around them, picked up a fallen branch and knocked it against the trunk.

Nearly immediately, the squirrel shrilled its scratchy call and dashed outside onto the branch nearest to the hole. *The animal looked down at them, made further noises, then disappeared upward into the thick branches.*

A true wolf might do as he did, Ryan knew, but not necessarily at this hour, and only if seeking prey to eat. He instead got back down on all fours, looked at Pete and nodded his approval of what he had done.

Pete laughed. "Cute. I might be able to find us something else to scare but I'd do better if I was shifted, too."

Once more, Ryan nodded. Perhaps he could find a fox or a snake next time to play with using methods that were even more human. He headed in a different direction now, making certain Pete followed.

What could he do next to make it clear to the young man how much human cognition he maintained? He sniffed at the air, figuring he would head toward the flat lawn of the park, perhaps demonstrating something near the podium where Maya had spoken.

Maya. What would she think if she saw him now and recognized who he was?

Too bad that he could not have agreed to allow her to participate. It was an important exercise for Alpha Force and needed to remain classified.

For the next minutes, he allowed his nose to lead him downward and in the direction of the park—until he suddenly heard a very soft but shrill noise, like a human cry of terror.

He stopped only for an instant to look up at Pete. Had the young shifter heard it, too?

Maybe. His expression appeared puzzled.

Ryan uttered a low growl and nodded his head in the direction from which the noise had come—just as he heard another one.

"What is that?" Pete asked softly.

With a small woof, Ryan began running in that direc-

tion, knowing Pete's footsteps would be louder and more conspicuous here than his own. But if a human was in trouble—well, there could be no better demonstration of the usefulness of the Alpha Force elixir than for him to use his human cognition to help that person.

Did he hear sounds from behind him? Perhaps Piers had indeed followed, despite agreement not to. But having backup here might be useful, and he undoubtedly would have Rocky with him.

Although—might it be someone else? There seemed to be more than one set of footsteps, and not just from one human and dog. Surely the older Sharans weren't following, as well.

Ryan could not stop to check now. He could only hope that, whoever it was, they did not add to what he suspected could become a dangerous situation.

As he ran, he listened and continued to smell the air. It would be better if he was alone. He did not want to lead Pete into danger.

And when he heard further sounds, voices and moans, he had no doubt that there was danger ahead of them.

There was also someone in trouble. It might be his human imagination, but the voice that moaned sounded like Maya, though that could not be. She was in her hotel room for the night.

But he knew her well enough to recognize that she was wherever she wanted to be—although of course, if it was her in danger, that had not been her goal.

"Please, just let me go. I won't tell anyone."

Damn. That was Maya's voice from somewhere in front of them. Ryan halted and turned to face Pete, to make him not only slow down and cease the sounds of human running footsteps through these woods, but also to stay back while Ryan scoped out what was there.

What was happening to Maya?

Who was with her, and who she was pleading with?

He quickly shook his head when he met Pete's eyes, gently knocking the hand that held the flashlight to convey that it needed to be shut off. When Pete understood and obeyed, Ryan sat down, nodding his head to convey that Pete was to do the same.

He was glad in many respects when Pete obeyed that, as well. This was a young man who was a shifter, who was smart and followed orders well. He recognized Ryan's human cognition and respected it.

He would make a fine asset as a member of Alpha Force—depending on what happened now.

While Pete sat there, Ryan turned back and crept forward on all fours, close to the ground. He continued to listen and take in the smells around him.

He heard nothing from Maya now. Was she all right? Had whoever it was listened to her and let her go?

Ryan wasn't naive enough in either form to believe that.

Slowly, slowly, he moved forward, wishing he could run until he saw what was happening. But that might be more dangerous to Maya if he was heard or spotted too soon. He needed to surveil her situation before determining how to act.

He slid along the dead leaves among the trees, trying to make as little sound as possible.

A small clearing opened in front of him.

There, off to his right, sat Maya. She must have been bound, since her hands were behind her.

In front of her was Morton Fritts, leaning down as if he wanted to strike her.

Carlo Silling stood beside Morton. His face appeared to be sliced open, and Ryan smelled the scent of blood.

But it probably wasn't Carlo's he smelled. No, lying off

*to Maya's side was someone else. Someone whose throat
had apparently been cut—gnawed?*

He wasn't sure, but it appeared to be that Trev guy.

Fortunately he saw no injuries on her...yet.

*He didn't even try to speculate why she was there. That
information would come in time.*

*But for now he had to determine the best way to save
her.*

*Vinnie Fritts was there as well, watching the men close
to Maya.*

*What would be his best course of action? Were those
men armed?*

*Might they shoot Maya first if he leaped in to try to
help her?*

*He hated to stay where he was, even for a few precious
seconds more. But if he wanted to do things right, he had
to observe and think and plan.*

Could he use Pete's help?

*Maybe. But he hated turning back to tell the young
man to join him.*

For now, he would wait. And watch.

Maya was terrified. What could she do?

Trev was clearly dead. The marks at his throat did look
astonishingly like bites. Wolf bites. And blood puddled on
the ground beneath him.

Vinnie had aimed a gun at her while they finished killing Trev. She had made Maya sit up afterward and checked
that her wrists were tightly bound. She wasn't sure what
they intended for her—but considering what she had seen,
she could guess.

Her phone remained in her pocket, but it was useless.
She'd screamed once as they killed Trev, but Vinnie had
kicked her and she'd immediately grown silent.

That had been a while ago now. The two men were huddled together over Trev's body, still arranging it, she thought. Clawing it more so it would appear the wolf had attacked other parts of him before going for the throat.

If only she could contact Ryan somehow, tell him what was happening, work with him to find an effective way after this to protect him and his kind, as well as feral wolves. Even before killing Trev, these miserable people had been creating injuries on themselves so they could blame wolves, the better for making claims that the animals should be killed.

And now they would have a dead body to demonstrate the worst that wolves could do.

If anyone deserved to really be attacked by wolves, it was these three. But she was the one in danger of being killed now.

Why wouldn't they kill her, considering that she'd seen what they had done to Trev? She knew the answer.

She knew what was coming.

Now she sat on the hard ground with her hands bound behind her back. She tried to keep her trembling from fear at a minimum. She didn't want to give any of them a further sense of triumph over her. In fact, they hadn't won... yet. She might be captured, but she wasn't done fighting.

She watched as Vinnie stood and joined Morton and the apparently injured Carlo. The group huddled together. Maya wished she could hear what they were saying.

Even more, she wished she could take this opportunity while none focused on her to run away. But though her legs were free, even if she managed to stand she recognized that at least Carlo, who faced her, would see it.

And they had guns. They probably didn't want to use them, since the wolves they wanted to blame for everything didn't shoot people, but she figured they would anyhow if she attempted to run. Even if they didn't shoot her, she doubted she'd be fleet enough, at least at first, to escape so far into the woods that they'd be unable to find her.

Those woods were dark despite the moon, though not quite full anymore, glowing above them. The light they had brought to this clearing wouldn't reach far. And she'd need her hands for balance.

Still, she worked on trying to pull them loose from the cords that bound them. She also attempted to look defeated as well as scared, even as she kept fidgeting slightly to try to find a way to stand and run.

At least the temperature was bearable, though chilly. She kept listening for sounds in the forest, any kind of distraction—like the appearance of a wolf.

Right.

Oh, sure, she heard some noises, like an owl hooting in a nearby tree, and some rustling thanks to rodents running on the dried leaves on the ground. None of those would help her.

If only she had some way of communicating with Ryan. She'd no doubt that he would try to help her. But just because she now had reason to believe in something she had considered unreal and supernatural just days ago—shapeshifting—she didn't yet believe that all such supposedly paranormal things were true...like extrasensory perception. She'd already considered recently if ESP could be real but doubted it. And she'd need ESP now to get through to Ryan.

Uh-oh. The conclave among her enemies appeared to be over. All three were standing, facing her, staring at her. And grinning.

That couldn't be a good sign.

Vinnie broke away from the men. Maya wished she could wipe the smugness off the woman's face. The woman's *scratched and scarred* face. Maya wasn't a malicious person, but right now she wished she was able to add to Vinnie's injuries, scratch her face up even more to distract her and the others, then run away.

But for now she couldn't, didn't, move.

As Vinnie approached Maya, her hands weren't visible. Was she hiding a gun? Did she intend to shoot Maya, then bury her out here where no one would ever think to look for her?

They would still have a body to show the world, one that arguably had been attacked by a wolf.

Boy, had she been dumb, Maya thought, not to at least have told Ryan what she was up to. But hindsight was, as usual, twenty-twenty.

She had to deal with things as they were now.

She had to survive, no matter what.

But then Vinnie pulled her hands from behind her back. She now grasped that clawlike gadget Morton had been using to maul Carlo—and that he'd then used to murder Trev. Of course.

Vinnie thrust it toward Maya, manipulating its handle so the claws at the end, mock nails as sharp as knives, opened and closed ominously.

"You know," Vinnie said, "I'd already figured it was a terrible shame that the wolves around here attacked first Morton, then me and poor Carlo, too. And after that, they even managed to kill that Trevor/Tim guy." She turned slightly in the men's direction but immediately faced Maya once more. "But they're not done. They're dangerous. Very dangerous. So dangerous that the one about to attack you will go for your throat, bite and claw it till you bleed to death just like Trevor did. Not just one death here tonight, but two. It won't be hard at all for us to convince the authorities that all wolves, no matter what their origin, have to be rounded up and killed."

As scared as Maya was, her thoughts focused momentarily on Vinnie's words *no matter what their origin*.

Then this group knew about shifters? Believed in them?

Wanted to get rid of them along with any feral wolves? Why?

They should at least answer her questions, shouldn't they, before they killed her?

And as she got those responses, maybe she'd come up with answers to the even more pressing problem: How was she going to get out of this?

"I don't really get it, Vinnie," she said quietly. "I know you feel strongly against wolves, but I'd like to know why, so I can fully understand why you killed Trev and intend to kill me, too. Surely, you can grant me that, can't you? And…well, what did you mean by 'no matter what their origin'?"

"You know!" Vinnie spat furiously, taking more steps toward her intended victim. "Don't try to play games with us. You've gotten close to that guy Ryan. I can't be sure he's a shapeshifter, but some of the people who moved here recently are shifters."

Would playing dumb help or hurt her? Maya determined to approach the subject as carefully as she could. "Shapeshifters? Even if there are such things, why do you dislike them so much?"

She was growing extremely uncomfortable kneeling there—physically. Mentally she knew she was a mess but had to keep smiling in a sympathetic manner.

"You mean you don't know?" shouted Vinnie. "Didn't you do your research on this area before you came like the eco-monster you are and began patting yourself and all other tree huggers—no, make that wolf-huggers—on the back for encouraging those killers to hang around here?"

"Sorry." Maya tried to sound humble as she looked down at the ground. She actually had researched the area both before and after her arrival and had no idea what Vinnie was talking about.

At least the two men stayed where they were, taking in this conversation without approaching. But that still didn't mean Maya could do anything to help herself.

"I'll tell you what they did. And it wasn't here in Fritts Corner but a distance away, up in the mountains overlooking the Pacific. I've got something in common with that Trevor guy, and not just because I was sliced with our little claw gadget here. No, it wasn't just my brother but the rest of my family, too—my parents and brother, Odell—who got killed a few years ago, not long after wolves started to be seen more in the western part of the state. My dear Morton was very close to my family, too, and Carlo was their neighbor. We'd thought Odell was crazy when he told us he'd seen a person turn into a wolf under a full moon, just like the old tales said. He wanted to prove it was true and my parents, though they thought him nuts, promised to go along…and they were all killed. No pictures or anything but they were mauled to death under a full moon."

That didn't necessarily mean the animals were shifters, Maya thought, though she wasn't going to say anything now. It could have been coincidence—or not.

And as she had been telling people in her talks, wild animals were wild. Even shifters, apparently.

It was safer to avoid all of them…right?

"We did some more research," Morton said from where he still stood. "Learned that it was likely that those damned shifters did exist, were present in that area, but it really doesn't matter. Her family was found mauled, sure, but their bodies were at the base of a cliff and the authorities said it was just a bad accident, a fall, that caused their injuries and death. We knew better thanks to the types of wounds they had. Wolves, bite marks and more, and the coroner didn't deny it exactly, just came up with multiple explanations."

"That's right," Vinnie added. "We kept pressing, saying we knew it was wolves, but people kept laughing at us, said we were crazy to make such allegations. They may have all been shapeshifters themselves, damn them."

"Wolves, whether human in origin or not, are dangerous," Morton said. "They kill people. The ones who mauled our family are probably still out there and we never learned who they are. So people should kill all wolves first." He paused, but only for an instant. "Go to it, Vinnie!" he exclaimed.

And Vinnie, still several strides away, rushed toward Maya with the claw gadget pointed toward her throat.

Chapter 24

"No!" Maya screamed as she tried wildly to yank her wrists loose, attempting to get free to push the claw away—or, better yet, run.

Fruitless. She wanted to close her eyes as the inevitable happened. She was about to die. Painfully.

And then, she heard a bark followed by a growl and opened her eyes as a large gray wolf leaped onto Vinnie, grabbing her neck in his mouth and closing his teeth into it.

Ryan. It had to be him in shifted form.

He was here to save her.

But she saw, beyond him, that Morton and Carlo had rushed toward them, both brandishing guns.

"Ryan!" she screamed. "Look out!"

Fortunately he was too connected with Vinnie for them to shoot without fear of hurting her, or so Maya believed. But they'd find a way. She was certain of it.

Meantime, Ryan had clearly heard her warning. Without lifting his mouth from Vinnie's throat or his body from partly covering hers now on the ground, he managed to look in the men's direction.

What was he going to do? Oh, lord, he couldn't die because of her.

He had reacted immediately because he'd no choice. He would not allow them to harm Maya. He would not allow them to kill her.

But now they would kill him, and if so they might yet do the unthinkable with Maya.

Wouldn't they be thrilled? A second dead human along with the corpse of a wolf, assuming he didn't change back. They would get away with all this and still be able to make claims that could lead to the murders of shifters as well as the death of feral wolves.

Revenge? Maybe. He had been listening before leaping in. But they should have found those who had killed Vinnie's family, not taken out their fury against all wolves... or shifters.

At least now he could harbor no further doubt that Pete wasn't the one to attack Vinnie Fritts.

What could he do? If he stayed as he was, they might not shoot since they would hit the human woman with whom he had entwined his body. But this could not last forever.

Even with his human cognition, he did not come up with an immediate solution. Yet this sort of standoff could not last long.

But then—he saw another form bound out of the forest, a wolf who resembled him. No, a wolf-dog. Rocky.

His cover dog had no weapons to fight off the attackers except his teeth, which would do no good against guns. Yet maybe he could act as enough of a distraction...

"Get them!" That was Piers, who now appeared at

the edge of the forest from which Rocky had emerged. He was a soldier, a member of Alpha Force, yet he probably had brought no weaponry here into the forest. Why would he? But he was giving Rocky commands that might lead to the dog's death.

"Yeah, get 'em," cried another human voice. Pete was suddenly there at Piers's side, still in human form, holding up a phone to take pictures.

But the photos would only show him, in shifted form, and possibly Rocky attacking humans—unless Maya could turn and show how she was bound.

The situation was pure confusion now. Who would get hurt—or killed? Who would survive?

He had to pull away, take charge, act like the Alpha Force member, the alpha member of his allied pack, that he was. Yet what would happen if he moved away from this miserable excuse for a human who now smelled like terror but would undoubtedly do all she could to kill him if he backed off?

And then—two more wolves appeared from behind the two human men, leaping into the clearing, each heading straight for those miserable humans with guns.

The Sharan parents, shifted? The scent told Ryan the answer. He appreciated that they wanted to help. Without human cognition, they would hopefully follow the lead of other members of this canine pack, including Rocky... and him.

But would they, too, get killed?

He could not allow that. He could not allow any of his current pack to be harmed in any major way.

He had to ensure that Maya remained all right.

The guns were suddenly pointed away from him. Oh, yes, he had to take charge immediately to save those brave older shifters. With a growl, he bit down once more be-

fore releasing the throat of the woman beneath him, hoping he had provided enough of an injury, and a warning, to stay where she was.

He sprang into action.

Thanks to Piers's commands, Rocky was now behind the men they all had to bring down. The men now facing the Sharans with their weapons.

Ryan began barking as he leaped forward toward the armed thugs, causing Rocky to bark, too, even as he followed Ryan's lead and bounded toward their enemies from behind.

They turned and fired their guns. Ryan felt a pain in his right side as he soared sideways to minimize their ability to target him. No matter. He was alive. And he saw no indication in that fleeting moment that anyone else had been hurt—except for Trev.

He crouched down momentarily as if badly injured, while Rocky hurled himself onto Morton's back and brought him down.

Ryan showed their other shifted pack members what to do, jumping up once more and grabbing Carlo's gun hand in his mouth, biting down. Hard. Shaking his head until the man, bloodied and shouting, released the gun.

One of the Sharans—Kathie?—hurled herself onto Carlo's back, ensuring that the man could no longer rise.

The other, Burt, jumped on top of Morton, holding him facedown.

Had they won?

No—Vinnie had not accepted his warning. She now had her arm around Maya's throat. "Let them all go!" she screamed. "I'll kill her!"

"You'll do it on camera," Pete yelled, aiming his phone toward her.

Vinnie appeared not to care. Maya was clearly attempt-

ing to break away, sagging and twisting as her eyes looked furious and frightened. But Vinnie's hands moved to clutch her throat.

At least that clawing weapon was on the ground, out of the way. But Vinnie obviously intended to choke the life out of Maya.

He had to count on the shifted Kathie and the fact that Piers was near them, crouching as if picking up one of the guns.

Ryan broke away from Carlo, feeling the injury he had suffered in his side and ignoring the pain. He wished for this moment that he was not in shifted form, that he could grab a gun and aim it at the fiend who was hurting the woman he loved.

Loved? He dared not think about that now.

He crouched once more as if in pain and crawled along the hard ground covered with leaves—and blood. His blood. But no matter.

He drew closer until—

"Stay there, you filthy creature!" Vinnie shrieked, obviously tugging harder at Maya's throat. Maya appeared ready to lose consciousness.

To die?

No!

Ryan lay on the ground for another second, as if giving in, obeying, giving up—

And then he sprang forward right at Maya, who, wonderful woman, had also been playing at submission. She pulled sideways and down, allowing Ryan to leap right at Vinnie, grab her throat once more in his teeth and go into worrying mode, shaking and tearing more at the flesh and what was inside.

He did not want to kill her, but one human here had already died thanks to injuries to his throat.

"No!" Vinnie's scream turned into a choked wail. She suddenly released Maya, clutching at her own throat even as she fell to the ground gagging and crying as Ryan held on.

In moments, Piers was there. He held a gun so its muzzle touched the top of Vinnie's head. "I've got her," he told Ryan. "It's okay to let go."

Ryan gave one more shake, then obeyed. He backed off slowly, making sure he saw what he hoped to: Piers in control of Vinnie.

The other canines were obeying commands Pete yelled at them, restraining one of the two formerly armed men: Carlo. Pete had put down his phone and had grabbed a leash—Rocky's?—and bound Morton's hands behind his back.

All was under control...now.

Only then did Ryan allow himself to fall to the ground and lose consciousness.

No. Oh, no. It was all supposed to be over. The bad guys were now under control, and sirens sounded in the distance. Pete must have already called the cops, and they'd be here soon to arrest the people who'd attacked her— and Ryan.

But Maya was a wreck. Her hands now free, she sat on the ground beside poor Ryan. At least he was still breathing. Still alive, with his eyes closed.

But how could his wounds be tended to? What physician would know what to do with a shapeshifter in animal form? Or should it be a veterinarian? And how could they keep it all a secret?

"We'll be back soon," Pete said and led two of the wolves back into the woods. The way he had been talking to them, they had to be his parents. Was he a shapeshifter, too? Maya would find out later, she figured. Right now, Pete held his phone in his hands and seemed to be looking at the screen even as he led the shifted wolves away.

Piers remained there, at least, holding what must be one of their own guns on the three evil people who'd started all this: Vinnie, Morton and Carlo. Rocky sat on the ground beside him, ears up and head edged forward, clearly ready to spring if any of those horrible humans dared to move.

Sirens drew closer as if cop cars raced toward the parking lot below them. As the noise stopped, Piers looked toward Maya.

"We need your help," he said.

"Of course."

In moments, she was the one to hold the gun aimed at the Frittses and Carlo. Piers dashed off for a very short while and returned with a backpack in his arms. He removed some rope from it, quickly bound the arms of their captives, then tied them together. Finally, he made them sit down, tied their legs together as well, then bound them tightly to a nearby large tree—not far from Trev's body.

"I'll leave Rocky with you. We'll be back soon."

He pulled a large lantern from his backpack and turned it on, and the light in the clearing was immediately enhanced. Then he put the backpack over his shoulders, hefted Ryan the wolf carefully into his arms, and hurried off into the forest, another, smaller light tied to his chest leading the way.

What was Piers doing? Would he leave injured Ryan hidden around here when the authorities arrived so as not to show anyone the truth of what Ryan was?

Could Ryan survive?

Maya wanted to cry, but of course she didn't dare do anything to keep her attention from the people in front of her. Sure, they were tied up, but that didn't mean they couldn't escape.

No way would she let them. They'd killed a man. They had tried to kill her.

They'd shot Ryan, the hero who had saved her from them.

She was relieved when a short time later Pete returned. With him were his parents—in human form.

Instead of staring at his cell phone now, Pete lifted it to his ear although Maya hadn't heard it ring. Maybe it had vibrated. He spoke into it, turned to tell his folks to remain there and help Maya if she needed it, and handed his father a gun—presumably the other one that had been aimed by either Morton or Carlo.

"I'll be back in a few minutes with the cops," he said.

Kathie and Burt stood beside Maya, and Burt kept his gun trained on the others despite their still being bound. Sweet and obedient Rocky stayed there, pacing a bit behind them, and Maya felt sure that he was as scared as she about what was going on with Ryan.

She had no idea about how much time passed, but soon Pete was back, leading some uniformed officers from the Fritts Corner PD. "Okay," said the tall man in front who appeared to be in charge. "Tell us what's going on here."

"These people jumped us, Officers," cried Vinnie from where she was tied on the ground. "They brought some wolves here, said they were werewolves. One of them mauled poor Carlo and then killed Trevor."

She motioned toward the dead body lying on the ground as Carlo, that supposedly poor, mauled man, jutted his head forward, obviously hoping to emphasize the cuts on his face.

"The gadget they used to make all the cuts, including the fatal ones, is over there," Maya said, nodding toward one side of the clearing. "They did it themselves to make it look like wolf attacks. Then they tied me up and said they were going to use it to slash my throat, to kill me in a way to look like a wolf did it."

"No way, Officer," Vinnie cried out. "She's just saying that to protect herself. It's them that—"

"I've got some photos on my phone to help show what happened here," Pete said. "And before you ask, yes, this wonderful dog, Rocky, is in some of them. He was trying to help us stop those jerks from hurting Maya or any of us."

Maya wondered if he'd done anything while taking his parents away to shift back to human form to edit the photos on his phone—or put them in another file or somehow conceal evidence that there had been four canines here instead of one. There hadn't been much time. But in her very limited experience, she'd been impressed to see what shifters did to protect themselves and each other.

If only that could have helped Ryan…

"Officers, so glad you're here," said a familiar voice from the edge of the forest. She couldn't help looking in that direction and smiling. Could her thoughts of him actually have conjured up Ryan?

He stood there in human form. Very human form, standing tall and straight, his face a bit pale but perhaps that was just the minimal illumination from the moon above and the fading artificial light.

He must have shifted back after Piers carried him off. Had the shift somehow cured his wounds, as well?

She doubted it, but at least for this moment he appeared okay.

Piers stood behind him on his right side, the side that had been shot. They must have intended to hide that he'd been a shifter in wolf form who'd been shot by this group of horrible people.

Sure, they might have a reason to hate certain shifters but to take it out on as many shifters, or even regular wolves, as they could put themselves in contact with?

To take it out on the perfectly innocent Ryan?

Horrible!

"Okay, look," said the officer in charge, who called
himself Sergeant Pass. "We aren't going to be able to sort
this all out here in the middle of nowhere. We've already
called the medical examiner's office to send someone for
the body. One of us will stay here, and all the rest of us
will head to the station." His fellow cops started herding
everyone together, weapons drawn, after slicing off the
ropes binding the Frittses and Carlo.

The Frittses and Carlo. They were locals. Would they
receive special treatment?

But at least some of the photos Pete had taken would
show what those horrible people had been up to.

The ones that could be shown to the cops and become
evidence, though, would only show Ryan in wolf form,
possibly injured.

He had saved her.

With the help of the others, he'd brought this group of
crazed anti-wolf people down.

He'd therefore potentially saved a lot of wolves, both
the usual type and shifters.

No matter what else happened, Maya would do all she
could to make sure the world, including WHaM members
and everyone else, knew what a hero Ryan Blaiddinger
really was.

As long as she could do it without revealing any secrets.

Chapter 25

His side hurt like the devil. But Ryan knew that Maya, the angel, was waiting for him in this medical office's waiting room, so he simply gritted his teeth while the doctor finished cleansing his wound and bandaging it. He tried not to inhale deeply since the room smelled of antiseptics and other medical aromas—including the odor of his own wound—and he definitely did not want to throw up.

At least now, since he was in human form, his wound was probably easier to deal with than if he'd still been shifted.

Plus, he'd be able to control better when he took the necessary antibiotics to prevent the injury from festering and becoming infected.

The Sharans had brought him here, to a medical doctor they'd been using since their arrival in Fritts Corner, a good guy who only cared about his patients becoming, and staying, healthy. The Sharans hadn't been the only ones

to use his services, either. Apparently this nice, skilled
Dr. Delmert had a perfect bedside manner with people,
even though he'd asked questions of the Sharans—and
now Ryan—indicating his suspicions that they weren't
just run-of-the-mill human beings. But he was kind and
discreet, and clearly wanted to help cure his patients and
keep them healthy while doing no harm—or revealing his
suspicions to the world.

When he first looked at Ryan and his wound, he'd suggested a hospital visit but had been willing to treat Ryan
here when the injured man had requested that instead.

"There." Dr. Delmert had dark-toned skin and gentle
hands, and he hadn't asked questions about the wound.
Fortunately, the bullet had passed through Ryan while he
was shifted but had caused an ugly, painful and bloody
wound. "This should start healing now. Just make sure to
keep it clean and don't do any heavy lifting for a while."

Then he wouldn't be able to lift Maya in bed—not that
she was particularly heavy.

And not that he would really get another opportunity
to be alone with her the way he had a few nights back.

"Sure thing," Ryan responded. "Thanks, Doc."

Then he left, heading for the waiting room, where he'd
pay his bill—and meet up with Maya.

Maya sat on a small, stiff chair in the compact and
nearly empty waiting room. She'd picked up a magazine from an end table and had been thumbing through
it, though she wasn't interested in the private lives of ce-
lebrities.

She'd much rather they had reading material about wildlife.

The reception desk was along the far wall and opened
into the area containing the medical facilities. A couple

of women governed it, checking in the arrivals and taking payment from those who were through.

Piers was with her, too. He had driven Ryan and Maya here, then took Rocky back to the hotel. He'd just returned alone, and Maya had to keep biting her tongue to avoid asking all the questions she had about what had really happened back there on the hillside, and what was going to happen now.

Assuming Ryan did all right. He'd clearly been in pain since he returned as a human, and it had been a while before they'd been able to come here. First, they'd needed to head down to the parking lot, then drive to the police station and answer questions. Fortunately, that hadn't taken too long and the cops had released them— for now. They'd said they would have more questions.

Through all of that, Ryan had been brave—not surprising, of course. And that pain…he had pretended it wasn't there, but she could see it in his eyes and slow, precise movements. At least his bleeding hadn't been heavy or the cops would have noticed. But he wore a jacket over his shirt so no one could easily see the bulge beneath it where he held things against his wound to absorb the blood.

Maya knew his wound had still been bleeding. When the interrogation was over she had quietly offered her hoodie to help staunch the flow of blood. Before that, he and Piers had used a T-shirt Piers had had in his backpack along with Ryan's clothes—and the other stuff he carried. Her hoodie had been larger and had absorbed a lot more blood than the shirt—but could only be used when they weren't around the cops any longer.

When they had finally come here.

But even if she couldn't talk about what she wanted to while waiting, there were a few questions she could ask

Piers now that they could discuss. "Piers, do you know where the Sharans are now? Did they just go home?"

"No, they said they were staying at the police station for now in case there were more questions. They said a few friends were on their way for backup, if needed."

Most likely more shifters. Even so, they were probably recent arrivals at Fritts Corner, too. Would the cops continue to accept the word of newcomers instead of members of the Fritts family, as they seemed to be doing?

Pete's photos helped with that, she knew. She also hadn't had an opportunity to check to see whether they'd been pared down to not show how many canines had actually been present before the cops' arrival, but she hoped so.

Questions about that would be hard to answer.

Piers didn't seem inclined to talk. In fact, he picked up a magazine from a nearby table, too—one on sports.

Muffling her sigh, Maya started looking once more through the magazine still on her lap. Maybe she could stand reading about a TV news reporter's elevation to anchor on the national network. At least it was better than who was sleeping with whom.

But she looked up when, from the corner of her eye, she noticed the door into the medical area open.

Ryan walked out. He was smiling.

She stood immediately and started walking toward him, as did Piers. She wanted to run, to hug him, to tell him how happy she was to see him.

Instead, she kept her pace moderate and then just stood there. "How are you?" she asked.

"Real good." He grinned at her, then turned it toward Piers. "Let's get out of here."

Ryan stood in the hotel parking lot, putting the last of his belongings into the rental car's trunk.

It was daytime now, a pleasant Friday in late September, several days since the bringing down of the Frittses and Silling. He had learned that they would be charged with the homicide of Tim Grant, as well as assault with a deadly weapon and more. Ryan had given his initial statement, and so had Piers, Maya and the Sharans. He'd have to return to this area eventually to testify at their trial—and he would be happy to do it.

It was cool today but not too cold. A good day to drive, and to fly.

He looked around the parking lot. Only a few cars were parked there right now but he figured more hotel guests would arrive later in the day to spend the weekend in Fritts Corner. Probably not a lot, though. The town hadn't exactly turned into a tourist spot, which remained a good thing.

At the moment, he was the only person in the lot. Piers had already finished packing his stuff and stowed it in the trunk, including his prized backpack and its vital contents. Now, he was giving Rocky a final walk before they left.

The Sharans had managed to put together a very brief meeting in their office yesterday, where the other people in town they knew to be shifters—Buck Lesterman and John and Georgia Maheus—were invited and told the truth about the Frittses and how they'd "claimed" to be trying to harm shapeshifters, of all things. No one gave them any credence, of course.

Of course. But that was enough information for those in that room, and they all promised to stay in close touch without talking about any secrets that had resulted in their invitation there that day.

And they weren't informed about the biggest secret of all: Alpha Force.

Now, Ryan kept looking around. Maya had said she

was leaving later that day. He'd told her what time he'd be packing up his car, hoping she would come to say goodbye.

She hadn't.

Maybe it was better that way but he nevertheless felt a bit…well, hurt. This was likely to be the last time they would see one another, unless they made plans otherwise. Piers and he were about to drive to Sea-Tac Airport to return the rental car—and to head back east to Fort Lukman, the military headquarters of Alpha Force.

They'd see the Sharans again, though. All three members of that family would meet them at the airport and join them on the flight and beyond. Once they were at the military base on Maryland's Eastern Shore, Ryan would introduce all of them to his commanding officers who would then also interview Pete.

He remained clearly eager to join the covert unit. Ryan believed he would be a great asset. The young man was smart, had even developed his own version of a shifting formula. Sure, it was far from perfect, but it worked enough for Pete and his parents the other night. They'd changed to help Ryan save Maya and bring down those bad guys who'd been collaborating to remove federal and state protection of wolves and get them all killed, shifters or not. The Sharans might not have had human cognition while shifted but their canine cognition was enough to get them to follow their son's commands.

Plus, Pete had been wise enough not only to take pictures of what had been going on during the tumult up on the hillside, but also to quickly download them onto a tablet computer his parents had carried into the woods. He'd left only those that would be helpful against the Frittses and Carlo on his phone, which he'd turned over to the cops as evidence after their promise to return it soon.

He'd told Ryan and the others later that he'd also fixed

things so that there'd be no evidence he'd taken those additional photos. Good guy—a whole lot more tech savvy than Ryan.

Well, some good had come out of this trip. Quite a lot, actually. Wolves—and most likely some shifters—had been saved. There would still be some observation of the area by Fish and Wildlife and other organizations thanks to all the newly arrived wolves that most people wouldn't know included shifters.

A new member of Alpha Force may have been recruited, one who was not only a shifter but also had some pretty valuable skills.

Ryan supposed that was enough. Yet—

There. He'd glanced toward the rear door of the hotel just as Maya came out. She peered around as if looking for someone, and when her gaze caught his she smiled and began hurrying in his direction.

Okay. They'd at least be able to say goodbye.

That would be enough. It had to be.

"Hi," she said breathlessly as she reached him. She looked up with her hazel eyes aglow, and he wanted in the worst way to bend down and give her a kiss that wouldn't quit.

But that would only make their parting harder. He'd give her a quick kiss goodbye as Piers and he got ready to go.

That had to be enough.

She looked dressed for traveling, too—a pale green shirt tucked into beige pants, dressy but flat brown shoes, nicer than hiking garb. But she looked good in everything. Too good.

And in nothing…

He nearly shook his head with disgust at himself.

"Hi," he said. "Glad to see you. I'm just waiting for Piers and Rocky, then we're going to leave."

A look of sadness seemed to cross her lovely face, making him want to reach out to comfort her. But then it disappeared.

"I'm leaving soon, too. But I wanted to invite you and any members of—you know—to come visit our facility in Colorado. We don't rescue wolves per se, though we help support organizations that do, and we've a lot of educational materials and classes available. Plus, there's all the information we collect and share with appropriate parties."

"Sounds good," he said. "Maybe someday…soon." He hoped.

But the reality of it was most likely different.

"Okay. Great." Her tone suggested she recognized that he was just being kind without committing. Then she perked up but kept her voice low. "So how are you feeling?" She glanced toward his side, which remained bandaged beneath his clothes. Most of the world didn't know he'd been hurt, and he needed to keep it that way. His wound had been cleaned well by that doctor, Ryan was on antibiotics to avoid infection and he seemed to be healing fine.

"Quite well, thanks." And he really did owe her thanks for helping him that night.

"So—any word about what's going to happen next with those horrible anti-wolf people?" She didn't mention what kind of wolves, which was a good thing, but he already knew she was tactful as well as caring.

Even so, he had to keep himself from pulling her close.

Instead, he said, "Things aren't resolved yet, whether it'll be the feds or locals who prosecute them, or maybe both. They're all still in custody here at the Fritts Corner Police Department but will be moved soon to the Tacoma authorities, at least for a while. It's hard to keep people whose names are the same as the town in jail there."

"I figured. But—well, since they murdered Trev, I assume they'll be imprisoned for a long time, maybe the rest of their lives. Justice should be served, and that should also prevent them from ever going after or hurting wolves or other wildlife. Right?"

"That's what I think, too. And besides our testimony, there's a lot of evidence against them for other crimes. Apparently they may even have admitted to leaving a patch of blood up on the hillside when Morton was first mauled but still claimed it was a wolf who attacked him. There's been some media coverage of their arrest and why, so that might help to at least keep the public's interest in protecting, and not harming, wildlife. Plus, though I'm not really with US Fish and Wildlife," he said softly, "some of my...er, bosses, have connections that will allow me to testify as if I am. I am an employee of the federal government, after all."

"What kind of charges besides murder will be brought against them?" She looked concerned, as if nothing could be punishment enough.

"That's the big one, of course, but the rest is still being worked out, too. They might be tried locally for conspiracy to commit fraud, thanks to their fake attempts to appear like they were injured by protected wolves. And they certainly can be brought up on charges for assaulting you, and your testimony then would be crucial. They could even be charged by the federal government for killing protected wildlife."

"Killing?" Maya asked, clearly worried.

He quickly mentioned the injured wolf whose body hadn't been found—actually, him—that had been the subject of some of Pete's pictures. Rocky and he both had been in some of them. But Pete had purposely not taken pictures of his parents. "He's got lots of other good photos of that night, too, that could help bring those SOBs down for any or all of those charges. Then there's the crime of fraud and false statements, claiming some of the wolves they were after to be shapeshifters." He kept his tone light but maintained a somewhat serious expression as Maya looked at him skeptically. "As long as the truth isn't revealed," he whispered, which made her smile again.

"It sounds as if they should get what's due to them," she said.

Ryan saw Piers enter the far end of the parking lot with Rocky. They would leave soon.

He had to say goodbye. Now.

He couldn't say goodbye.

A thought crossed his mind. He pulled his phone out of his pocket and checked the time.

"I think we can spend another ten minutes here," he told Maya. "Can you join me for coffee?"

"Sure." Her face lit up with what appeared to be hope. Or was he the one who was seeing things because he was hopeful?

"I'll let Piers know."

Which he did after striding across the parking lot to his aide and cover dog.

"You saying goodbye to her?" Piers looked dubious, as if he expected Ryan to do something else.

Actually he wasn't sure.

But he had an idea.

He would suggest it to her during coffee, which he'd buy and they'd carry on a private walk around the hotel area.

He hoped the result would make his goodbye temporary, at least for now.

Coffee with Ryan, and a last walk with him before they said goodbye.

It was better than nothing, Maya thought. At the coffee shop near the hotel she ordered just some brewed stuff with cream, hoping to somehow coat her insides to help alleviate the sorrow she knew she'd feel.

But as they walked back onto the street and headed around the block in the opposite direction from the hotel, she listened carefully and pondered the possibilities of what Ryan suggested.

When he stopped talking and looked down at her as they still strolled, she didn't return his gaze for a minute while she thought. And then she stopped walking and looked up at him. "I think it'll work," she said. "In fact, I love it!"

"And I love you," Ryan said. His eyebrows rose as if he was shocked at what he'd said. But then they lowered, and his smile grew wide and sexy and definitely inviting.

How could she resist? Especially because it was the truth.

"I love you, too."

Chapter 26

Maya was excited. She was thrilled.

A week had passed since she'd last seen Ryan, and they had stayed in close touch.

She was now in the main administration building at Fort Lukman.

The home of Alpha Force.

Ryan had picked her up at BWI Airport in Baltimore. He was dressed in military fatigues in camo style, greens and browns and altogether official-looking.

He looked great in it, though no better than he'd looked in the casual clothes he'd worn around Fritts Corner.

She had dressed up a bit, in a gray suit and heels. This was, after all, going to be an interview of sorts. She had checked a suitcase with several additional outfits in case more than one day was needed here to get things settled, which was what she hoped. It was now in the trunk of Ryan's car. He'd said he had booked her a room in nearby Mary Glen.

Ryan had driven her here to Maryland's Eastern Shore. He'd talked nearly all the way about who she would be meeting, and what she should expect.

Lots of interesting people she gathered—some who were shifters.

And lots of questions, too.

They'd eventually reached the facility, and Ryan had pulled his car up to a kiosk at a gate beside a large black metal fence that undoubtedly kept the place private. He talked to a guard there whom he appeared to know and was permitted to drive inside and park. Then he'd led Maya into this small but official-looking building.

Now, they were in a waiting room of an office on the top floor. Piers joined them with Rocky, who leaped over to Maya and wagged his tail. "Great to see you, guys," she said, patting the wolf-dog on his head and behind his ears. And it was.

Not just because he reminded her of a shifted Ryan, either. She simply loved canines that were, or resembled, wolves.

"And great to see you," Piers said. "Ryan told me what's going on, and I think the idea's a good one."

So did Maya. But would these guys' commanding officers agree?

Another soldier in camo, probably in his early forties, entered the reception area from the office door. He was tall, with dark hair that had lines of silver within it. His eyes were golden, his eyebrows dark and he had a hint of dark beard on his nice-looking face.

She couldn't be sure, but Maya believed he could be a shifter. He at least had some features with coloration resembling a wolf.

Ryan and Piers both rose to greet him. No salutes, but

Ryan had said that generally Alpha Force tended to be less formal than most military units, at least in that way.

"Maya, I'd like you to meet Major Drew Connell," Ryan said, motioning for her to join them, which she did. She offered her hand, and the major shook it. "Drew, this is Maya Everton."

"Ah, yes. I've heard a lot about you, and I've liked WHaM for a long time." That statement somehow convinced Maya even more that this man was a shifter.

She'd anticipated meeting quite a few of Ryan's kind here.

They all went into the room behind the door, and she was introduced to the man whose office it was—and quite an office it turned out to be, with bookshelves lining the wall behind the main desk. Its featured contents appeared to be classics, and in the center, under glass, was what appeared to be an original script of the movie *The Wolf Man*, starring Lon Chaney, Jr.

It belonged to General Greg Yarrow, who apparently was the driving force in the military behind Alpha Force. He knew and helped to select its members, even though Maya gathered that he wasn't a shifter himself.

The general sat behind the desk, rising to shake her hand. Like the other military men here, he wore a camo uniform. He also appeared fairly senior.

"Welcome, Ms. Everton," he said. He introduced the other men who sat in chairs facing his desk.

Then Drew introduced her to Lieutenant Patrick Worley, his second in command at Alpha Force, as well as Drew's wife, Dr. Melanie Harding Connell, a veterinarian—and, apparently, not a shifter, Maya gathered.

"Welcome," Melanie said. "I think we'll have lots to talk about if all goes well here."

Which it seemed to do.

Ryan's idea had been to form an alliance between Alpha Force and WHaM. Although the fact that many of Alpha Force's troops were shifters was definitely private, its reputation was now being allowed to grow as a unit that used K-9s and other animals for military purposes.

Many of them appeared to be wild animals, like wolves and cougars and birds of prey.

Having an organization like WHaM as an unofficial partner in the protection of wildlife seemed like an excellent idea.

Giving one of the founders of WHaM an office at Fort Lukman could only add to the cover story. That's what Ryan had suggested, and his commanding officers seemed willing to give it a try.

They seemed to like and respect Ryan. In fact, he'd promised that Pete Sharan would meet them when they left here. His parents had come, too, but had left for home. Pete definitely was joining Alpha Force in the near future.

It didn't take long before an initial agreement was reached with the others in the room with her. They'd need to come up with a more detailed plan before putting it into effect, but everyone seemed pleased with the idea of an alliance, at least to some extent, with WHaM.

Maya soon said goodbye to her new friends here, except for Ryan, who walked out the office door with her.

She felt a bit overwhelmed, but definitely delighted.

Especially since she would get the opportunity to see more of Ryan. Potentially a lot more.

As they exited the building, Ryan said to her, "This is a great beginning."

"It sure is," Maya agreed, grabbing his hand and squeezing it, but only for a moment. They both had to act professional, especially here.

"Now, I'd like to show you more of Fort Lukman," Ryan

continued, "like the kennels and training facilities for our cover dogs, the labs where our elixir is made and improved, and more."

"Sounds wonderful," Maya said.

"We can grab dinner a little later at the cafeteria—and then, if you'd like, I'll show you around our Bachelor Officers Quarters, my apartment in particular."

His smile grew wide and suggestive, and Maya could only grin back. "I'd love to see it now—and visit it in the future when I move here, too."

"Count on it," Ryan said, putting an arm around her shoulders and, despite the fact that other soldiers were out there on the grounds of the military facility, he pulled her close.

She didn't object. In fact, she did the same with him.

And definitely looked forward to the future.

* * * * *

MILLS & BOON®